The Long Stretch

The Long Stretch

A NOVEL

LINDEN MACINTYRE

HARPER ● PERENNIAL

HARPER ● PERENNIAL

The Long Stretch
© 1999 by Linden MacIntyre.
P.S. Section © 2006 by Linden MacIntyre.
All rights reserved.

Published by Harper Perennial, an imprint of HarperCollins Publishers Ltd

First published in hardcover by Stoddart Publishing Co. Ltd: 1999
This Harper Perennial trade paperback edition: 2006

HarperCollins books may be purchased for educational, business, or sales promo-
tional use through our Special Markets Department.

HarperCollins Publishers Ltd
2 Bloor Street East, 20th Floor
Toronto, Ontario, Canada
M4W 1A8

www.harpercollins.ca

Library and Archives Canada Cataloguing in Publication

MacIntyre, Linden

The long stretch : a novel / Linden MacIntyre.

First published: Toronto : Stoddart, 1999.

ISBN-13: 978-0-00-639583-6
ISBN-10: 0-00-639583-X

I. Title.

PS8575.I655L66 2006   C813'.54   C2005-905577-4

HC 9 8 7 6 5 4 3 2 1

Printed and bound in the United States
Design by Sharon Kish / Set in Sabon

for
Dan Rory MacIntyre

'*A chuid de Phàras dà*'

"Canadian army to open up the supply route
to the north through Arnhem, and then to
operate to clear Northeast Holland, the coastal
belt eastward to the Elbe, and West Holland."

*Item #8, orders of Field Marshal Bernard Montgomery,
Commander 21 Army Group, 28 March 1945*

Part 1

1

Sextus was standing just in front of the liquor store, a bag of booze under his arm, squinting. I was coming from the drug store, keeping close to the brick because there was a wicked rain dashing against the pavement. A typical Saturday. November 19, 1983. I remember the date because it's close to an anniversary I don't often forget . . . though I wish I could.

Until that moment, my plan had been simple and not unusual for a Saturday: buy a flask, call Millie, drop by for supper, watch the hockey game, maybe go home, maybe stay. Depending on her cheer.

Well, I said to myself. *There's* a bunch of options all shot to hell.

The style of him caught my attention first. The overcoat was practically dragging on the ground. Flapping open. Belt tied casually behind. First I thought: a politician. Then I saw that familiar, unmistakable profile. Jesus. Look at him. I felt a great knotted ball of fear and anger and excitement.

There was nothing stopping me from turning on my heels right then and there. Pretending I never saw him. Just carry on the way I have for thirteen years, recovering from the last time. But I was in the grip of something stronger. Curiosity. And, yes, pride. I wanted him to see that I haven't just survived these thirteen years. I have grown.

He plucked his little reading glasses from his face, flipped the overcoat open, and plunged them into the breast pocket of a fancy camelhair jacket. As he turned to walk away he spotted me.

"Johnny," he said, amazed.

I looked, trying to act like I didn't recognize him, but I could feel the flush on my cheeks.

He, of course, pretended not to see my reaction. There are people like that, who know how to project whatever they want, no matter what they feel. I just go blank, which is useful in my work. I work with people. Or personnel, as they're called now.

Just look at the bugger as he strides toward me, not a doubt showing. The onus is on me. It would only take a word, a hesitation of the hand. But already shamed, I blurt recognition and catch his hand with a studied firmness.

It is soft. He couldn't miss the scratchy hardness of mine. I have one of those Scandinavian woodstoves in the living room for extra heat. I split my own wood. I'm bony and fit because I've been running and sober for seven years.

"You look great," he says. "Life's obviously good to you."

"No complaints," I say. "You're looking," I begin, searching for a truthful word, "prosperous." And in a gesture of self-confidence that makes my knees watery, I pat the bulge of flesh swelling over his belt like dough.

He laughs and sucks it in.

Sextus is my cousin. First cousin. Around here that's about as close as a brother. Closer, in a lot of cases. He's the only son of my father's only brother. The late Jack Gillis. Uncle Jack. Finest man that ever lived.

Because there were only the two, each named the first-born after the other. I'm named after Uncle Jack. This fellow is named after my old man. Not the Sextus part. That's actually the second part of his name. His first name is Alexander. That was the old man's name. Sandy for short. He's been dead now for years, since November 22, 1963. The day they shot Kennedy. Almost twenty years ago.

Our name is common around here. But none of the other Gillises are related to us. So seeing him brings back memories. Most of them bad because of everything.

He's really been gone longer than thirteen years. Last time I saw him was just after Uncle Jack's funeral. But he'd been gone a long time before that. He'd already made a name for himself away, writing on newspapers. Then he wrote a scandalous book. And then he stole my life and ran with it. For a long time I had to block everything out when I heard his name. But I rebuilt and eventually he just blended into the miserable part of the memory. It means nothing to me now.

But here he is. He shifts his hand to my arm, clutching my coat just above the elbow.

"Long weekend," he says, by way of explanation.

I remember. He's a teacher now. Or something.

"Just got in. Jesus. It's good to see you."

I am suddenly speechless.

"I was planning to drop in on you, out at the old place. You're still there, of course? We'd have a drink. Jesus Christ. Wow," he says, face animated. "Just look at you."

I half laugh. Allow a look of surprise.

His smile holds firm, though I know he's reading my mind.

"No, no, no," he says. "We'll have lots of time to talk about all the old stuff."

The rain is staining the shoulders of the overcoat black. I'm wearing my woods jacket.

"Christ, what a coincidence." Laughing and wagging his

head, unaware of the pounding sleety rain. "Man, you're just the guy I wanted to see."

The words keep rushing at me and I'm studying the face for some connection with the real world. Like remorse maybe.

Then he blushes, removes the clutching hand from my arm and thrusts it into his pocket. Fumbling with something there. Keys probably.

"Look," he says, as if reconsidering. "If you just want to . . . ," and the busy hand comes back out of the pocket, fluttering. "I mean, I wouldn't blame you."

"No, it's all right. What were you going to say?"

"Well." He clears his throat. "I was over at the graveyard. The old man's grave. There's no stone."

"No," I say. "Uncle Jack has no stone. None of them have."

He searches my face with those eyes that show none of the uncertainty in the voice. Hard con-man eyes. The hand flutters to his face.

"Would you believe," he says, "I don't remember where we put him? Sandy I can vaguely remember. Angus, of course, I wasn't here. But my own father?"

The we laugh, both flushed, eyes engaged.

"You must think," he says. "God. I can't imagine what."

2

They named him Alexander Sextus because he was the first-born in the sixth generation of Gillises living here. And the sixth Alexander. Names used to be important around here. The county we live in is Inverness, named for the county I guess most of the people came from in Scotland. Everybody knows Nova Scotia means New Scotland. A Latin name, like Sextus. The Sextus idea came from his mother. Something new. Tired of the repetition—Sandy, Sandy, Sandy. That's Aunt Jessie, ahead of her time. Today the place is up to its arse in Shanes and Shaunas, Jasons and Kyles. Anything to be different. Not so long ago everybody was John or Sandy or Angus.

But that's the least of the changes. It's become pretty much like any other place on this side of the ocean. Which is almost funny, considering how intense everybody now seems to be about the past, that mythical time when, compared to the present, everybody was poor and proud and happy. Now you hear them going on about roots and connections. Placing tartans and bagpipes in obvious places to fool the tourists. The way I remember it, though, the old people in our family couldn't have cared less. They'd say where they got to was more important than where they came from.

During the wars a lot from here got over there, visited the old country, saw how backward things were. Reported back. Made the old people feel better.

My old man was all over Europe during the Second World War but didn't even bother going to Scotland. Claimed he was never interested. Spoke Gaelic like the rest of them before the war, but never after. Something about his memory. He was wounded. In the head. Took away the piece of his memory that held the Gaelic and a lot of other things, like feelings. People around here admired my old man for his hardness and for what happened to him. Getting shot. A wound that would have killed an ordinary man. You had to live with him to know the truth: that hardness is often just a shell. And that there's more than one way to be killed.

Angus MacAskill was a different story. Went away from here the same time as the old man. Joined up together. But Angus came back from the war with a Scottish wife, one kid and another on the way. More or less intact, except for what you couldn't see. Angus was with my old man when he was shot. They were in a barn in the north of Holland. Outside a place called Dokkum.

You don't forget something like that. Not just that it was so dramatic: somebody getting shot. It was a war, people getting shot all the time. And the old man survived it. What gave this story a life was the weird coincidence that put them in that barn at that moment. The odds of that happening were practically zero, since they'd basically been through different wars, in two different parts of Europe. And, of course, the consequences of that get-together, which are still making life difficult. Not least of all for me and the fellow standing in front of me with the rain running down his face, through the grooves beside his nose, like tears.

I'd have expected, if I had ever anticipated seeing him again, seeing an outsider. But except for the clothes and the smooth manners, he's more like us than ever. Like the Gillises. Big shouldered and dark faced, with deep lurking eyes and a complexion like bark, an unready smile that dominates.

He used to complain about his name. But it always made him seem special. And he was good at the books. Good talker. Seemed physically strong so never had to prove much. And he lived up to expectations, becoming special. Writing, away. When we were kids, away was the place you went if you had worth, or wanted to get ahead. He was always bound for away.

"Were you going to get something inside?" he asks.

"Oh, just a pint of vodka for later," I say.

"Never mind," he says, gesturing to the bag under his arm. "I have one here. Will you come with me, then?"

I nod. Can't tell him the vodka was for Millie.

Millie and I are both AA. That's where we met. But now and then she allows herself a little treat. And I seldom object. I'm strong in some ways but Millie is stronger when it comes to having the odd drink. Millie can be a lot of fun.

It is raining harder as we hurry across the parking lot to my car. Water is pooling on the asphalt. I'm wearing my work-boots. He has dress shoes on, flecked with wet grass from his earlier trip to the cemetery. Inside the car, with the rain rattling on the roof, he asks permission to smoke. Lights up his last one, then drops the empty pack over the back of the seat, onto the floor.

It isn't far to the cemetery but he says he needs more cigarettes first. I take him to Langley's. He dashes inside, hunched against the rain as if it hurts. When he comes back he has a can of Sprite and some plastic glasses. As I'm pulling onto the street he's pouring two long shots of vodka into the glasses. He tops them up with the soft drink and hands me one. Like old times. I feel a blast of guilt. AA reflex. But what can I do? I take it and immediately notice the blue and white flash of a police cruiser hissing by. I can feel the Mountie staring at the incriminating plastic glass.

"Shit," I say. I brush the condensation from my side window and peer after him into the side mirror. He is gone quickly into the shower.

"What?" says Sextus.

"The Mounties."

"Oh," he says with a half-laugh.

"It isn't like the old days," I say. He was always too cocky.

"Sure isn't," he says.

Old days you were drinking in the car all the time. There wasn't anywhere else. It's always been like that. Alcohol and recreation: you can't have one without the other. Men in the old man's generation were the same, though they probably didn't have as much access. Alcohol was probably the root of all the problems. Especially the old man and Angus. Even the old man getting shot. Nobody has ever denied it. They were well into some found booze when it all happened.

You started drinking early because there wasn't anything else to do. Sixteen. Seventeen. Just about when you got the driver's licence. Driving around trying to pull in hit parade music on the radio. You could get a lot of American stations, stuck as we are out in the water, an island. Cape Breton. Canada's little toe. That's how the grade one teacher would explain it, pointing with a long stick at the Neilson's candy map on the wall of our two-room schoolhouse.

A good radio would get New York City clear as a bell. Or Wheeling, West Virginia. Local stations were boring. Then, when you'd be feeling good you'd roar into a dance somewhere, which was mostly fiddle music. You'd leave the New York music behind and bluster into the jolly hall, head suddenly filled with the squeal of jigs, heart pounding in time with the reels, ready for anything. The girls sitting along the walls on the hard chairs waiting to be asked; the hard guys hanging back near the door eyeballing everybody. The booze smoothed out any rough spots that might have created resistance on the slide toward happiness. Later on in your life, when you needed something to help through a hard patch, you knew where to turn. It takes a while to realize that if there is happiness, the booze will never help you get there. I found out the hard way.

3

"I was ninety-nine per cent positive there was a tombstone," he says, brooding.

The cemetery gate is open and I turn in.

"I thought it was over there." He wipes the inside of the windshield with the back of his hand the way I tell people not to. He leaves a smear.

"No," I correct. "He's on the other side."

We're driving slowly along a narrow road that loops around the perimeter.

"It was a day like this," he says. "But a lot colder."

Rain lashing, wind trying to tear the pages out of Father Duncan's prayer book. Father Duncan helped Father Hughie with the funeral Mass for Uncle Jack. Sextus looking dark and doomed, holding on to his mother, Aunt Jessie. Us remembering and grieving. Him planning ahead. The last time I saw either one of them . . . him or Effie. The day of Jack's funeral. Thirteen years ago. Last February.

What else. My mother's arm is looped tightly through mine. Effie, my wife, is on the other side of me, keeping up appearances but making stealthy eye contact with him. Plotting with him. Near consummation of all their wicked plans. I'm in the dark, but not for much longer.

Effie's brother, Duncan, the priest, is shouting into the wind. I'm hoping there's a short version of the prayers for the dead. I'm frozen. Wet. Rumsick. And remembering Jack.

If there is a shorter prayer, Duncan doesn't know it. I distract myself from Effie and the cold, reviewing the homily in my head. It was by the parish priest, Father Hughie. Uncle Jack was one of the Peters of the world, Father Hughie said. Jesus had a special affection for people like him. Working people. Blue-collar Apostles.

I remember making a little rhyme from it:

The twelve were all, save Matthew, working class.
The priest finds relevance in this coincidence at Mass.

Angus MacAskill was there. Looking grim. Angus the Giant they called him sometimes in his later years. The *fuamhair*. Even young ones at the tavern, Billy Joe's, not knowing a word of Gaelic, would say: "The old foyer." There was a real giant named Angus MacAskill in Cape Breton once. Biggest man in the world, I guess. But they called this Angus MacAskill the giant because he was so shrivelled, and weakened by the booze. Irony. I've heard that people called him Monty after the war because, in his better days, he looked like the famous field marshal. They say Angus actually spoke with Montgomery once. Spoke right up during an inspection. That was in Holland too, just before the end. They'd say Angus was bold as brass—useless as tits on a bull, but full of gall. People couldn't understand the connection between himself and Sandy Gillis, my old man. My father was low key. Solid. Except, of course, when the devil was in control. Which people rarely saw. That's Angus buried over the fence. No stone there either but I know where he is. I helped put him there. Angus was Duncan's father. And Effie's.

Sextus rolls the window down, almost all the way. The rain slashes at his face. "I can't make head or tail of it."

"Take it easy," I say. "I know where he is."

We swing slowly around the loop. I have my window down, peering into the rain, feeling the lightning of the vodka in my veins and a gust of sentiment reading the names on the stones. Reynolds. Ryan. MacIsaac. MacNeil.

"Jack's right over there," I say, pointing ahead and to my left.

Sextus is silent. You can feel his dread. I stop the car and cut the ignition. We sit for a moment, listening to the weather revving up outside. He pours more vodka into his cup. I decline. He swallows it all quickly, then opens the car door and slides out into the rain. I follow.

"Just over here," I say and I walk at an angle between the stones, careful to step over the grave mounds as if my footfall might disturb what's below.

I know his coordinates. Head to foot he is between Jack Ryan and John Alex MacNeil. On either side, his neighbours are old Jimmy Charlie Fraser and Dougald MacDonald. My father is due south, one mound beyond John Joe MacFarlane. All war veterans, except Uncle Jack. You can tell Uncle Jack's exact gravesite by a shallow subsidence. Even without a stone.

Sextus stares hard but still doesn't weep. At least, you can't tell in the rain. The furious face is more haggard than I had first observed. Hair coursing with the rain into the eyes. I'd hardly recognize him now.

He blesses himself. I instinctively do the same. In the name of the Father and the Son and the Holy Ghost. Then he sinks to his knees on the soaked earth.

I'm thinking: Millie lives just over there, in the Heights. She'll probably see the car in the graveyard and she'll be asking. Oh well.

4

Around cemeteries I'm always conscious that somewhere, there's a grave waiting for each of us. I will postpone my appointment for as long as I can. It's all about time and decay. These three, my father, Uncle Jack, and Angus, I watched their decay, not knowing what I was witnessing until much later. The old man breaking down quietly from within. Angus, slowly and deliberately destroying himself with outside help, until his last pathetic moments on the side of a road. And poor Uncle Jack: victim of forces he could never even have considered. Economics, history. Life itself.

I was heading in the same direction but I decided to be different. I've learned how to minimize the effects of time passing. That's how I survive. Except when I run, I have abolished time. There is only change. What somebody called entropy. That's what I'm fighting.

A lot has changed since we buried Uncle Jack. And I am certain that I am better now than I was then. Healthier. In control. So much for time and entropy. Looking at my cousin kneeling on the wet ground beside me, head and shoulders bent as if by time, the shaggy soaked hair showing wisps of grey, I can only think: Thank Christ I saw the light when I did. And thank Millie. But you can't let your guard down. You can't let people drag you back.

The words return from the shadows of memory, like leaves in the wind:

The twelve were all, save Matthew, working class.
The priest finds relevance in this coincidence at Mass.

But what did Matthew do?
There were eleven working men like us;
And Matthew pushed a pencil, just like you.

That was a long time ago, long before I became a pencil-pusher myself.

From here in the graveyard, you could once see where I work, over at the pulp mill. Now the poplars and silver maples are too high. But you can still see the whirling clouds of vapour from the mill's smokestacks whipping high over the trees and the new houses and the Protestant graveyard across the road.

The mill was a godsend. Jobs for hundreds, thousands if you count the woods. One thing this place has is woods. Fly over it sometime, Halifax to Sydney, and you'll see. Woods clambering up and down the rocky hills, striding across ravines, wrapping the broad lakes as if to suffocate even them, contained only by the nudging sea. Mile after rugged, ragged, rolling mile. Trees. Black and green and blue-jade. You'd hardly think anybody lived here.

Generations fought the woods, an endless war for the nourishing ground. The ground fed us and our animals. The woods were the enemy, and, for some of us, worse. Imprisonment. A dense sound barrier, cutting us off from the world outside, tolerant only of its own sounds. Sounds of loneliness. Especially if you lived deep in the woods like we did, out the road they called the Long Stretch. Then the mill came. Thanks to the Swedes.

We call wood "fibre" now. And fibre means money. Money meant progress, a sudden leap into the twentieth century. At least that's how it felt. The woods between the Long Stretch and the village, Port Hastings, are all thinned out now. Almost gone. There's hardly a break between the village and Port Hawkesbury, three miles further along the Canso Strait.

Thousands of us live here now, as well as anybody lives anywhere, bombarded by the sounds and images of everywhere, and we owe it all to the woods and the Swedes who had the sense to see potential in the trees. Jack saw the potential too, but it takes more than vision to make something happen. It takes money and it takes drag. Jack didn't have much of either.

The mill came too late for Uncle Jack. Ten years sooner it might have made a big difference for him. Maybe he'd be alive now. Without it I don't know where I'd be. Maybe like him now, under the sod. All worked out and used up trying to get something going in life. Maybe a little independence and dignity. Like I have now, in spades.

I've put in more than fifteen years over there. But it's like yesterday I started working in the woodyard. Then moved inside. And when they built the high-yield, I got in there as an operator. Watching dials and pushing buttons. On my way then. Now I'm management.

Sometimes I wonder why I ever left shift work. We worked twelve-hour shifts, three of them a week, which left a lot of spare time. A lot of the shift workers have little businesses on the side. Taxis or trucking or woodlots. Imagine people with two paying jobs. It isn't such a long time ago when there were damned few around here with even one. That's why men like Uncle Jack were away so much. For me, one job was plenty. I'd put in my three twelve-hour shifts and then spend a lot of time on self-destruction.

Then I hooked up with Millie and got my act together. Got into fitness. Moved into the office, assistant personnel manager. Lots of talk when that happened, but I took the position. Fuck it. And anybody who didn't like it. I help people when they need it, but I cultivate a careful balance between being neighbourly and private. I learned to treasure privacy when everybody knew my business. There is no comfort in familiarity. But isolation is dangerous, so I have crafted a careful formula. A little bit of both. Millie helps. Two or three times a month.

5

He blesses himself again and stands up. We are both wet through by now. The chill is in my marrow.

"So where's Angus?" he asks.

"Over there."

"No stone either," he says.

"Not yet, anyway."

"You were there. When Angus," he says.

I just nod.

"Near the end of the Long Stretch, they said. His own worst enemy, Angus."

"I half thought, at least she would . . . come down, that time," I say.

"No way," he says. "She wouldn't even send flowers."

Her own father.

He looks at me, wondering what I know. About the real Angus. She wouldn't call him Angus the Giant. Or Monty. The Devil, she called him. But I reveal nothing. He has already taken enough of my privacy.

"Think of the three of them," he says. "These two and . . ." He looks at me again, inquiring.

I shake my head.

Angus and my father were together only when they were on the booze, but they were linked closer than brothers. It was always a mystery, Pa and Angus. Once friends who became like enemies, they remained bound by something closer than friendship. An unlikely experience that changed everything for them and their children. Effie. Me. Then Sextus.

They were in the war, but in different outfits. Different campaigns, for the most of it. But people say the war was a common experience for their generation and became a bond among those who were in it, stronger than brotherhood. For people who didn't know them as well as I do, that's usually enough to explain the mystery of their association. For me, there is no mystery. I know the bond. I know the unlikely story of how they came together somewhere over there. Of what happened. I know the truth.

Once Duncan wrote up a long account of his father's war experiences. It was after Angus died. There's a lot about Italy and Holland. No mention of what happened to my old man, though. Duncan tried to whitewash the truth by ignoring it. Sextus wrote a novel based on it, but he didn't even try to get near the truth.

A big word that, truth. It took me years and a lot of pain to get it. My personal possession now, not transferable, as they say. Of no relevance to anybody else.

Truth and time: you spend your whole life either searching for them or hiding from them.

"The three of them gone without a trace," he says.

"This one should be remembered," I say, bowing my head to Uncle Jack's grave.

"Not a stone among them," he says.

"Angus got a write-up," I say. "You've seen Duncan's manuscript."

No reaction.

"And of course, the old man. The stories just get bigger and better. There'll be a movie some day. Maybe with Sylvester Stallone. You'll be a rich man."

Not even a smile.

"They all deserve a stone," he says.

"Jack anyway," I say.

"We'll have to do something," he says.

"I'm game."

He's looking at me again, for some opening. I stare straight ahead.

"I'd like to see where Uncle Sandy . . ."

I turn away. "Some other time."

We return to the car, wordless. He swills vodka straight from the bottle. Passes it to me but I wave it off.

"Queer when you think of it," he says. "The five of us. Here we all are again. Too bad we can't all talk about. Things. Hey?"

The moment blows by with another rain rattle.

"So that's that," he says, lighting a cigarette. He sounds angry, or disappointed.

"I can look after the stone," I say.

"Makes sense," he says, looking down.

"Of course, I'd consult."

He just looks at me, then away.

"He is your father, after all," I say.

"A mere technicality."

"Oh, I wouldn't say that."

"You and he were closer than . . . anybody," he says.

I am listening for the undertones, but there aren't any.

"I think I was resentful," he says. "You and the old man. When you were working away together."

"I hardly think," I begin.

"I'd like to have known him better."

"What was he when he went?" I ask. A gesture of pity.

"Fifty-one," he says.

"Angus made what?"

"Fifty-seven. And how old was Uncle Sandy . . . ?"

"Forty-five," I say quickly.

He is studying the cigarette between his fingers. Then he spots something to pick at on his thumb. Nervous hands. Not like Uncle Jack's, thick and worn at the finger-ends, but steady.

"Fifty-one, the old man," he says. "Hard years. Not a lot of pleasure for poor old Jack. Or Angus. Or any of them, I guess."

"They had their time," I say.

"Fifty-one."

"Not very old when you think about it."

"You know Kennedy was only forty-six," he says.

I trace a line in the condensation on the side window.

"Wicked young," he says. "You realize that when you hit forty yourself." He is smiling.

"We could put both of them on the one stone," I say, finally.

"Assuming they're close enough. Their graves."

Closer in their graves than they ever were out of them.

"They're close enough," I say.

"You must think of him a lot. Uncle Sandy. These days. Being nearly twenty years, exactly."

"I find myself thinking more about Uncle Jack," I say. "I don't know why. I guess maybe there's more to think about there." I roll down my window a crack to let some smoke out.

"And how about yourself?" he asks.

"Doing okay," I say. "And yourself?"

He shrugs and spreads his hands, making a face. Then I take a deep breath and say: "So what about herself?" I watch closely. Then say the name. "Effie."

He looks at me carefully. Then he says, casually: "We're split. You know that."

There is no shock, no relief. No payoff.

"Say something," he says. "Or hit me. Just don't look stupid."

"No skin off my arse," I say. I look him in the eye to confirm.

"Can we shake on it, then?" he says, lifting his hand.

I can't. Shake. Or let the moment pass. I keep my hands on the wheel. "How long are you here for?"

"It depends."

"I suppose."

"Wouldn't be right if I didn't put in an appearance in Judique," he says. "Face the old woman. It's been quite a while."

"She'll be glad to see you," I say, carelessly.

"You think?"

"Well, I would think so. It's been what since you left here?"

"Thirteen years," he says. "Give or take. Queer how you let the days slide and they become years like that." He snaps his fingers. "Then you figure it doesn't matter any more. But of course that's wrong. It never goes away. The nagging, missing. But the longer it goes on, the harder it gets to face. So you push it further away. You know what I mean?"

I look out the side window.

"Not that I haven't seen Ma now and than during that time. But seeing her on a few short visits to Toronto, you don't really get much of an impression."

"I can imagine." Then I say: "You should come out to the old place, have something to eat."

He looks at me hard, showing surprise. "I'd better check into the motel. Take a shower. Get to bed early. I'm pretty bushed from the drive down. Anyway, I wouldn't expect you'd want to talk a whole lot to me."

But maybe listen.

"Suit yourself," I say. "I've got no plans. Was just going to watch the hockey game. You're welcome to come out. The place has a shower. You could stay the night."

"Can't stand hockey," he says, laughing.

"Not that interested myself," I say. "Just something to occupy a Saturday night."

He is thinking about it, staring at me, searching my face, I suppose, for motives. I look straight at his eyes. The sockets have grown deeper and darker. The liquor taking hold.

"I have a bag in the car," he says quietly.

6

I live alone in the old Gillis place on the Long Stretch. The family's been there nearly 150 years. I'm the last. Some would say I have the worst of two worlds: there's the loneliness, but the place is still occupied by the ghosts. Grandmother. Grandfather. Mother. Father. Uncle Jack. Effie. Sometimes you catch yourself waiting for people to come home.

The Long Stretch used to be just a backroad off a backroad going nowhere in particular. Now it's almost part of the village, Port Hastings, which grew a lot after the causeway changed everything.

It's nearly thirty years since they built the causeway across the Canso Strait, which separated us from Nova Scotia and everything else. Then they built the Trans-Canada right through here. Port Hastings was a dead little village before. Now it's motels and restaurants. All-night gas stations where shift workers from the pulp mill can buy milk and bread and skin magazines and smokes any hour of the day or night. There's even a little airport. Port Hawkesbury has a radio station now, blasting out American-sounding music twenty-four hours a day. One shopping mall and talk of another. And a couple of weekly papers. Everybody has TV. I've got one of those new VCR gadgets and can watch any movie I can get my hands on. Yet still, it's the old things and the ghosts that define the space I live in no matter how the place changes.

I used to go on real benders when I was alone at first, like after Uncle Jack died and Effie left. Almost sold the place during one twister. I eventually got over the binges with a bit of help and a thirty-day rest at the Monastery. The Monastery is a detox. Of course I'd never get away with it now, in this job.

Once I asked Millie if she wanted to move out here with me.

"You gotta be kidding," she said. But then she laughed and gave me a big hug. She was right.

Running was my salvation. I do about four miles a day along the dirt roads that go forever out and back. Once a week I'll do a twelve-mile loop, through Sugar Camp and the Crandall Road, through Pleasant Hill to the main drag between Hastings and Hawkesbury, back through Hastings and out the Trans-Canada and up the Long Stretch to home. People would tease me at first. Now there are a lot running, races and marathons. But I like to run alone.

It's hard to tell now that the place was ever a farm. The barn is a jumble of hand-hewn beams and grass tangled in a wind weave. It was once quite a structure. There wasn't a nail in the frame, just wooden pegs. I feel guilty for letting it go. It was one of those projects that slipped away from me. Weathered barnboards were stylish for a while. People noticed and asked for some, and before long one side was open to the elements. One night during a high wind the roof went. That was the end of it.

I've taken better care of the house. It's a fine old place. My great-grandfather built it. Millie's tried to talk me into tearing down an ugly porch at the back. It's out of character, she says. My father and Uncle Jack put it there, just after the war, before they drifted apart. It's where I keep work clothes and the clothes I run in. It helps keep the place warm in the winter. It breaks the wind.

Millie's especially fond of the enormous stone fireplace in the kitchen. That was one of my biggest projects, restoring it. My grandfather sealed it off during the war. After a lot of wallpapering and rearranging, the old fireplace was eventually forgotten except, occasionally, during a burst of reminiscence about one thing or another. That's how I came to know about it.

Then a couple of years after Effie left I'm sitting in the kitchen. I'm working on the bottom half of a bottle of Scotch and I start thinking of Jack. How he got sick here as a small boy. No doctors then. How the sickness kept him from school until he was too old or embarrassed to start. But this place didn't kill Jack. It was his leaving and not being allowed back.

Screw it, I said. And I went straight to the cellar, got a hammer and a drawbar, and went at the wall that hid the fireplace.

Then Millie came along.

About Millie. You don't have to know much. Her folks were immigrants after the war. The whole family came over from Holland, including the grandfather. I don't remember her, growing up. She was from near Dundee, on the Lakes, well out of our circuit. She went away to Toronto young, worked in a bank, drank a bit too much. Around the mid-seventies said piss on it, pitched everything, and moved back. Got a job in the bank here. That's about it.

So I'm tearing up my kitchen when I notice a large envelope held together by a string, full of letters and newspaper clippings, crumbling at the folds. Glorified accounts of what was going on overseas, mostly in '44 and '45. The letters, in a faded, laboured scrawl, were mostly from Angus to my father, soldier to soldier. One of them stood out. Something about the tone. It was more formal. Then I realized it was written by Angus to my grandfather, *about* my father, about how he was wounded. Shot. But was doing well. Dated May 1945.

Near Dokkum, the letter said, Sandy was hit by a sniper's bullet. The two biggest dangers, Angus said, were snipers and shrapnel from the shelling.

Millie told me years later where Dokkum is. Showed me on a map. Not all that far from where she was born. But then nothing in Holland is.

It was the early seventies when I found the stuff. Not long after Angus went, drunk and frozen on the roadside. Things Effie had told me about him were suddenly swirling and I was tempted to shove the letters into the garbage bags with the other junk. But I poured myself another drink. Packed the letters and clippings neatly and went back to work. I eventually gave it all to Duncan. Figured it might have some value to him. Not having a clue what he'd do with it.

7

"Jesus," says Sextus, gaping around the kitchen. "You've made a few changes."

He goes to the fireplace and bends over.

"Where the hell did this come from?" he asks, pushing at one of the iron cooking rods. It moves, squealing.

"It was here all along," I say. "You didn't know?"

"No," he says, crouched and practically inside the firebox.

"Uncle Jack must have known about it," I say.

"The old man and I never talked much about the old place." He squeals the rod again. "Never talked much, period."

He looks younger with his hair slicked back and his face flushed from the hot shower. He still has a good hairline. He is tall, and the designer cords and expensive sweater hide the lard.

"So what's the plan?" he asks, straightening up, rubbing his hands together.

"I'm thawing a couple of steaks," I say. "We'll have a dram or two. And who knows."

"I heard you were on the wagon."

"I am," I say.

He laughs. "My kind of wagon."

My real problem with Sextus is simple. I had a wife named Effie. She ditched me for him. Simple as that. And at a time when we were all stupefied by a book he wrote, the old wounds it opened. *The Day They Killed Kennedy*. It came out shortly before his own father died. A lot of people were saying it was the book that killed Jack. Then afterwards they were saying if the book hadn't killed him, the next shock would have: those two running off together. Leaving poor Johnny in the lurch.

I used to have lots of questions, like why Effie and I got together in the first place, what she saw in me, and why it changed; why he would have had any interest in her, considering his success away, her just ordinary, from here; why they did it like thieves, and right after Uncle Jack. I'd come up with answers, but Millie told me, years afterwards, Your answers are all bullshit.

"I hear you and herself had a kid," I say. "A girl?"

"Hardly a secret," he says. "What else did you hear?"

"That you broke up, Aunt Jessie was saying."

"Divorced, annulled, prorogued, cancelled. Kaput," he says.

"So," I say, "she'd be what now?"

"Twelvish," he says warily.

"What did you call her?" I ask, knowing already.

"You don't know?" he says, disbelief barely hidden.

"No."

"Cassandra." He looks at me hard. "Mostly we called her Sandy."

"Hey," I say. "The old man'd be proud."

"Her mother wanted to call her Jacqueline. After my old man. I declined."

"I think I'd've liked that better," I say, quickly adding: "If I was her. The kid, I mean."

"She likes her name. She's more of a Sandy than a Jackie."

"So do you see much of her?"

"No."

"And herself?"

"No more than I have to."

"So you drove down just for a long weekend."

"Well," he says, shifting his weight on the chair, "I have a little longer than that."

"Oh."

"Got in a little scrape," he says. "School thought I should take a week off."

"A scrape."

"Young fellow, a student. Told me to go fuck myself over something. I guess I didn't react with the kind of restraint you're supposed to have these days. Gave him a little . . . push."

I bet.

"He's out for the rest of the term, of course." He reaches for a cigarette. "Anyway, I'm figuring on packing in the teaching after this year. Not my cuppa anymore."

"So what'll you do?"

He shrugs.

"Funny," I say. "Never thought I'd see you on the shitty end of the stick for a change."

"You want to talk about it?" he asks.

"No."

He says: "Really. I want to straighten things out with all the people who matter to me around here."

"There's nothing to straighten out."

"Well," he says. "Maybe the fact she and I went . . . you know . . . aren't . . . anymore. That clears one thing out of the way maybe."

"It's been out of the way a long time now. If you'd checked before," I say.

"Well, that's good," he says. Smiling, waiting.

I'm setting the table. The storm is building a wall around the house. Trees raising an uproar, like waves breaking on shore.

"I know there's a lot more," he says.

"I read the book."

"There is the book." He nods. "And there's also the day itself."

"A school day like all the others," I say. "It was Aggie Mac-Neil told me. Aggie, who taught you everything you know about writing. She was the one that told me. 'Poor President Kennedy.'"

"I don't mean that," he says quietly. "I mean what happened at Ceiteag's place that afternoon. What happened to—"

"Leave it alone," I bark.

"I know you've thought a lot about it," he persists. "Where it originated. Something between himself and Angus. And the war. And a woman."

"But I don't have to talk about it," I say. "I don't *want* to talk about it. Nobody wants to talk about it since you wrote about it. It's all behind us."

"Some of us have a responsibility to the future."

"Well, good luck to you and your future."

Bringing him here was a mistake. Bringing him and her and all the rest of them with him. People I thought to be safely away or secure in cemeteries. Future, my arse.

"Let's just let sleeping dogs lie," I say.

Then he smiles, the one that got him all the things he has, all the places he has been, and is.

"Pour me something and then let's get those steaks under way."

You have to laugh.

Part 2

1

He ate supper like a starved person, face close to his food. Finally shoved his plate away, straightened up, sighed, burped, then tilted his chair back.

"A regular five-star chef," he says. "You must do something with the calories, to look that fit."

"I run a bit," I say.

"You gotta like . . . isolation," he says.

"Maybe."

The wine goes down like water. You forget how much you enjoy a good glass of wine.

"*Loneliness and the Long-Distance Runner.* You must have read that?"

I never heard of it.

"Believe it or not, I slept with a woman who slept with the guy who wrote that."

I should care.

"About five years ago."

"Effie slept with him?"

He laughs. "No, no, no. Somebody else. Just after I left Effie. In '78."

"It's been that long." I am surprised.

"Five years," he says. "You must have laughed your hole out."

"Didn't mean much by then."

He stares at me for a moment.

"Alex something," he says.

"Who?"

"That writer. I had a whole bunch of short relationships after I . . . moved on."

"Yes," I say. Cutting it off.

"It's good that we can talk about it."

"It was a long time ago," I say. I avoid his eyes.

"Alan . . . something. Stivel or . . . Stiletto. No."

I look back at him blankly.

"That writer's name. It'll come to me."

———

Out in Hastings, down below his place, there was the remains of an old coal pier. Near where the railway station used to be. It's all gone now. In my time it was a high black rickety structure of old timbers, great for jumping off in the summer, if you knew how to swim, or wanted to learn quickly. Once in, it was hard to get out. You had to climb up the splintery creosote. Hard to believe today but you could swim in the strait back then. That was before the Swedes came with the pulp mill. Before we pumped the strait full of old fibre and chemical crap. Making a living at it.

Uncle Jack said he and my old man worked at that coal pier in the busy days. Practically boys, they were. First paying job. Them and Angus. Shovelling coal onto boats. Coal from down north when there were mines in Port Hood and Inverness. Middle of the thirties. Jack building his strength after being sickly for years.

One day they were loading coal on a boat bound for a place

called St. Lawrence on the south coast of Newfoundland. Wicked hard times there but some American fellow was trying to start an underground mine. The place was going to take off, they were told. They knew nothing about Newfoundland or mining but this was a chance. Get out. Earn some real money. When the coal boat sailed, they went with it. That was the start of their mining.

That's how he remembered it, Uncle Jack. The beginning of liberation. By my time, the coal pier was a tumbledown relic of when the village had a purpose. A place to go swimming. Even though the old man forbade it.

"Somebody's going to get drowned there," he'd say, anger and anxiety in his face.

There was a public wharf right next to the old pier. Some of the old fellows kept little rowboats there. They'd pull a few lobster traps in the season, maybe a herring net in the summer. Some groundfish in autumn. Jack Reynolds got a nasty-looking shark in his net once. It was in the papers. We'd steal his boat when there wasn't anybody around and row out into the strait, Sextus and me, Effie, her brother, Duncan, hunting shark or whatever. One day it was just Sextus and me. Down along the shore. It was early November, I think. I was arsing around, and fell in.

I remember my hand kind of grabbing the air, and then the water closing over my head. And the jolt of terror. Afterwards you wonder: Where does the terror come from? Certainly not from reason. And something stronger than reason makes you struggle.

I bobbed briefly to the surface but could feel my feet dragging me down. My new rubber boots. Instinct said kick them off. But Pa would kill me if I lost them. So I struggled against the downward drag. Then thinking: Pa is going to kill me anyway. The sky broke over me again for just a moment, disappeared again. That's when I became aware of the underwater silence.

———

"She wasn't the only one," he says.

"The reporter," I say.

"There were a few reporters," he says. "Plus a TV personality and a social worker. And a politician. An elected member, actually."

"I guess you got around quite a bit."

"The seventies were pretty wild," he says. "They talk about the sixties, but that was just . . . experimentation. The seventies were life."

"I can't remember much about the seventies," I say. But he just motors on.

"Took a lot of chances before I left her. Fooling around on the side. Quickies on the road. One-night stands. Punishing her, I guess."

"What for?"

"Don't go looking for logic."

She'd know, had it been me. She could always read me. And I'd want her to read my anger. You'd want her to know your mind and soul so she'd know they were full of her.

"Then one night, out of the blue she says, 'We have to have a talk.' And I knew what was coming."

"So she knew."

"No. That was the killer. She was all defensive. Uptight. Said there was a friend and the friendship was getting out of control . . . handy the threshold. So I go into indignation gear. 'Where's the threshold?' I ask. 'Before or after the pants come down?' That's when I blew it."

All right, I say to myself. This is okay.

"She had me then," he says. "Didn't have to say another word. Just stared at me. I grab my coat and a pack of smokes and out the door. Excpecting her to shout something. Stop me."

"She must have known something."

"No way," he says. "She'd have used it if she did. You know her."

With me it was a brief note. Life sentence.

He says, "You must have been saying 'Serves the bastard right' when you heard."

"To tell the truth, I can't even remember how I found out."

He stares into the cigarette smoke, the way his father used to. Then says brightly, "I think it's great. You and me here. Grownups. Scars and all. But no hard feelings."

"But that's not why you're here."

"I suppose not," he says, smiling.

I'm not sure what I should say next. Don't provoke.

Eventually, he says: "Bottom line, I guess. I don't know why the fuck I'm here." He spreads his hands, preacher-like.

"I think we've grown up a bit," he says, with that smile again.

Some more than others, I'm thinking, absorbed into the sounds of the storm outside, and the vastness of the history around us. All grown up and not even looking at each other. Speaking in parables.

The loneliness of the long-distance runner, he said. Good line.

"Some grim out there," he says, tilting his head toward the outside.

The wind is rattling furiously at the latch on the porch door. Trying to get in.

"So you should have come in summer," I say.

He drains the glass. "It was hard this afternoon. The three of them there . . . planted in different, random spots. You'd never know any one of them ever had anything to do with the others."

———

Next time I surfaced, I stayed. I heard myself shouting, and the water splashing and the bump of the boat, where my arm must have been hitting. Then he had me by the hair. "Hang on!" he was shouting, but it was himself that was hanging on. Then he must have lifted me up or something, because I got my hand over the side. That's how he became special. The first time. Gave me life, a piece of his own, if only to take it away again when it was finally worth something.

2

"Home," says Millie. "Home is where they have to let you in."

And so, you go home, fear following closely like a dog. Fever starting. Like Jack got once. Romantic fever, he called it. Chilled to the core. But fear dominant. If Mother Nature doesn't get you, the old man will. So straight through the kitchen to bed. Ma there in the gloom later, hand extended to my brow.

"You're burning up."

"I'm good."

"I'll bring something."

"No. Where's Pa?"

"Down there."

"Don't tell."

"What's wrong?"

But I'm under the water again. Warm and silent. Ma told me later I was gone for three days, into the fever. Temperature over a hundred and four. It was touch and go for at least another week. I remember faces. Sextus looking anxious. Whispering something. Don't say anything. About what? The first sorrowful mystery of the agony in the garden. Duncan kneeling where Sextus had just been. Hail Mary full of grace, the Lord is with thee. I'm wanting to laugh. What am I not to say? Feeling a small hot hand on my hand under the blanket. Effie's round face, blue eyes wide and frightened, on the edge of the bed. Saying: Don't die.

"Die?"

The old man gave me a reprieve. It must have been bad. Ma said he talked about Jack all the time. Almost like he cared about Jack again.

———

"So we're here," I say helpfully.

"The way we were. More like brothers then . . . for quite a while."

I nod.

"But you were Sandy the Lineman's boy." He laughs and leans back. "Took after him too."

"Uh. No," I say, smiling at his transparent insincerity.

"Old Sandy," he says, oblivious. "There was a man. Larger than life. What I wouldn't have given . . ." Then, through the smoke, he asks: "What happened?"

I act out my confusion, raising a hand to my temple, half

closing one eye quizzically, struggling to speak. Finally uttering: "What?"

He studies my face steadily for some seconds, then says: "Shit. Who knows what? What happened to Sandy. And my father. What happened to us."

———

The face I've been dreaming and dreading looms a final time, pale as snow, eyes dark forest green. Unmistakably different from other fathers' faces. Or Uncle Jack's. Even Angus MacAskill's. Then he puts his hand on my head and it is trembling.

Even he could be gentle in the presence of death.

"Pa. What's that?"

"What's what?" he says.

I extend my hand carefully toward his head.

He laughs, touches his shattered and bloodied temple.

"Snake," he says.

I stare.

"The worst kind of snake," he says.

"Rattlesnake," I say.

"No."

"Asp," I say, remembering a comic. Little Orphan Annie.

"No," he says.

I am out of snakes.

"Two-legged snake," he says. "Worst kind there is."

Then the eyes go dark again but he laughs.

———

"The best years," Sextus is saying, "were the few years there when we were all kids. It's all downhill after . . . puberty." He smiles.

"I had the impression you kind of enjoyed your puberty," I say.

He laughs. "The novelty wears off."

"Wears off what?" I say.

He rocks back, laughing louder.

Some of us didn't even notice puberty when it happened. Just a new layer of confusion.

He's poured another rum. Determined to be grave again.

"You know she doesn't go by Effie anymore," he says.

I didn't know. "What do you call her now?"

"Me? Still Effie. But everybody else, Faye."

———

Recovery happens first in the eyes of the others. Relief that they no longer have to be concerned. Not in that particular way. The old man returns into the shelter of his shell.

I see him now clear and present. Sitting in the living room, where the woodstove is now, back to the corner. Reading the newspaper. A daily ritual with him.

"Pa. How did the snake get you?" I ask, begging an extension of the pardon granted in my moment of peril.

"What snake, for Christ's sake?" he said.

"I thought you said a snake. Bit your head."

"Oh, that snake." Silent for a while. "Caught me napping," he said finally, folding the paper.

"Oh."

"Never let a snake catch you napping."

———

"Try to picture her as Faye," Sextus says.

Hard enough to picture her as a wife—or ex—when she was, for such a long time, like a sister.

"How old were you when they came here?"

"I don't know," I say. "Seven or something."

It was in the early fifties, when people were talking about starting work on the causeway. We were an island, part of a North Atlantic archipelago. Prince Edward Island, Newfoundland, us. Every island proudly alienated from the others, and from the blob of uniformity called the mainland. To justify the loss of our uniqueness, this new causeway had to be unique. Was going to be the deepest causeway in the world, they said. Two hundred and forty feet deep in the middle. Road to the Isles, they were calling it. After some Scottish song. Road to the future and everything modern. Prosperity. Jobs for everybody. Tearing rock from the mountain called Cape Porcupine to make the magic link. Then erecting cities and factories and institutions. This is what they promised.

And I remember them at the kitchen table, pale and silent. With their coats on. Their mother was dead. It made them more grown-up than I was. Independent. Both had red hair, his cropped close to his skull. Angus had clippers, and a shaky hand. Her hair was bushy then. Angus trying to be jolly, smelling of wine. Pa with his arms folded, acting cautious. Because Angus smelled of wine, I thought.

"You've been doing all right," Angus was saying, seeming satisfied by that.

Pa nodding.

"I'm real glad," Angus was saying. "Real glad."

"Yourself?" Pa said.

"Ah well," Angus said.

You hear the details later, after they become neighbours. Disconnected bits floating free. Angus took his wife and Duncan and Effie to Sydney after the war. Got a job at the steel plant. Effie was nine months older than I was. No trouble getting work then. Angus had the credentials, had some relatives over there, in the city. He was all set, they'd say. You get the whole picture if you're interested in any part of it. And I was. In her. From day one, now that I look back on it.

Or maybe I just think that, because of later.

Angus grew up here, on the Long Stretch. Born in the city but his mother couldn't look after him after his father was killed. Put him in the orphanage. An old couple here needed a boy. Got Angus. That's how he grew up here, up the road from our place. A bit older than Pa and Uncle Jack, but they became like brothers. Until the war. In the kitchen that day, when Angus moved back, he and Pa didn't seem like brothers.

Of course it was the wintertime.

Pa looked sour when Ma offered tea. Milk and cookies for Effie and Duncan.

"Well, I don't mind if I do," Angus said warmly.

"Yes, please," the kids said in unison.

Angus reached out then, ran his fingers into Effie's hair. Looked at Pa searchingly.

"So you're going to resurrect the old place," Pa said.

Angus shrugged. "For the time being."

"Must be pretty bad over there," Pa said.

"Not so bad. They put a new roof on in '45."

"I ga'e them a hand," Grandpa said. "I and old Willie. Shingled 'er ourselves."

Then they died, one after the other. In a matter of months, Willie and the Wife. Left everything to Angus.

But he went straight to Sydney after the war. Until he had to come back.

"We got a lot of catching up to do," Angus said.

Pa made a funny kind of a laugh and turned away. When he turned like that, you could see the scarred depression near the temple, where the bullet tore a piece of his skull away.

"What's that?" Effie said, pointing.

Pa looked at her with a half-smile. His dangerous look. "You ask your papa."

Life would have been so much simpler if Angus had stayed put in Sydney. Or gone to California. Or anywhere.

There was a lot of talk in the kitchen those days. Ma and Grandma. How was Angus going to manage with two children? Then he'd come by whenever he was drinking. Usually two bottles of wine in a bag. You'd know he'd started with three. Bright's wine. I got to know the label well. I'm sure they knew it even better. They'd be with him, quiet and frightened as he sat at the kitchen table with my father talking. About the war, you'd think, and you'd want to hear everything. Everything was about war, those days. Newspapers. Comic books. Radio. There was war all over the place. Joe Larter from Hastings just home from Korea. Ma and Grandma working to distract us kids from the loud talk. But we couldn't stop watching and listening. They were our fathers talking about times past and people they knew then. Pa drinking too. Until they could hardly stand up. Endless stories. Boring stories, it soon became obvious, even to us. They never told a story that was familiar to us. Nothing like the war comics or battles, snipers or ambushes. More about shafts and drifts and crosscuts and raises. Bunkhouses. Cookhouses. Merits of trucks. Cars. Must have been a different kind of war they were in. A boring war with a lot of men like them sitting around drinking. No shooting. Except Pa got shot somehow.

Then you'd realize they weren't talking about the war at all. Not with us around.

We'd go outdoors, Duncan, Effie, and me. Leave them to it, blabbing on. Until Angus would take them home. Eventually they'd come by themselves. Then just her.

Sometimes Pa would visit their father. I'd go with him. We three kids would be outside. Which was better because we wouldn't have to listen to the same stories again. But often you'd hear them shouting inside the house. Crazy. You'd hear things smashing. Effie would put her hands over her ears and make faces. Duncan would run over, climb on a bucket or something, look in the window, his face angry and afraid and excited at the same time. Then we'd run to our place. Tell Ma, who'd just look away.

They started once in our barn, not realizing I was there. Loud talk first, then they jumped up from where they were sitting drinking. Angus tried to say something back to Pa, but his arm blurred and there was a solid wet splat and Angus went over clumsily backward. His face was all twisted, eyes closed. Then there was another sound, even more terrible. My father, face red, gasping, tears pouring down the lines of his face. I never forgot the sound. I never cry.

If we were near them when they were like that, in their warp madness, she'd stay close to me. Sometimes hanging on to my sleeve. Even holding my hand.

And I remember this. Or dreamed it.

It is summer. We are lying in a hayfield behind our barn, warm in sunshine, talking about unknown places above the clouds, beyond the bend in the road. Suddenly she jabs my armpit. Giggles and rolls away. Lightning swift, I dig her ribs before she is out of reach. She rolls back shrieking, pokes at me again but I am jabbing and grabbing for all her ticklish places. Touching flesh. Scrambling and laughing until we are touching everywhere. And then a sleepy kind of thing rises out of the warm earth and wraps around us.

"Hey!"

A sweeping foot catches my wrist, throws my hand away from her. She sits up quickly.

My father. Towering, white as a birch, turbaned with cloud. A storybook figure.

3

"Christ, you should see her highness now," he says. "You'd never know where she came from."

"She did all right, then."

"Better than all right."

"Good for her."

"Oh, yes," he says. "Way better than all right."

"And when did the Faye start?"

"A few years back. I'm surprised you never heard."

"Faye what?"

He laughs. "Get this. Faye MacAskill fucking hyphen Gillis."

"So she stayed on her own," I say. "After you."

"She was mixed up with this oldish lawyer for a while.

Irishman, full of Old Country charm and bullshit. I think
he christened her Faye. Anyway, he had a shitload of money.
Owned a couple of health clubs. Keels over one day, leaves her
the bundle and a nice house on the Kingsway, mind you."

"Health clubs?"

"See," he says, pointing at me. "There's no guarantee, no
matter how fit you think you are." He lights another cigarette.
"Some posh house she wound up with."

Long pause. Wind. Rain rattling.

"Anyway," he says finally. "Enough of that." And takes a
longer drink. But he can't leave it alone. "I remember the old
lady mentioning about you two. Early '65. I just couldn't see
it. I guess it really started, for you . . . Christmas '64?" Draws
deeply on the cigarette. Waiting for me. Finally says: "Of
course, when I saw her, the next summer I think it was, I said
to myself: Hoo-wee, that Johnny."

I don't think he expects me to answer.

"Only later, you understand. Later, when you could say the
same about myself. But by the time she had her hooks in me
. . . you say the only thing we have in common is where we're
from but . . . that's more than enough. It's only later. You start
to notice what's missing." He tests the drink.

"That's how it was, was it?" I don't look at him. "Her hooks
in you?"

"Well," he says. "You know what I mean."

I pour water into the teapot.

I remember once asking Millie, coming right out with it:
"What was wrong with me?"

"Who knows," she said.

"You know me better than she did," I said.

She took a long time lighting a cigarette. Millie still smokes.

"What's wrong with you is the same thing that was wrong with what's-his-face, your cousin with the name. Probably wrong with a lot of people."

"What would that be?"

"The same thing that's probably wrong with me and Effie and most everybody else." Dragged another big lungful through the fag and said: "Nothin'. When you get right down to it, absolutely nothin'.'"

And people wonder what I see in Millie.

I often wonder: If Angus had stayed in Sydney. Or gone to California. Or if my father had only had the sense to avoid him after he resurfaced. But the awful thing between them kept bringing them together. As if they thought that being in the same place, blending their common memories, they could somehow defeat that thing that was eating them. Find some understanding. Of course they only made it worse. And we all spent years dealing with the fallout.

Millie thinks we still are.

4

"Your father is a hero," Ma said.

I can still see her face. White as flour. Blue crescents beneath her eyes. Eyes a little crazy. The way they were before everything happened.

"How do you know?"

"He just is. An article of faith. Like the Blessed Trinity. I'll never forget when he came home. From the war. There was a party. The biggest bash the village ever had. For him. And they had a fiddler. The Germans shot him in the head and still couldn't kill him. People came from miles around. Filled the hall."

"What hall?"

"The community hall. The one you kids burned down."

"Oh. That one."

If he'd only had the brains to stay away from Angus.

Looking at Angus you'd never guess what lay within. He was dapper. That's the word you'd hear most. Always wore a necktie. "No harm in Angus," they'd always say. And he looked like a general or a field marshal. Maybe five nine or ten. Wiry. You could believe he actually talked to Montgomery once. Shortly before the end of the war, when Montgomery visited the Cape Breton Highlanders. Right after they went from Italy to Holland. I believe it. My father was hard on the outside. But you got the impression Angus was hard on the inside.

The army had a big impact on Angus. Hair always trimmed. Swore he'd never go a day without shaving. Had a tidy little moustache along the edge of his lip. Until the later days, he'd walk poker straight, shoulders back. All this, of course, eclipsed in the memory by the image from the last time I saw him. Pleading. Out near the end of the Long Stretch.

5

I remember the community hall as a big old shell, all weathered and full of ghosts. Grandpa told a story about people playing cards there one night. A stranger off the Boston boat was winning all the money. And somebody dropped a card. And when they bent to pick it up saw cloven hooves. You'd shiver, the way he told it.

There was an old piano on the second floor but you couldn't get a sound out of it. Not that you would anyway. We'd always be quiet. We weren't supposed to be in there. The place was condemned, they said. Because of the devil, I thought. Other than that piano there was nothing. Just empty bottles, and old dried-up stools of shit with bits of newspaper where people would go. I guess the older guys drank in there. And that's where I saw my first French safe. Mostly we'd go in there to sneak a smoke.

I know the fire happened in May. Sometime near the long weekend. After school. I was staying in, hanging around the village. Donald Campbell had a pack of cigarettes. Sweet Caps. I remember Donald had a new bike then. His father was the railway station agent. Duncan, Effie, Donald, and I and Sextus were there. Donald was handing out the smokes and I took one.

"I didn't know you smoked," Effie said to me.

"Sure," I said impatiently.

"Oh." Superior. By then she was developing a certain tone.

Then we lit up.

She was nine months older than I was, and beginning to enjoy it.

———

"The definitive moment of change," Sextus says, "when you think back was . . . what? What was it for you?"

"I don't know," I say. "Opening of the causeway. The mill. Lots of big moments." I concentrate on my tea.

"How about the old dancehall? The day she burned," he says. "Something poetic happened there."

"Compared to?" I ask.

"Symbolically," he says. "It was the official end of the old. Everything after that is new. People now don't have the same . . . connection with the place."

"How would you know?" I say patiently.

He laughs, flushes a little. "I suppose. I have been gone quite a while. But you do have to admit, the place has lost something."

A dancehall?

I pour another cup of tea.

The wind is making a rocking sound around the house. The rain fills our silences, slashing against the window. A cardboard box scratches as it moves along the side again. I'm tempted to bring it in but it's just too miserable out there.

"And I guess the Gaelic is gone," he says.

"A few old people," I say.

He laughs. "Wasn't it always 'a few old people'?"

———

Duncan finally took a cigarette too, lit it. He'd hesitated. Duncan was becoming holier every day. Effie was inhaling.

"You'll make yourself sick," I said.

"You're not my boss," she said.

"Well I am," said Duncan, and he plucked the cigarette from her fingers and threw it aside.

"Hey," she said, trying to see where the cigarette went.

Then Donald noticed the condom.

"Hey, look." He touched it carefully with the toe of his rubber boot.

"I wonder who that was," said Sextus.

"What is it? I said.

They almost threw up laughing at me. Except Effie.

She was staring at it, figuring it out for herself.

———

"The causeway I suppose is the true symbol of change," Sextus says. "From island to peninsula."

"Whatever."

"God made us insular," he says. "The politicians made us peninsular." He chuckles.

"That's an improvement," I say.

"You sound like the old man."

I take my cup to the stove, top it up. Whose old man?

———

Donald was squatting, poking at the condom with a stick.

"I'm pretty sure who it was," he said. "I saw Alex Joe at the garage and he had a whole bagful of these things."

"And who do you think the girl was? It wouldn't be . . ."

"Theresa," said Donald.

Theresa was in grade ten. The smart one.

Then I finally figured it out.

Effie was giggling.

"What are you laughing at, for Christ's sake?" said Duncan.

"I know what it is," she said.

"We're getting out of here." Duncan ground out his cigarette, grabbed her by the arm.

"Wait," she said.

He gave the arm a yank.

"You said Christ," she accused.

———

"Remember building the causeway? It was wild," he says. "You'd be sitting in school. The ground would shake. Real slow. You'd look out the big windows and the side would be heaving off the cape, like in slow motion. There'd be dust and smoke for an hour after, it seemed."

"What are you driving at, anyway?" So what if aggravation shows.

"Don't take it the wrong way," he says. "But thinking back to all that, the causeway and the hall and all, led me to thinking about Uncle Sandy, and all the talk. After the Swedes moved in with the mill." His face is a study in managed sincerity. He should have my job.

"We all know what that kind of talk is worth," I say.

"It's wicked the way people get speculating," he agrees.

"A lot of the speculation came from the story you told in your book."

He avoids my eyes. "Well, if you want to get into all that, we both know the speculation was rife long, long before the book." He is studying me closely now, eye to eye. And I realize I have been lured into a place he intends to revisit. No matter what I want.

———

Donald was the first to see the flames.

"Holy Jesus," he said.

I looked and the fire was curling around some old newspaper, licking at the dry wall. Sextus jumped at it, kicking it away from the wall. But it was too late. Crackling happily.

Donald beat it with a board. It roared angry then.

———

I look out the window. "If it wasn't so stormy, I'd take you in to Billy Joe's tavern, have a couple of beers . . ." Making sure my tone is light. Then I turn and smile at him. But he's looking away.

"When I was little there wasn't even pavement. Then, overnight, we're on the main drag. A truck stop on the road from St. John's to Vancouver. Whoopee shit."

"A little bit more than that," I say, sitting down again.

"True." He splashes a bit more rum into his glass. "We're also . . . what did the sign say? 'The Largest Ice-Free Deepwater Harbour on the Atlantic Seaboard' or something. What the fuck does that mean?" Though he smiles.

"We've had some pretty big supertankers."

"Oh, yes," he says. "There was a refinery. For a while. Whatever happened to that?"

"Who knows," I say. "The Americans pulled the plug."

"Wasn't there a heavy water plant as well?"

"That's gone too."

He laughs.

———

The fire truck from Hawkesbury poured water on the wreckage all night. When they first arrived the fire was leaping high into the late-afternoon sky, smoke billowing almost all the way to town on a gale that carried embers in all directions. They ran a fat hose up from the strait and kept pumping water on the roof of the Reynolds' house and Clough's store. If the store went, they said, the village was gone. Not realizing then that the old village was already gone anyway, fire or no fire. Soon to be replaced by the new roads and the world passing through.

6

I knew my father knew. Word got around. He didn't say anything at first. You just knew by the way he looked at you. Half a smile on his gaunt face.

"Too bad about young Campbell's bike," my father said.

"Yes," I said. "It got burned."

"I know it got burned," he said. "Gaddam lucky thing he didn't get burned with it."

He was looking at me too closely. Waiting for something to betray me.

My father was tough. You're a hard man, Uncle Jack would tell him. Gotta be hard to be good, the old man would snap back.

He had a lot of sayings like that. Takes a hard man for the hard road. Harder y'are, easier things go.

He was staring at me.

Sextus had that wise look, enjoying my fear.

Donald was there, standing sort of behind him, smirking.

Then my father laughed, made a fist, pressed his knuckles to the side of my head and pushed gently. I shut my eyes tightly.

"You're a bad bunch," he said.

After he drove away I said: "I wouldn't tell."

"Yeah, you better not," said Donald. "He don't kill you, we will." He looked to Sextus, who was bigger: "Right?"

"Right," said Sextus.

———

"I'm still struggling with the Faye," I say.

"You should have seen her, when she went after me. During the breakup. Fwoof."

"Hard to imagine."

"Like I was a piece of shit!"

"Take it easy," I say.

"I'm sorry," he says. "If I ever got started . . . talking about her."

"Never mind." I slide the forty-ouncer toward him.

He fumbles with the cap, hand shaking, pours into his glass. "I made a shitty husband," he says. "But I was going to be a good parent. Father. Going to be everything mine wasn't."

"Hard to blame somebody for something he isn't or wasn't," I say.

"I didn't say I was blaming," he says.

We just stare at each other. Then he smiles.

"This is her worst nightmare happening," he says. "The two of us talking. She'd shit herself."

"She knows you came down?"

"She knows everything."

I take a mouthful of tea, waiting for a real answer.

"Fucking Faye," he says. Laughing. An ugly sound, as if he's talking to himself. "Connecting up with her was the worst thing that ever fucking happened to either one of us."

"Speak for yourself," I say.

He studies my face. Then: "Things were nearly perfect in my life, you know. Free and easy. Then I got mixed up with her." Sighs, takes a drink. "Remember when we torched the old dancehall?"

"I was just thinking about it."

"It was her cigarette that did it," he says. "Her and Duncan bickering about something. I got the shit for it."

"Oh, yeah?"

"You probably didn't know. The old man found out. Then I ran away. You remember? I come in late one night, shortly after the fire. He says he's putting me on a curfew. Says he knows how the fire started, et cetera. Says, 'When the eight-o'clock siren goes off in Mulgrave'—remember how it used to every evening in the summer? You could hear it at home—he says, 'I want you in your room.'

"I just ignored him. I remember going to the fridge. He says, 'I'm talking to you.' I just pretend I'm not hearing. Then he says, 'Take that cap off your head when you're in the house.' He had a thing about caps. Would always be telling me, 'Tip your cap to a lady' or to an old person or 'Tip your cap going by the church.' Me just shaking my head. Cap on.

"Then he says it again. Something like, 'Get that gaddamned cap off your head while you're in the house.'

"I say something like, 'You can bite my arse, you're only a visitor here anyway.'"

The wind blows up outside again.

"People talk about the lights going out when you get hit. I never saw him move but it was like every light in the universe suddenly came on. And me on my arse in the corner."

"He hit you?"

"Something did. Anyway, I scramble out of there like a four-legged spider. Never stopped running till . . . Well, you know."

He was gone for three days. Nobody knew why. Everybody out looking for him, even the Mounties. Day two I found him hiding in our barn. But didn't tell. I owed him. He saved my life once. From drowning. He persuaded me that Jack was try-ing to kill him. So I helped him hide until Grandpa accidentally discovered him. I remember Jack hugging him closely after-wards, saying nothing.

"You look back now," he says, "it was a big turning point. We never got close after that." He slowly blows out smoke. "There was something about him. All of them. They really didn't seem to . . . fit. Nothing prepared them for families," he says. "It wasn't just my own old man. They were all like that. That generation. Always seemed kind of out of place around the wife and kids. Uncomfortable, like. Then it was kind of natural to assume, when he was always gone, that it was be-cause there was something about us."

"It's beyond me," I say. "I just know Jack cared. About you."

"Maybe, but I never knew it. So what the hell?"

7

I know it wouldn't kill me to share with him the things that I know. But, God forgive me, it feels good sitting here with something that he craves. After all he took away from me.

He joins me at the sink.

"Enough heavy stuff," he says. Opens a cupboard door look-ing for a dishtowel, spies a fresh forty-ouncer of rum. Brightens conspicuously. "For a guy on the wagon you've got a pretty good supply."

"That's the secret," I say. "You'll always have it if you don't use it."

"What do you say, huh?"

I look at the bottle.

"What the hell," he says, plucking two clean glasses from a shelf. Uncaps the bottle, pouring free-hand, singing: "Oh mein papa, to me you ver so vunderful." He hands me my glass, raises his own, taps mine with a clink. "Down the hatch," he says. Tosses it off in one gulp.

Then: "You can't imagine how weird it is, being here. I'm talking to little Johnny. But I can't get it out of my head how much you've become . . . both of them. You're the image of Uncle Sandy, but you're so much like the old man. Must have been all the time you two spent together. In the bush. When was it you two went away? Nineteen . . . ?"

"Sixty-four."

"Of course," he says. "Just after Uncle Sandy . . ."

8

"What really happened to Pa's head?" I asked Ma.

"What did he tell you?" she asked back.

"Snakes," I said, smiling. "Two-legged snakes."

"I suppose you're old enough to know," she said.

I don't remember how old I was.

"It was in the war. There were people called snipers. They sat up in trees. Or high up in church steeples. Or in the upper windows of houses. And they shot people who were just going about their business."

"But they couldn't kill Pa," I said.

"That they couldn't," she said.

"And did Pa get the guy?"

"I'm afraid not," she said.

Part 3

1

A stranger driving the Long Stretch wouldn't see much. Dense dumb trees jostling in spaces that were once fields. A sodden marsh. Cords of pulpwood stacked, awaiting a trucker's whim. A few unwelcoming houses.

The sun in winter struggles just above the woods, weakly tinting the grey with a rosy glow and, sometimes, in the evenings, igniting small fires of light in frozen puddles. Summer shines, but only briefly. The Long Stretch is mostly a winter memory.

Belonging to the place you see more.

My father, Jack, and Angus grew up here, closer than brothers. Jack would never say something like "closer than brothers." He'd say *t'ihck* as t'ieves. "We were *ahll t'ihck* as t'ieves around there." He'd say it with a little smile. Exaggerating his accent. Because of speaking Gaelic when he was young. Talking Gaelic left them handicapped, Jack used to say. Every time you opened your mouth. *Mouht.*

They lasted in Newfoundland about a year after their first flight from home, on the coal boat. Hellish work, Jack said. A bunch of Newfoundlanders digging a hardrock mine with their bare hands practically. Working for nothing, or next to nothing. Soaked and cold all the time. Wet rag over your face to keep the dust out. Working for hope—that this would turn into something. And it did, later, "after the three stooges left," Jack said. Turned into a real mine.

They left for Quebec in '38. First to Senneterre, then to Bourlamaque, which was great. Close to Val-d'Or. Good times then. Bought an old rattletrap of a car in Amos. Then the war started and they went home to celebrate for a while. Then drove to Sydney to join up. The Cape Breton Highlanders took two of them. Turned Jack down. "Bad wind," he said, tapping his chest with his big middle finger. "Something they didn't like in there."

Romantic fever.

So my father and Angus went to war, and Jack went back to Newfoundland. It was the same as service, they told him. Mining fluorospar in St. Lawrence. Strategic material, for making aluminum. And he joined the militia. Got some kind of uniform at least. But he wasn't a soldier, he was a miner.

The old man called Jack a zombie once. Drinking at the kitchen table long ago. During the causeway construction, when everybody was around. I barely remember it but I have this image of Jack going over the table after him. Pa, scrambling back, laughing. Grandpa caught Jack halfway and held him. I remember the sound of the table cracking.

The old man could get away with a lot since he was a vet. Wounded in action. People wondering, of course: What kind of action?

Jack worked in St. Lawrence right through the war, his destiny taking root.

Coming back from the war, my father didn't even have the accent. Talked like from away, at least in my memory. Except when he said "hard." The *r* would stick in your ear. Lost everything else, it seems.

A car drives by the end of the lane. I instinctively look to the place on the wall where light would reflect when my father would be coming home. There is nothing.

Then the phone rings, like an alarm. We both jump.

"Hello."

"Hello. Which one of you is this?"

I put my hand over the receiver. "It's your mother," I whisper. No reaction.

To the phone I say: "It's John. Is this you, Jessie?"

"Let me speak to the other fellow," she says.

I hear him say "Hello, Mom" like he does it every day. Not like somebody who's had hardly any contact in thirteen years.

Then a long silence, letting her talk.

There was a huge celebration the day they opened the World's Deepest Causeway, and the Deepest Ice-Free Harbour on the Atlantic Seaboard. Thousands of people swarmed over Port Hastings. Birth of a new metropolis on the shores of the Canso Strait. HMCS *Quebec,* lolling like a great grey sea serpent, relaxed after its wars, fired lazy shots in salute to the future. Booom-ooom-oom-ooom rolling down the flat black fjord, vanishing behind the point of land where the Swedes would build their big new pulp mill. Bless them. Air full of the fragrance of broiled wieners, and car exhaust. And fiddle music. Always fiddle music. Somebody at school drew a mural, pinned it to the big door between the two schoolrooms, showing skyscrapers. Then all the dignitaries from God-knows-where led a march across the new link, and at the head of the crowd a hundred men in kilts playing bagpipes. You knew you'd never forget it.

Jack was at our place in the evening that day, with Pa and Angus. At the kitchen table. Having a few. Pa behaving now, a special day. Jack had been working at home for nearly two years then. Like hundreds of others, home building the causeway. Driving truck.

"You'll be away again soon, I expect," Pa said.

"No," said Jack. "Going to hang around for a while. See what's next."

"The place is going to take off," Angus said. Angus always sounded sinusy and head-stuffed when he was on the bottle, which was almost always.

Pa scoffed. "We should all go," he said. "I hear there's big money to be made in Elliot Lake."

Jack kind of laughed. "You got her made right here, boy," he said. "Made in the shade."

"I'd go quick," said Pa.

Angus was silent, after making his point. Pulling at the little moustache.

Jack thinking deeply. Making plans.

―――――

"Is there another phone?" he asks.

"Up in my bedroom."

"You mind if I use it," he says, standing a little unsteadily.

"Go ahead," I say.

And he heads for the stairs. I take the rum bottle and pour a good shot into the teacup. What the hell. Drinking from the teacup doesn't seem as dangerous. Not like the old days when I'd be sucking it out of the neck of the bottle.

2

I'm thinking: They were the days of wrath. *Dies irae*. A song you hear at all the funerals around here. I heard it first at the old man's. Then after Jack's I asked Father Duncan, What's that about?

Days of wrath, he said. And I said, Perfect.

Jack tried to get established here, after the causeway. But there were no jobs for a fellow who'd never gone to school, never served overseas, didn't know anybody important. Somebody incapable of sucking up. Jack knew he'd have to make his own job.

My father was on the power commission, since shortly after he returned from the war. The Masons and the war vets had all the power commission jobs and the railway jobs. Anything to do with the government. Jack wasn't a Mason either.

This defines the difference between me and people like Sextus.

People treated me like I was lucky having a father with steady work, home.

People here used to say: Maybe if Jack had been more like his brother. Sandy, my old man. Hard. He'd have been home more. Would have been more of a father to poor Sextus. Only saying this, of course, after Sextus had become a stranger and a bit of a scandal to the place. They'd say: Poor Jack lost control of him early on. Now, you look at Johnny and see the difference. Having a man around.

Here's the memory. I come home from school with a bruised cheekbone, blood on my sleeve where I wiped my nose.

"What happened?" he wanted to know.

"Nothing," I said.

He had his hand on the top of my head, turning my face to the light.

"Never mind the snivelling. Just tell me what happened."

But I can't.

"Donald Campbell did it," Effie said.

He didn't even look in her direction. "Go home," he said. She left.

He always wanted me to be somebody other than who I was. Hard, like him.

———

There's Donald Campbell jabbing me, goading me on about Effie. Half the school standing around close. Me doing nothing. Standing there, head down, eyes on fire. "Johnny sissy, Johnny sissy," he shouts, a nickname with the awful potential of sticking to you. Like the one stuck to Hughie the Slut. And Ebenezer Lemonsqueezer. Johnny Sissy. I could be an old man, them calling me that.

Donald is jolting my shoulder with the heel of his hand, not satisfied with the effect of his verbal taunt, but it bounces off, slams into my ear, deafening me for a moment. My hand comes up suddenly, an automatic spasm, more fear than aggression. Grazes his arm, high, close to his face. Provocation. Then the nauseating smack of his fists against my face. Quick thumps. And then the smells in your nostrils. Then the taste, sweet salted blood, snot, and tears.

"I'm telling Sextus and Duncan," Effie was saying, scrambling along beside me coming home, walking fast to keep up. "They'll fix him."

"Don't tell anybody," I'm saying, thinking of Pa.

———

"What happened!"

But how do you explain that to the father who survived a thousand thumps? Delivered thousands more. Shook off a sniper's bullet, and a whole war. Who could never understand.

The hand went swiftly to my chin, thumb and forefinger rough on the jawbone.

"Come on," he said, voice quieter. "I don't care who did it. I just want to know what you did back."

Eyes locked on mine.

"See," he said, "you let somebody walk over you once, they never stop. You hear what I say?"

Me nodding against his hand.

"You can get a black eye or a bloody nose. That's nothing. But you let them get away with it . . . you never get over that."

He let go of my face, which tilted instantly to the ground.

Then: "It's my own fault . . . I never toughened you up soon enough. What are you now?"

"Nine," I think I said.

"Here, give me one, hard as you can. Right in the guts. Let me see what you've got."

I couldn't even lift my gaze from the ground.

3

I hear his footsteps. Stops in the bathroom. Toilet flush. Now I can hear the creak of floorboards in the living room. He's exploring.

He calls, "I have a photograph here. The old man's sawmill. Him in it."

"I watched him build it," I say, impatient. Where did he find that?

He shuffles into the kitchen with a photograph in his hand.

"So what about the phone call?" I ask.

"What about it?" he says.

"Like when did Aunt Jessie find out you were around?"

"Well, what's the difference," he says. "It just means now I'll have to go see her tomorrow." Something evasive in his voice, the averted face.

"Wasn't that your plan?"

"Well, yes," he says. "But you never knew how a fellow will feel tomorrow. Anyway. Look at this."

He drops the photo on the table between us. Black and white. Uncle Jack standing by the big circular saw. Hand on the long lever that controlled the carriage. Him looking like he has the rest of his life under his hand.

"He gambled everything on that old mill. Everything he saved up working on the causeway. Lost his shirt."

"I don't want to harp on it," I say. "But how many people know you're here?"

"Couple," he says with a shrug.

"Like?"

"Well. Ma, obviously."

"And who else?"

"Well," he says. "Effie knows. That's the point, eh? Make her sweat. Worrying what we'll be talking about."

"So what did you tell Effie you were coming down here for?"

"I told her I wanted to see Ma . . . maybe you."

See me.

"She thought that was pretty funny. Said I'd better make sure there aren't any firearms in the old place."

I snort. "So you're on pretty good terms," I say.

He laughs a long chortling "Nooooooho. I wanted to take the kid with me. Sandy. See the place. Let her meet people. Expecially Ma."

"So?"

"She laughed."

I couldn't stay away from the sawmill. I'd head there straight from school. Hang around until near dark. Jack would often drive me home. Running interference. Telling them I'd been helping. Now and then he'd give me some change or a dollar so I could prove that I was really working with him. I watched Jack digging in for the long haul. Not counting on anybody.

I remember Uncle Jack saying that he wanted to get the mill running by winter. The best time for cutting and hauling logs. The earth was frozen. You could get the truck a long way back into the woods. People who lived out there would cut the logs for him and haul them to the woodroads with their horses.

I take the photo from Sextus. I haven't looked at this stuff for a long time. Not since I culled just about everything with him or Effie in it. A wonderful purge. To look at him now in the photograph, I realize Jack always knew he was living short term. Maybe he got that way working in the mines. Mining exhausts itself. Miners are always moving. Standing beside the big saw, Jack could see the causeway. Once he remarked: Funny looking at something that permanent.

Roadway to a place called the future. A place that only exists if you do.

The old man would stop by the mill occasionally and watch. Even when Jack was setting it up, working alone, except for me and sometimes Sextus and Duncan. Helping. Setting up crib-work, machinery, his future. The old man would just watch Jack, hands on his hips. Jack would ask him if he'd like to take a turn running the carriage, making a cut on a log. He'd shake his head, kind of laughing. His face would be saying: This project is doomed. He was negative like that.

That didn't bother Uncle Jack.

Angus showed up, asked Jack if he needed a hand. Jack said sure. Put him down at the end of the carriageway, on the trim-mer. He'd take the slabs of wood that were cut away when the log was being squared and chop them into stove lengths. People would pay for them. Jack told him he could have anything they made from selling slabs. But Angus showed up pissed af-ter about a week and almost cut his own hand off. Jack told him to stay away.

Even though Angus MacAskill was a veteran, he never had a steady job after the causeway. Because of the drinking. And he had some deafness, I think. From the big guns. In Italy. They'd be talking about Coriano Ridge. Ortona. I saw a movie about Monte Cassin once. They said Angus would eventually be stone deaf. Duncan wrote about it later.

Ma said it was a shame Angus couldn't wear a hearing aid. He got one from Veterans Affairs. But he wouldn't wear it. There was a roar in his head and the hearing aid would make it worse. Eventually the noise inside his head would drown out everything else.

"Angus is bad news," Jack said once. The worst thing I ever heard him say about anyone.

Jack always made me feel equal, even while wrestling with the logs at one end of the mill. He'd flip them easily, pretending not to notice my struggle. As the winter settled in, the pile of logs diminished and the piles of lumber and slab grew on the other end. Two-by-fours. Two-by-sixes. Only cutting boards when somebody would come asking for them.

Then Jack would shut down for a day or two, heading back to the woods with the truck, replenishing the pile of logs.

Always working alone, unless he had me with him. My father in the background, waiting, wearing his yellow power commission hardhat. Jack wore a ballcap.

4

Remembrance Days were bad. First, they were always grim looking. The sky thick with rain or sleet, cold. It was a day off back then. The old man would be up early. Barn chores done, he'd wash up and shave. When I was really small I loved to watch him shaving. He'd stand there in his barn pants and undershirt, his arms brown to the elbow. Then creamy white up over the shoulders. When he moved his arms, muscles would thicken and swell under the skin. When you stood on his left, looking at him standing sideways, you couldn't see the mess on the right side of his forehead. I liked the smell of the lather. Hearing the scratchy sound of him sharpening an old blade by rubbing it around the inside of a drinking glass. He'd always get a couple of extra days out of it that way.

Then he'd put on his good pants and Legion blazer, the poppy and the bar of medals. He explained what they all were but I've forgotten. Gave them to the museum in Hastings after Ma moved out. He'd carefully comb his hair across the top of his head, the right side combed forward to cover the blasted patch where nothing grew. Then he'd put on the beret he wore only on that day or for Legion funerals. We'd all go in. Him, Ma, and Grandma in the cab. Myself and Grandpa, and Angus in the back, on an old car seat. Sometimes Effie and Duncan. And we'd watch the parade. He'd be in it, near the front, carrying a flag. Looking grim like the rest of them. And Angus, farther back. They'd march along the main drag in Hawkesbury, to where the war memorial used to be, at the Old Post Office. There would be quite a crowd of them back then and up into the early sixties, when I quit going. The last one I went to was November 11, 1963, only eleven days before they killed Kennedy.

After the causeway and the pulp mill, the main street pretty well died. The memorial and the Legion are up on the by-pass now. The new main street built around shopping malls. The day comes and goes now and I hardly notice. Just people pestering you to buy a poppy. Then you notice the wreaths and stuff when you're driving by.

They had the Sea Cadets in Hawkesbury for a couple of years and I joined. I figured the old man would be pleased, seeing me in a uniform. But the first time I put it on he kind of chuckled and said, "Come here and let me look at that."

I stood in front of him for inspection.

He said: "Well, well. Popeye the sailor man." Kind of singing it.

I dropped out after a few months.

After the parade he and Angus and the other vets would go to the Legion Hall. Jessie would drive the rest of us home, everybody jammed into her car.

Remembrance Days were bad because you always knew something was going to happen. Him and Angus getting hammered.

Uncle Jack shut the mill down Remembrance Day in '57. Out of respect, he said. And I could understand just by the way he said it. By the next Remembrance Day of course the mill was a dead duck.

———

The sawmill was a big mistake, Jack told me years later.

"Should have listened to Sandy. And the wife," he said. "They told me all along: 'You got no head for business.'"

He was a little bit drunk, remembering.

"Your timing was bad, that's all."

"The causeway was good. Good timing," he said. "Got me home for about three years there. Longest stretch I ever had in the place."

"But it was just a construction project. Temporary."

"But they were saying there would be lots of work afterwards. New industry."

"I guess it was too . . . small scale. Your little mill."

"I planned to expand. When I got on my feet."

"Maybe you were in the wrong place."

"You can say that again."

Jack would stand by that terrifying saw, hand on the lever that controlled the carriage, like an admiral on the bridge of his flagship. Clothes flecked with sawdust, eyes squinting against the spray of splintered wood, wincing, cigarette clenched between his lips, as the saw screamed through the log. The carriage then raced back, ready for another run. Boards and plank falling away, perfect objects of art. More than revenue. Each turn of the saw was another bite at the future. Never mind the world's deepest causeway and the big political plans. I'd come after school, help him roll big frozen logs from the pile onto the carriage. Using a peavey tall as myself. Jack using bare hands. Talking to me like I was somebody.

"You ever been to Sydney?" Uncle Jack said to me one day.

"No," I said. Thinking: Sydney, a city, huge steel mill, a massive smoking, steaming place. Pictures of it often on television.

"Ya want to go?"

"When?" I asked, blood pounding.

"Tomorrow," he said. "Going to take a load of lumber down to the Co-op."

Heart sunk. "There's school."

"School shmool," he said. "Look at me. I never went to school a day in my life."

"They won't let me."

"Leave that to me."

And the next day we went. And it was exactly as the TV showed it, except louder. Cars streaming along King's Road and red plumes of ore dust staining the sky over the crash and rumble of machinery. White steam billowing high above stinking coke batteries. People hurrying by. Confusion, but everybody knowing exactly where they're heading. Saying nothing. Small boys shouting "Post Rrrrrecord!" skinny shoulders hauled down by heavy bagfuls of newspaper.

Our first stop was at a Co-op lumber yard. Jack parked close to the door of a building with offices. Beyond it you could see huge piles of lumber, stacked precisely, saturating the air with a sour freshness. A man wearing a white shirt and necktie came out and walked around the truck. Then he and Jack talked, Jack looking at the ground, hands in his pockets. The guy went back inside. Jack jumped in behind the wheel and started the engine.

We went to two more lumber yards before they started unloading. Then we went to a restaurant. I'd never before been in one. Everything looking and smelling delicious, even the name. Diana Sweets. Everybody looking important, except Jack and me. Was too nervous to take my coat off because I had egg yolk on my shirt from the morning. From hurrying to leave before dawn. Jack smiled, told me to leave the coat on.

I devoured a massive plate of spaghetti. Jack ordered a sandwich but only ate half.

"It's a hard grind, boy," he said, smoking, watching me eat the other half of his sandwich. "They don't get you coming, they get you going."

———

"Everything was against him," Sextus says, pouring unsteadily into the glass, drinking straight liquor now. "Nobody in the village gave him one little bit of encouragement. An eyesore. That was the exact word. Mainly because of the sawdust pile. With all the other crap that was around here."

"Today he'd need an environmental impact study," I say, sympathetic.

"Fucking assholes."

Dreams die hard, people say. You read about "the death of a dream" as if a dream ever really ceases to exist. Life would be so much simpler if dreams did die. But they don't. No way. They sit somewhere in the darkness, ready to resurface in some simple recollection. And ruin everything. That was Jack's problem. And I think part of my father's problem too.

5

The kitbag always told you when Uncle Jack was coming or going. He'd never take it into the house. You'd see it on the doorstep or in the porch. A filthy canvas laundry bag, jammed full of the boots and belts, woollens and waterproof clothes he wore working in the mine. Stuff too dirty to wash. The hard-hat would be on top, a bit of scratched brown crown showing where the drawstring didn't quite close. You could see the out-line of the lamp bracket. He usually kept the kitbag in the barn when he was home. If you saw it on the porch, you knew he'd either just arrived home or was just going away. Sometime in May '58 I saw the kitbag in the porch.

Sextus says, "So he packs in the sawmill venture in . . . what was it?"

"Around '58."

"Machinery was always breaking down. Then you couldn't get a price for the lumber. Was losing money on it. Figured all along he'd have to get work somewhere, get a bit more money to put into it. Of course, he was hardly gone when the government showed up. When you think about it now, it was a blessing. The best thing that could have happened. The Trans-Canada."

It was inevitable. Part of the Future. The new causeway was attached to a road that ran clear to the other end of Canada. Naturally they'd want to build a proper highway on our side too, cross Cape Breton, then Newfoundland. Sea to sea. Just like John A. Macdonald did with the railway. But before long they're bulldozing the old houses and Mrs. George's orchard. Tearing up the fields. The new highway ran smack through the middle of Jack's little sawmill. He could see it coming and packed up before it got to him. Sold the machinery to somebody but managed to be gone before they came for it. "Didn't want to give them the satisfaction," he said.

"He was never cut out for business. Should have settled for an ordinary job like everybody else. But he had to be different."

"Don't see where he had a lot of choice in the matter," I say.

"Funny thing," he says. "One of the last times I talked to him. When was it, '69 or '70, just before the end. You'd never guess what he was talking about."

I heard it a hundred times.

"Another sawmill. Would you believe it?"

———

So I'm looking at the kitbag, when he said: "Well, young fellow . . . I'm putting you in charge of the women. Expecting you to be dropping in here regular to make sure everything is copasthetic."

Aunt Jessie jumped up from the table where they'd been sitting. Headed into the pantry rattling dishes and stuff.

He was sitting with one forearm across his knee, an elbow on the table. And he reached into his pocket and pulled out a dollar bill and handed it to me.

"Here's an advance on your wages," he said.

"Thanks," I said. "Where are you going?"

He stood up stiffly then, like an old man. And Jessie was suddenly there.

"We're just going out for a few minutes, dear," she said. "I'm driving Jack to the train. You can wait here till I get back."

Like she wanted me to.

As soon as their car was out of sight, I streaked for home.

Around that time it became clear, at least to me, that one day I'd be going with him. Predictions of prosperity weren't for the likes of me and Uncle Jack. Something false in all the promises.

Ma once asked: "What do you think you'll be when you grow up?"

My response was quick: "A miner like Uncle Jack."

I heard the old man laugh.

Uncle Jack was gone for the best part of three years after he went away in 1958. Flin Flon, Manitoba. I'm sure it was '58. It was after the causeway but before the pulp mill. He went to Tilt Cove late in '60. Maybe it was '61. That's where I hooked up with him in '64.

"We got the '58 Chev," Sextus says, "just before he left the last time. For, where was it? Flin Flon? Yeah. I remember by the car. Almost new."

Remembering by association with large events. Like buying cars.

Sextus learned to drive the '53 Ford before they got the Chev. For my money, the Ford was the nicest car ever made. Sextus just couldn't wait to get behind the wheel. "Car crazy," Uncle Jack said he was. And he seemed to have the car whenever he wanted it. Aunt Jessie was like that.

"Young people need to get around," she'd say.

And there was a lot of territory to get around in unless you wanted to be doing the same thing night after night. The fun could be just about anywhere in a radius of fifty miles. That's how lots of us got killed. Gas was cheap then, about fifty cents a gallon. If you could scrape together three or four dollars you were good for the evening. And Uncle Jack was sending money home, once he got work in Flin Flon.

He called Aunt Jessie from somewhere one evening a week after he left. He was still on his way. I could tell by the way she was talking to him that he was drunk. When she got off she said, "That was poor Jack, in Winnipeg."

"Wow," I said. "That's halfway across the country."

"Just about," she said.

"What's he doing there?"

"Having a few, I think," she said wryly. "I don't mind. I know when he's in there, where he's going . . . he'll have nothing to do but work. He never drinks when he's working away."

I guess they all told the wives that.

Jack used to joke about it: I was so far in the hole in '58 I had to go down another hole to get out of it. Meaning Flin Flon. Laughing and gagging over his own irony. Whenever he laughed it usually ended in a spasm of coughing violent enough to blow his head off.

The Trans-Canada went through where his mill was. I watched them bulldoze the sawdust pile and a lot of trash wood left behind. There had been a lot of firewood there, slabs cut into stove lengths. He'd been selling them there for ten dollars a truckload, but after he was gone people just took the wood. Filling the trunks of cars, or the backs of their half-tons. Sometimes in armloads. The last of the slabs went the night before the bulldozers came. Aunt Jessie took a picture.

The new road ate through the place and you'd think the country would never heal. It was all charred tree stumps and mud banks and big boulders with the dust and the sour smell of the blasting still on them. Today it looks like it was always there, a natural thing bright with lupins and wild roses in summer, the new spruce crowding close again.

———

"We just never clicked. Don't ask me. There are people like that. Warm, kind-hearted, good people. Draw you in, all right. But you never really know the real person. You know what I mean? I mean, your gut tells you nobody is as great as those folks seem to be. So you always wonder, what's up with them?"

"But your gut can be wrong," I say.

He looks at me, measuring.

"He wrote to me in the spring of '61, said if I needed work he'd get me something in . . . where was it? Tilt Cove. I was calling it Tit Cove. Underground labour, he said. Jesus Christ, I thought. Said no, thank ya. Got on at the pulp mill. Electrician's helper. Good money, great summer. Couldn't picture the two of use . . . bumping around in a place like that."

I say: "He never mentioned."

"Then, a few years later, you went. Hung in for what? Years." Shakes his head slowly. "Christ, that must have been an experience."

He fishes out another cigarette, waiting for me to move the subject forward. Open up some space for exploring all the unanswered questions about my father.

6

Here's truth. Duncan and Effie, white-faced in their barely managed panic, tumbling through that door, gasping: "I think Uncle Sandy is going to kill Pa."

They called him uncle too, though he wasn't.

Ma, as always, calm. Drying her hands at the sink, barely turning, saying, "John, you and Duncan go over and take the truck home so they won't go anywhere else."

Duncan looking hopeless, not having a clue how to drive. Me knowing the theory, taking the keys like I knew more, the two of us sprinting over. Duncan speaking quickly: "They came home late. We had supper in the oven. We all sat down to eat. And Uncle Sandy shouted 'Jeeeeesus!' Flipped the table up on end and everything slid down and onto Papa."

That was how it often started.

———

Duncan and I climb into a truck neither of us knows how to drive. I am too afraid to enjoy the look of helplessness in Duncan's face as he watches me turn the key and start the engine, then put the truck in gear; then stall it, popping the clutch and giving too much acceleration. And the instant terror when we see a giant figure looming through a sudden splash of light, carrying a rifle.

Duncan and I dashing home and telling Ma and hearing her say, "That's okay. I called the Mounties."

Jesus Christ. The Mounties!

But the truth is that Ma looks half ready to murder me for telling her: "They're saying Pa smashed the window out of the school porch." Saying it like I heard it, with cautious levity, people looking at me askance in the schoolyard that day. Me looking askance at her.

"At the dance? Grabbed Paddy Fox by the throat and drove him through the window? Nearly took the eye out of him? You should see it. Looks like a big blood clot?"

Her face pink with shame. "Don't you be listening to that. They just love to start stories."

"But did he?"

"Just never mind!"

"But Paddy's eye?"

"He could have got that anywhere . . . and good enough for him. The things he'll be . . . Get away with you now. With that foolish talk about your own father."

———

"We had a dog once. Effie, Duncan, and I. You must remember."

"Called Sandy," he says, smiling, "after Little Orphan Annie's dog."

"Do you remember what happened to it?"

He frowns for a moment, then says, "Killed by a car, I think he was."

"No," I say. "He was shot."

"That's right," he says. "Now I remember. Some hunter."

That's what everybody thought. But the war hero killed him. I knew right away, when I found the corpse in the ditch, looking like a discarded cardboard box at first, the colour of winter-flattened hay after the snow goes. Thinking he was killed by a passing car but seeing, as Duncan picked him up, the large ragged black hole a bullet made. Then noticing my father, leaning against a fence post near the barn, the .303 resting on the top of the fence, half-covered by his arm. Remembrance Day '58. After Jack was gone.

Should I tell him this? Perhaps, for his own good.

"Everything goes to ratshit, sooner or later," he says wearily.

To agree is to comply.

"Three guys, like brothers. Come the war, they become strangers . . . two of them like enemies, actually." Turning then, and to the side of my face: "Four of us like family. Then . . . herself and Duncan, you and I. But no mysteries there, eh? No war."

"That's true," I say.

"What, then?"

"It doesn't matter," I say. "Even ratshit goes away, in time."

He laughs softly. "When was the last time you saw Duncan?"

"Must have been around Christmas," I say. "Yes. He was over helping out the priest in Hawkesbury. I talked to him after midnight Mass."

"So what do you talk about?" he asks.

"Not much. Work. A bit of politics. Getting older."

"Did he ever give you his take on me and herself? The split?"

"He asks," I say. "Now and then. Do I ever hear?" I look at him, questioning.

He grabs the bottle then and sloshes a splash of rum into my teacup.

"Easy," I say.

"So Duncan still calls her Effie. No Faye there, eh!"

"Actually he never mentions her by name."

He laughs and says, "No wonder." Pours another splash before I can stop him. "I'm trying to get you pissed now," he says. "Trying to corrupt you."

"That's not so difficult," I say, moving my cup out of his reach.

"Because," he says, "I'm working up to a confession here."

I just stare into his face.

"My being here," he says, "wasn't the big coincidence I made it out to be." Watching me carefully. "Actually docked late yesterday. Stayed with the old woman in her little apartment in

Judique last night. Sorry I lied," he says. "Just. I wasn't ready for it. When you popped up like that. Kind of panicked." Smiles. "Quite an evening we had, Ma and me," he says. "Spent half the night talking about things."

"What things?" I say.

"We talked through a lot of stuff, Ma and me," he says. "A lot of stuff we haven't got into yet . . . you and I."

Part 4

1

I can't avoid the ripple of annoyance. Not about the silly lie. Compared to all the others he's invented, this one's pitiful. My annoyance is based on this: he has caused another shift in my scaled-down, manageable world with its tiny population. What will he do next? Sleep with Millie? I wouldn't put it past him. At least to try. But then, he'll never know about Millie. Not many do. Not even Jessie.

For a while in the early seventies, Jessie knew everything about me. In a few days, both our lives were reinvented by the same disasters: Jack going to his grave and Effie and Sextus running off together. That bonded us for a couple of years. Then, in early 1972 she swallowed a lot of pride and reservations and visited Toronto, presumably to see her grandchild.

"What do you think?" she asked me.

"Looks like a baby," I said, handing the pictures back.

"In the flesh," she said, "she's the spit of yourself."

That seemed to be staring at me, waiting.

I just laughed.

It took me longer to move on. Which is why I became progressively more crazy over the course of about five years. Until I discovered AA and Millie. Haven't seen much of Jessie since.

"Everything changes," she told me once. "From the minute we're born."

Uncle Jack's life changed the way a soft stone changes under the corrosive stroking of the wind. Mine changed in a single afternoon, in November 1963, the way a bottle changes dropped upon a stone floor. Then, in 1964, I went away with Jack. Looking for another change, hoping to become him.

It never happened. I got distracted. Aunt Jessie always said she saw it starting. Claimed it made her apprehensive, right from day one.

2

Christmas 1964. Jack and I came home from Newfoundland, from the mine in Tilt Cove where we'd been working. He'd been there for years by then. I'd been there for eight months. Jack was frightened flying, so we had to get drunk first. "A couple of rivets to hold the courage together," he'd say. It took about a dozen. Nine o'clock in the morning. We flew from La Scie to Springdale in a seaplane. Car to Badger. Train to Port aux Basques. I can't remember the boat over Cabot Strait. Or getting home.

By that Christmas, home was changing radically. Just Ma and Grandma at home by then. Pa gone more than a year. And Aunt Jessie out from Hastings at least once every day, checking. I had been away only a short time and I could see the differences. Grandpa was gone by then too, practically lost in the darker longer shadow left by my father. They were fading fast. Nothing but women left on the Long Stretch. If you didn't count Angus.

Christmas '64 was on a Friday. We got home sometime in the afternoon of the Sunday before. Had a nap. Effie came over in the evening. I couldn't believe how she'd grown up over the summer.

And she threw her arms around me. Right there. In front of Ma. Grandma too. Right around my neck. Standing on her toes. Didn't kiss me or anything. But her cool face against mine. I half jumped. And the smell. Some kind of cologne that went right to the core.

That was the beginning of it.

It still feels weird, just remembering. Her clinging to you. The tone of voice, the energy, the fullness in your arms, against your body, all strike edgy sparks at the base of all sensations. But in your head she is innocence and vulnerability. Little Effie. Orphan Annie. Nine months older than you are, but still the little sister, looking for the safety of a sibling. How could I have known, when she folded those long arms around my neck, pressed her cheek to mine? This was no embrace. This was a collision. Needs crashing up against each other.

My first trip away was in '64. And my first trip back, Christmas. The old man was gone, and you could feel his absence. And Squint MacDougall was hanging around. Another war vet. Served overseas with Angus MacAskill. Made you uneasy, the way he'd look at you. But there was Effie.

I can't believe she's changed her name to Faye.

Uncle Jack was in a funk, just sitting around the house. Sextus was in Bermuda. Bermuda? Where was it, anyway?

"Down south."

"You're sure?"

"Yes. Way south. All black people, they say."

"And what's he doing there?"

"Him and a friend."

"Friend?"

"Somebody from away."

Duncan had decided to become a priest and spent the whole time in church, or staying at the glebe house. But there was Effie.

I laughed a lot. A new sensation. Everything she said was funny. And every time I'd laugh, she'd laugh at the sound of it. Everything around us was fresh. New building everywhere, new roads. From Port Hastings, looking down the strait, you could see tall stacks with smoke and steam billowing. The future taking hold. Full of promise.

Christmas Eve, Effie and I went to town to buy each other gifts. Coming home afterwards, sitting over on my side of the truck, she said: "You don't *have* to go back there. To that Tilt Cove place."

I didn't answer. But she was right.

"It sounds so boring there. You could stay home. There's work here now."

"You never know," I said. Wondering what Jack would think.

She'd finished school while I was away. Had a job. Working at a new motel that was almost on the site of the old community hall. The place she worked was called the Skye Motel. I laughed when I realized it was almost on the ashes of the place we burned.

On our third night out, coming home from a movie, she said to me: "Take me parking." She slid across the seat, close to me, and slipped an arm behind my neck. "Come on," she said. Her voice was strange. Low.

"Where do they usually go?" I asked, feeling hot.

"What," she said, "you don't know?"

I said, quickly, "I never had anybody out from here."

"Well, it's about time," she said. And told me to drive down by the railway station and over to the old coal pier.

The station is gone now too.

I remember there would be half a dozen people on the platform when the train arrived each afternoon around five. People going nowhere, meeting nobody. Just there to feel the heat and power of the machine. Potential for change.

There was soft music murmuring from the radio. Bobby Darrin, voice like dark syrup.

I knoooow, beyond a doubt, youch, my heart . . . will lead me there.

"Used to play around here all the time, didn't we," I said.

Then she leaned into me, face very close.

My lover stands on golden saaaaands and watches the ships that go saaaailing . . .

"So let's play around again," she said, smiling gravely. Nose almost touching mine.

Before I could reply, her mouth was spread wetly upon mine.

Her kissing was enough to consume everything. Hauling the tongue out of me. Eyeballs. The breath from my lungs. Like nothing I'd ever imagined. All through my guts and groin. Almost abandonment. Could feel my arms responding as if automatically, my hands cupping her shoulderblades.

By the station platform, near the old coal pier, we were all over each other, gasping between the whispers. Car radio urging us on with slow suggestive music. Raw ecstasy mixed with the terrified knowledge that it will take an act of my own will to stop this magical flight.

I said: "I think we should go."

She started to extract herself, lightly giggling. A white flash of bra and firm bulging flesh. Her fingers fumbled slowly with the buttons. Her face resumed its weary smile.

"That's probably wise," she said.

And we went home in silence, wondering what was happening.

Suddenly glad Sextus was away somewhere. And Duncan wrapped in his own anxieties. And our parents lost to us.

New Year's Eve, the last day of 1964, Jack said: "Seen your half-ton on the road today but it couldn't have been you at the wheel."

"No? How come?"

"The driver had two heads."

Trying to be funny, but the disapproval like a bruise.

3

She was almost as tall as I was, shoulders boyishly broad, giving her a deceptively flat-chested appearance. She wasn't glamorous, but there was energy in her expression, starting with the eyes. It could make you nervous. What else? The down on her upper lip, soft as a breath. I think we found an excuse to be together every day and night that holiday. I remember there was a lot of snow and it was cold. But we'd find places to park the old man's truck and we'd talk about things. Inevitably some emotion would blow up out of nowhere and one or the other of us would reach out and we'd fuse. Naturally as anything.

————

"Something made them both crazy," she said. "Our fathers."

It was at Christmas '64 she introduced me to the worst of the demons. It came up casually. A weird joke. Her father's nerves were going, she said. A combination of the war and the drink. He'd wander around at night. Sometimes straight into her room.

"When he sleeps," she said, "which isn't very often, he has these nightmares. And he shouts out people's names. Often your father's. He'll scream 'Sandy' at the top of his lungs. He seems to be terrified of the dark," she said. "Just wanders around. Only sleeps when he flakes out. Then he wakes up angry."

It was the night before Jack and I went back to Tilt Cove. Just after New Year's. There was a party somewhere. She was invited. Had talked for days about going, taking me. Our first public appearance. A formal coupling of sorts. But when the time came, she just wanted to talk.

"Maybe if somebody talked to him," I said.

Grabbing my wrist tightly, she said: "Never. You've got to promise."

"Maybe it has something to do with the old man's problem. What drove him to—"

"No," she said quickly. "I can tell you for a fact. He hasn't a clue. I asked him a hundred times. About what he knew."

"Okay, okay," I said. "It's just that he's the only one left."

"It doesn't really matter," she said. "What's done is done."

"You can't help wondering, though," I said.

———

In January I found Jack's company disturbing. He seemed restless. Talking about heading out somewhere else. Had a bellyful of Tilt Cove. Never wanted to spend another winter in Newfoundland.

"Maybe we'll head for Bermouda," he said.

I laughed.

"Sure they could use a coupla good raisemen in Bermouda," he said. "Good raisemen are hard to find. And shaftmen."

Jack was famous in the shaft.

"But I don't suppose there's a lot going on in Bermuda," I said, smiling. Knowing more about Bermuda than he did, thanks to the TV.

"We could always ask the Bermouda expert," he said.

He didn't even call at Christmas.

Christmas was a drag, he said. Didn't even have a car. Sextus had demolished the Chev a month earlier. Home for a weekend visit. Somewhere down north, beyond Judique. Passing someone at a hundred miles an hour, the cars just nudged and he lost control. Ran a hundred yards in the ditch, then flipped. Lucky the snow was early. Two brothers from Port Hood killed in exactly the same kind of accident the summer before. Sextus and Duncan and a bunch from Hawkesbury, just touring around. Not a scratch on anybody.

It was easy to believe that Sextus was the cause of his anxiety. But that, of course, was not the whole story. Jack could see the future taking shape. Didn't like it.

Train rattling over the long railway bridge at Grand Narrows, getting near North Sydney and the boat to Newfoundland.

Uncle Jack lost in the scenery. Mountains of snow. The air in the coach hot and sleepy, stinging from cigarette smoke.

"You're dreaming about some place warm," I said, keeping it going, hoping to engage him. Badly had to talk to someone. About bigger things than Bermuda.

No answer. Train sounds a noise trench between us.

"What about Arizona," I said. "How about if we went there?" Knowing he'd worked there once, sinking a shaft with Paddy Harrison.

"What would you think of that? Going back."

No reply.

"I'd be game," I say.

The hair on the back of his neck is curly. He didn't even get a haircut while he was home.

"Pat Bellefleur was saying the Congo," I said. "They're screaming for people."

A shrug of the shoulders, meaningless from behind.

"It's in Africa," I said. "Hot."

"Big place, Africa," he said.

"I'm up for anything," I said. Settling back in the seat, giving up on him. "Just let me know." Feeling a queer restlessness.

I was equally reluctant to be going back to Tilt Cove. But for a different reason. I was planning ahead, to when I'd be back home again. I was overwhelmed by the complexity of what we had between us, Effie and me. My future paralyzed by the last night home. Out with Effie. Hearing her talk about her father. Who had been invisible to me so much of the time when he wasn't being troublesome.

The Bermuda shaftman speaks.

"I hear MacIsaac is sinking a shaft in Sudbury," he said as the train slowed down for Boisdale. "A fellow could always go there."

"Sudbury has a nice climate," I said.

4

You'd never have known she was terrified of her father. Loyalty. That's what she and Duncan always had in spades. To old Angus and to each other. She'd be holding Angus by the hand like he was survival itself. She'd be at his knee for the whole visit. His hand would go to her head as he spoke. Smoky fingers vanishing into her burnt curls. *M'eudail,* he called her. Darling. And it just seemed natural. When she was little. A lot of old people called kids *m'eudail.*

Then at about twelve, you could see a change. Whenever he was around she'd stay close to me, watching everything with that expression of indifference that she never lost. Not even after she grew up. I'd notice his face, cold and miserable. But then he'd wink and smile. Insinuating: Sandy's boy and his little *m'eudail.* Proper thing. She'd look nervously at me. But never betray any ambiguity of feeling toward him.

But after that Christmas, sitting in Pa's truck down near the old coal pier where the three of them had once worked, she talked about her terror of night. Waking to cigarette smoke, seeing the glow of his cigarette in the corner of her bedroom, then the outline of himself. In her room, her most private place. Then, discovered, he'd disappear for days. And she didn't know which was worse. The fear when he was there or the guilt when he wasn't.

"Jesus Christ," I said. "I could never have guessed it."

"I was probably fourteen," she said, "when it started to get serious. I never noticed anything funny before. Just that he always seemed more concerned about me than about Duncan. I thought that was natural. Then he started treating me different, like I was a stranger. That was tough.

"And then one night we were in the kitchen, after supper. I got up from the table to clean up. I dropped a knife on the floor. A big one. He jumped up and stared at it and then at me. And he cringed up against the wall. I'll never forget the look on his face. Like panic. And hate. I tried to talk to him. He couldn't hear very well anyway, but this was different. He was somewhere else and didn't have a clue who I was. And I just had the feeling that he was going to make a grab for the knife. He just kept looking at it on the floor, his eyes wild. But I got it first, put it in the cupboard. Then he started to cry."

"Was he drinking?"

"Less than usual."

"What did you do?"

"I put my coat on and left. After that he was always watching."

I waited, left her to say it in her own time.

"Then I'd catch him . . . he'd sneak into my room, just stand and watch me. It would wake me up. But after that, I was really scared. He'd just be standing there, in the dark. Sometimes you'd only know by the glow of his cigarette.

"Then after Sandy," she said. "After the day . . . last year. I had this queer feeling. That everything was connected. All the strangeness, in the both of them." Squeezed my hand again. "And if that was true, he might be a bigger menace to himself . . . than to me."

I studied my hands. They were trembling slightly.

"I was sure, after. Your dad. He'd be next."

She clasped her two hands on mine then, hard as she could, emphasizing her words with the pressure, imprinting them: "I'll tell you everything. But you mustn't get the wrong idea." Her face was full of entreaty. "He wasn't what you think. I know now."

"I know," I said.

"But maybe worse," she said.

I repeated it: I know. To reassure her. But I knew something different. Something that stirred anger and nausea, mingling in the gut, put a burning in my throat. I know. What he was up to. Bunkhouse education covered that. Sick stories, jokes you'd laugh at nervously, about perversions. And here we had our own. On the Long Stretch.

"You've got to get out of there," I said.

"Sure," she said. "And where to?"

"Let me think."

"That's okay," she said, moving back, wiping her face.

"I could speak to Ma . . . maybe our place."

"No," she said. "Your ma has enough, taking care of your grandma, getting her own life together."

"I suppose so."

"I'll be all right," she said. "Worse comes to worse, there's a gun there. A big rifle. Duncan showed me how it works." Then giggled and sniffed. Asked if I have a Kleenex.

"Does Duncan know about this?"

"No," she said. "I couldn't tell Duncan."

"I just want to face him," I said. "Put it right to him. What's wrong with him. What the hell was it with those two."

"Oh, no," she said. "You can never do that. He can never know I told you."

The sorrow in her voice. It never left me. Nor sharp imagined images. One dominant: A cigarette glowing in the dark. Cauterizing something in me, that ember, leaving a little black hole of intolerance.

Jack would say: A fella can't judge. Jack's way of condemning him by reverse judgment. "Poor Angus." Codewords, full of denunciation by understatement, which is common around here. Before that I might have been defensive about him. There seemed to be this tendency to blame everything on Angus. But the same people were protective of Sandy Gillis. Maybe out of fear of him. Afterwards I had a stronger feeling about Angus than Jack did. I felt disgust.

5

I close my eyes, slide down into the motion of the train, drift back to my favourite place. Running with the wind to wherever it took us. The little dog dashing close among our flying legs. Heading into the woods and becoming soldiers among the trees. Playing war, I'd be North Novies like Pa was. That was his outfit eventually, after they joined the army. North Nova Scotia Highlanders. Angus stayed in the Cape Breton Highlanders. She'd be the CBH.

And sometimes when we were sheltering from the wet or cold, within the rustly, quiet warmth of the barn, we'd talk. Mostly of the fabulous future. Some day, far off. Snuggle in the warm hay.

She'd say: "When we've finished school, we'll go to Boston. Or Toronto. Or Detroit." I'd laugh and say: "We won't have to go to those places. This place will be just as big. Or bigger." And she'd shake her head, curls blurry, and say: "It doesn't matter. I want to go somewhere else. And you have to come too."

Jack's head is rolling with the train's motion. It is just as well to leave him there. He'd be no help.

Growing up, the chemistry was different when Sextus was around. He and Duncan dominant. Older. Visitors from their own place, adolescence, making reconnaissance forays into the grown-up world. When it was just the two of us, Effie and me, that world didn't exist. We'd wander miles through the dark woods, pushing through dense thickets of spruce, with starved lower branches tearing at us. Effie right behind me. When she was in front, she had a habit of letting branches whip back where she went through.

In the open spaces, where the trees were tall and the trunks bare to halfway up, and the ground softened by a spongy moss, we'd run silently, crouched low, rifles loose in the ready hands, parallel and close to the ground. Swift and alert. Like the Indians in the show. Looking for Germans. And sometimes we'd see a real animal. A bounding rabbit, tic-tacking through the bush. And we'd start shooting. Pa-khew. Pa-khew. And argue over who saw it first. And sometimes a deer, staring with silent wary interest. We'd stare back. Usually it would be me, raising the rifle, taking steady aim. Pa-khew. It was a spy, she'd say. Or, I'd correct her, a sniper.

———

And then I am dreaming.

We are all standing in front of the barn at home. Angus and Duncan, Squint, who lived alone over the Crandall Road, Pa and Grandpa, and me. It is a cold morning. Snow not far off. There to kill a pig.

Effie isn't supposed to be here at all. Butchering the pig is men's work. Women boiled the water for cleaning up. But there she is, down by the corner of the barn, hanging over the pole fence. There is a little pen down there where we'd keep the cow sometimes, when she was freshening. Effie has her elbows over the top rail and she's watching intently. Duncan has his back to her and can't see her. Otherwise he'd have chased her away. Duncan is controlling one of the two big sliding doors. Angus has the other one. There is the hilt of a hunting knife sticking out of the top of his boot. You can hear the pig inside, thumping around on the threshing floor. I feel this great bubble of resentment toward the pig: He is stupid; he will be surprised by what will happen. Stupidity invites betrayal. Invites pity. I should have remembered.

Pa stands, legs spread, in front of the big doors hefting a sledgehammer. Duncan pulls his door open a crack. Suddenly you see the pig's snout, hear him snuffling. Duncan pulls the door a little more and the pig shoves his head and shoulders through. Grunting. Then Duncan and Angus jam him squealing there in that position. Pa swings the sledge hammer. Nails him in the forehead, almost between the ears. Whump. The pig roars and his legs go from under him. Then Angus moves quick with the knife, catches the snout, and in an effortless motion, slices his throat open.

Now the pig is struggling to get up. Wheezing. Blood gushing. Grandpa is there with a wash pan, trying to catch the blood, holding the pig by the ear. Squint helping. The pig is flopping on the ground, kicking. Squint grabs his hind legs so Grandpa can get the blood. For *maragan*. Grandpa loved *maragan*. The rest are standing watching. Angus holding the knife grimly, face red. Effie's face powder white, fascinated. Then I notice, below where she's leaning against the top rail, the tightness of her shirt under her open jacket. The start of breasts. Flesh replacing everything I knew of her.

The pig's struggle has subsided to quivering and twitching, the movements growing lazier. The eyes, however, full of accusation.

"What do you figure he's thinking?" I say to Duncan.

"Pigs can't think," he says.

Then he sees Effie and shouts: "Hey!"

And she says: "What." Defiantly.

Then they haul the pig into the barn and put a stake through the tendons on his hind legs and hoist him up off the floor. Hung upside down from a beam.

"Just like Mussolini," Angus says, laughing. Smear of blood on his pant leg where he wiped the knife. Everybody chuckles with him, knowing he'd been there. Squint had been in the CBH too. He was a sniper. A sharpshooter, they called it. That's how he got his name.

———

Besider her, leaning on the rail, "I saw them doing it last year."

"Once is enough for me," she says, sort of turning toward me. It is getting colder. Her jacket is zipped up now. She shoves her hands into the side pockets.

"What are you doing tonight?" I say.

"I don't know."

Her eyes scanning, looking for someone.

Then, motioning toward the barn door, she says, "I think they're going to town. Papa said. Did your father say anything?"

"No," I say. Then: "Who cares?"

"Well," she says, "it isn't very nice when they come home. Is it?"

I look away. Not knowing.

"Maybe it's all right for you," she says.

"No, it isn't," I say quickly. Seizing on something but not knowing what.

She looks like the least thing would make her cry.

And he says they call you Faye. How could you?

And later when everyone is gone, with the truck doors slamming and the engine starting, I am looking out the kitchen window and the two of them are in the cab as the truck lurches down the lane. The old man and Angus. Heading into town.

And Squint is staying around for a while, helping Grandpa clean up around the barn.

"Wicked with a knife, Angus is," says Grandpa.

"Aah haha," Squint says, putting another half-hitch in the rope suspending the pig.

Then the two of them coming in for tea.

The sun rouses me early the next morning, revealing through my window that his truck is neither home nor over at MacAskill's; downstairs, Ma sitting at the table, a mug of tea in front of her, just sitting there with her hand under her chin, like she's been there all night. Her face all red welts, as if slapped, but surely not. He isn't like that.

6

Sextus retrieves the photograph of Uncle Jack and the sawmill from the tabletop. Studying it, sadness in his face.

"Like day and night, they were," he says.

Tell me about it.

"Two fellows, cut from the same piece of cloth, set out in life down the same road. Come to a crossroads, go different directions."

Some crossroads.

————

Christmas Day 1964, Squint was at the house for dinner.

"You were in the war," I said.

"Uh-huh," he said, with a questioning look.

"With Angus and the old man?"

"Well," he said, "it's a complicated story."

"How complicated?"

Leaning forward, elbows on knees. "We were all in the CBH together . . . but your father . . . he transferred out. To the North Novies. You knew that?"

"No," I said. "I didn't know anything."

He shook his head slowly, studying the floor.

"So why did he transfer out?"

"Och . . . it's a long story."

Ma came into the room then and he changed the subject.

———

"The old man never really forgave me. For Christmas '64," he is saying.

"Not true," I say.

"He comes home. I'm off to Bermuda," he says, not listening to me. "He never forgave me, did he? You and him home from . . . where was it? Quebec? No. Newfoundland. Tilt Cove. Home from the salt mines. The two of you home. Special."

"Copper," I say.

"Wha'?"

"Copper mine. Tilt Cove."

"Whatever. The first normal Christmas after Uncle Sandy. And me in Bermuda. Imagine what was going through the old man's head." Swallows a mouthful. Sighs long. "What a prick I was."

Was?

"Nobody ever missed Christmas. Not if you didn't have to. A war or something. But I missed Christmas." He grinds out the cigarette, exhaling thin smoke. "Went to Bermuda with a broad from Halifax. You never met her?"

No!

"Boss's daughter. Slick like you never saw. Out of the blue she says, 'Let's go south for Christmas.' 'South where?' I say. 'Bermuda,' she says. 'Daddy's got a place there.' She was kind of the first, how shall I put it . . . mature relationship." He winks at me. "She couldn't get enough of it. So . . . how could I say no? Ma wasn't too pleased. But I half expected the old fellow would understand. I mean, he'd seen a few Christmases from away. Himself and Uncle Sandy. The mines and the war and all."

"Didn't seem to bother Jack one way or the other," I say, looking him in the eye.

He holds me there. Then: "When you get right down to it, by Christmas '64 there wasn't all that much between him and me. Not really." He laughs. "There was no dramatic breakdown. Just something gradual, over the years."

He's dabbing the cigarette in the pile of butts in the ashtray.

"Back when I was feeling sorry for myself, I'd tell anybody who cared to listen that it was because he got physical. Punched me out once. But thinking about it, honestly. It was just once. And, fuck, I sure asked for it. So. It was something else."

———

Going back to Tilt Cove after Christmas, it was clear I had to find out how much Uncle Jack knew. About Angus. About what Pa's problem had been. About their whole history. Maybe understand November 22, '63. I kept watching for an opportunity to ask him about them overseas. To intercept the proper mood, get access to their common memory. All night crossing Cabot Strait. All next day on the train. Struggling back to Tilt Cove. Looking for a chance, as the slow miles of snow and mournful spruce and silent rock crept by. But Jack was pretty sick all the way back. Wouldn't talk.

Ignorance cultivates nightmares.

Grandpa used to talk about the *cailleach oidhche,* the old woman of the night. She'll creep into your dreams, he'd say. Climb on top of you and try to crush the breath out of your lungs. Never let you see her face. Only way to get rid of her is call for the help of the Lord. Scream *Iosa Chriosd* for all you're worth. That'll get rid of her, he'd say. Faith.

"The *cailleach oidhche?*" Effie just laughed the first time I mentioned her. The *cailleach oidhche* is an owl," she said. "Grandpa was just pulling your leg."

But I know it's real.

Back in the bunkhouse, sometimes I'd wake up in the middle of the night and imagine a cigarette glowing in the dark. The sensation that I knew she felt. The steam whispering and clicking in the heat pipes.

Eventually it would be morning, the bunkhouse door slamming. Guys clumping down the front steps, heading through the frosts to the cookhouse. Or the headframe. Me still fagged out from lack of sleep.

It was then I started hanging around Itchy's on my own. Drinking with the hardcore. Sheltering in their rough company and their stories about worse.

One night I realized I was smelling real cigarette smoke. Sat up quickly. Snapped on the overhead light. He was by the door. Standing there in his underwear with his trousers in his hand.

"What are you doing?" I asked, too sharply.

He looked at me curiously for a moment, the cigarette between his lips.

"Hitting the sack," he said. "Stayed at Itchy's a little longer than I should . . ."

The end of the sentence lost in coughing.

I collapsed back on the bed.

"Something wrong with that?"

I didn't answer. Got up and went for a leak.

He was sitting on the side of his bed winding his watch when I got back. I sat facing him.

"Bunch heading for Grande Cache next week," he said. "Want me to go with them. I said I'd rather dig shit with a spoon than mine coal. But I'm going somewhere, that's for sure." Yawned. "So what's your problem?"

"Nothing worth talking about," I said.

"Maybe you're having a bit of feeemale trouble."

I pretended to laugh.

"I'll be noticing the mail coming in," he said.

"Nothing to worry about there," I said. The urge to seek his confidence suddenly diminished.

He looked at me, eyes a bit narrower than I was accustomed to.

"Anything you want to know, just ask me," I said. "You're the one told me never mind listening to the bullshit around home."

He flipped over on his back, finishing his smoke. Then said: "You should be careful before that one gets her hooks in you."

———

Her letters after that were cautious.

Things are pretty well the same, she'd say. But it's under control.

Then something like: Had my visitor again the other night. But now that you know I don't feel so spooked. Actually, I'm getting sick of it. I don't think it's sick or perverted. But you never know. Duncan doesn't know everything but I'll tell him if I have to.

She was handling it.

———

The next night over beer, Jack told me he was quitting at Easter. Take a week off. Go see MacIsaac in Sudbury. Am I interested? Better money in Sudbury. Big bonus money in the shaft if you're any good.

Guys got rich in Elliot Lake. Kirkland Lake. Timmins before that. Now it's Sudbury. I could maybe work there a few months, save everything. Go home, start something there. Maybe get serious with Effie. Start a life. You could work forever in a place like Tilt Cove and still have nothing. A scab mine, no union, no bonus, minimal pay, no benefits.

And, of course, at twenty-one, I'd have insurance coming. From the old man. Legion life insurance.

"They've got a union in Sudbury," I said.

"They have that," Jack said. "But that don't bother me."

Jack was against unions.

"Anyway, it's just time to move on."

I agreed.

Halfway down the third beer, my label peeled and piled in little balls, I said without looking: "About last night."

He looked uneasy.

"I've been going out with Effie some," I said.

"I noticed," he said.

"She's . . . not like Angus."

"The war did a lot of damage to people," he said. "Brought out the best in some. The worst in some others."

I just nodded.

"Maybe it will come up between you."

"Why would it?" I asked.

"There's *tihngs* you don't know," he said.

Tihngs.

Finally he asked: "Do you think you'll be coming with me? Or going home?"

Then his face contorted in a grimace.

My answer was lost as he folded up in a seizure of deep coughing.

Part 5

1

Effie and I are fooling around like we always did. Carrying on, Ma used to call it. I'm twelve. She must have turned thirteen. We each have pieces of wood and we're swordfighting. She dodges my thrust but loses balance, and spins away from me. Suddenly, this perfect round ass is filling the back of her jeans in a way I've never seen before. All slack and boniness, gone. And, buoyed on an adrenalin surge, I swing my wooden sword and whack the fleshy curve of her buttock more firmly than I'd have wanted to.

She freezes, then wheels to face me, "Grow up, for God's sake."

And the words sting.

I guess that's what happened when I was away with Uncle Jack. I started growing up. Effie grew up a long time before I did.

———

There was a fellow who'd bring oil to the school. Driving a big tanker truck. The girls thought he was the spit of Elvis Presley. She'd be glued to the windows with the rest of them. His name was Bobby Campbell. And there was another one named Jimmie who would park his car near the schoolgrounds and just sit there. Driving them crazy. He had shiny black hair with a few twists on front. Duck's arse on the back. They said he looked exactly like James Dean who died a few years before but whose movies were just getting here. He had the same half-closed semi-gawky mouth. And he knew who they thought he looked like. So when he sat there in the car, he slouched and smoked. And when he talked he tried to sound like an American. Kind of nasal. He'd been out of school a couple of years. Was waiting to go away to the uranium mines in Elliot Lake where all the young fellows were heading then. Anybody who wasn't away already was waiting to go away. That was what growing up looked like.

Duck's arse on the back of your head and waiting to go away.

Then the Swedes and the government announced the pulp mill. It was about 1960. And people started coming back again. Like when the causeway started. But not Jack this time. Stayed absent.

2

"So how's your ma?" I ask.

"A whole lot better than anticipated," he says, watching me warily. "I guess you haven't seen her lately."

"Drop down for a game of cards from time to time."

Realizing it's been months.

"She was pretty apprehensive about me bringing things up that might be a little upsetting."

"Like what?" I ask.

"Something about your ma and Squint?"

I got a letter from Ma. Around the same time Uncle Jack was talking about us moving on somewhere else. Sometime in February '65. Ma says she and Squint are going to get married at Easter. Don't take it wrong, says she. It's for the companionship. And he's a good man. Grandma is all for it.

I was floored. Not a year and a half passed since the day the old man . . . and her getting married again. And to Squint.

"Grandma says she can manage alone if I move over to Squint's. I don't know. Grandma's probably better off alone than with Squint here (ha, ha)."

First time she ever wrote to me in her life.

"Ah well," Jack said. "Sandy'd want that. I know that much about him."

Grandma used to call Squint the *gloichd*. In plain English, a creep.

"I suppose Squint will be moving in," Jack said with a sly look.

"No," I said. "I think she's moving to his place."

"Jaysus," Jack said. "They'll have to do a fumigation first."

"Grandma wants to live alone," I said.

Grandpa was gone by then just about a year. Since just before I went to Tilt Cove with Jack.

"Can't have that," Jack said, rubbing his chin. "Grandma is after getting a little *gliogach* herself."

"Grandma *gliogach*," I say, laughing. "Hard to imagine that."

"Dropping things," he said. "Forgetful. Wife was telling me in the last letter. Some day she'd fall down. Break a hip. Screwed then," he said. "Maybe we can get her to move out, stay with the wife."

"There isn't room at your place."

"Wife can move into the young fellow's room. Give the old

lady ours." Reaching then for his smokes. "For all I'm home," he said. "Wife doesn't need all that room by herself."

I knew Jack would take a couple of weeks to communicate his plan to Jessie, so I wrote to Effie write away: "Right after Ma and Squint, I'm going to want you to move in with Grandma. It'll be doing us a big favour. And of course, I'll be going home for it."

———

"You mind if I make some fresh tea?" he asks.

"Go ahead."

Over the sound of the water gushing he's saying, "Ma told me there'd been a bit of a . . . falling out. You and your mom. And Squint."

"Just a little something with Squint," I say.

He makes a face. "More than 'a little something,' I'd guess, to come between yourself and your mother."

"Nothing worth talking about," I say. "Anyway, how did that come up?"

He shrugs. "I mentioned to Ma that I might drop in on Squint while I'm here. Since he was overseas with Angus."

I hear myself saying: "So what if he was overseas with Angus. I've spent a long time forgetting it and I'm fucking sick of it."

"Hey hey hey," he says, holding a hand up like a traffic cop. "Take it easy. It's me. Sextus. Family. Calm down. Skip it. I'm just making conversation."

Family. That's what Squint said. As if it excused falsehood.

———

Effie wrote: "It's great, your ma and Squint getting married. She needs somebody. I feel terrible, even thinking about what you suggest. Moving in there, for your grandma's sake. But whatever happens, I'm going to have to get out of here. It just gets worse. The other night he went out and locked me in the house. He padlocked the storm door. I had to leave by the window."

———

"Ma said there was a falling out. You and Squint. I was only wondering," he said.

I say: "Sorry about that. Booze throws off my sugar. Makes me edgy."

Squint's insinuating know-all face in front of me; half smiling as he communicates gossip with the bogus authority of an eyewitness who saw nothing and knows nothing.

"What was it, then?" His voice is soothing.

"Nothing I want to go into," I say.

"Nothing to do with the Swede's wife," he says.

Then I lie: "No, no, no. Just something to do with herself. What did you say it was? Faye. Angus and Faye."

He persists. "But to alienate you from Mary. Your poor ma . . ."

"That's not true," I say. Another lie. "Ma and I stay in touch."

"I actually thought," he says, "driving up here this morning, the two of us would drop in on him. Bring a jug. Maybe get him talking."

"I don't think so," I say. "Squint's changed."

"Like. Who knows? It's nearly forty years now. If we got him talking we'd get to the crux of whatever it was with Uncle Sandy and Angus. Whaddaya say?"

I say: "Even if Squint had something to say—and I doubt it—what's the point? Like, what else is there to know?"

His face. Like Squint's was. Like everyone who has ever spoken to me with the attitude of superiority based on knowing what I don't know, assuming, as they must, that I know nothing.

"The kettle is boiling," I say.

He stands, walks to the stove. Then he heads for the door.

"Where are you off to?" I ask.

"I feel like taking a piss," he says, then stops, and looks back over his shoulder. "If that's all right with you."

———

Just before Easter '65, she wrote again to say she'd move in with Grandma as soon as we wanted her to. She knew there would be talk but didn't care. Didn't know how she'd keep the old fellow from hanging around there. But figured Grandma would control that. Grandma didn't put up with much. Would move in right after Ma and Squint, if we still wanted. They were getting married at Easter.

I broke the news to Jack, carefully. He looked at me for a long time, saying nothing. Making me want to wave a hand in front of his face, say, Hello there! Speak up! But he said nothing. Just pulled a matchstick out of his pocket, stuck it in his ear, and wiggled it around. When he extracted it there was a big brown gob on the end of it, which he examined. Then said: "Whatever you think yourself."

"I know what you're thinking," I said, feeling a trace of desperation.

"Well, that makes one of us," he said. Laughed. And walked off.

Heading for Itchy's. He was there, most every night those last few weeks in Tilt Cove.

Ma wrote once more. She thought Effie and Grandma was a great idea. You couldn't tell what Angus thought. He was on a bender at the time.

———

Leaving Tilt Cove felt like the last day of school used to. Cleaning my stuff out of the dry. Putting up with a lot of static from the guys. Tilt Cove was a place you stayed in because you had to. You lived to leave. And Jack and I were leaving. Our two kitbags packed and leaning side by side in a corner of my room, hardhats giving the top a rounded shape. Smelling like underground.

Then Jack's old buddy Black Angus MacDonald came by with a bottle of rum. Captain Morgan. I had a couple with them but he and Jack were speaking Gaelic. Stuff I couldn't follow.

Spent a few minutes in the card room, watching. There was a game going on pretty well nonstop. The usual crowd. A half-breed shift boss. The doctor. Itchy. Hubert the hoistman. A few others. Pretty intense about the cards so I didn't stay there long. Walked around outside for a while. Climbed the steep embankment behind the bunkhouse and prolonged sundown a few minutes that way. But it became instantly cold when the sun dropped.

We drove out. New road to Springdale pretty solid considering it was springtime. No talk in the car for hours. Jack seemed permanently down those days. Shaking hands with Black Angus as we left, you could see faint ripples along his jawline.

Jack bought a flask in Corner Brook. Saved it for the boat. Sipping it as we crossed the Cabot Strait, heading toward

North Sydney. Halfway through the flask, he made a few jokes about Angus. Me being almost related to him, going out with Effie. And Squint going to be my stepfather. Me retaliating: "He'll be almost like your brother-in-law." "No fucking way," Jack saying, half laughing.

He'd only recently started using "fuck" in front of me.

Aunt Jessie met the ferry. Hugged me, kissed Jack lightly on his cheek.

Ma and Squint got married quietly. A few people sitting around at our place the night before. Effie came over. Didn't stay long. Angus was there, pretty well elected.

He sobered up for the church part. It was only for family, but he was invited. He and Squint had spent a hard year together in Italy, and later in Holland. There was a little reception. And that set him off again. Got maudlin trying to propose a toast. Last seen leaning in a corner, singing "Molly Bond." *For sheee was taaall and sleeender, and gentle as a faaawn.* Then was gone for days. That's when we moved Effie into the old place.

Her first night there we sat up late talking mostly about childhood. How things change.

"There's something I have to tell you."

"What?" she said.

"The dog."

"What dog?"

"Sandy. I think my father shot him."

"Everybody knew that," she said quietly.

Everybody.

She kissed me softly on the forehead. Then shoved her hands through my hair.

"Enough about the past," she said. "If that's the worst you'll ever have to confess . . ."

And we went to our separate and chilly little rooms.
You could hear Grandma snoring.

3

The next day Uncle Jack and I drove to Ontario in Jack's car.
Straight through to Sudbury, taking turns at the wheel. Blew
through Ottawa in the middle of the night. Parliament Hill lit
up like a carnival. Made Sudbury in thirty hours. Stayed with
somebody Jack knew from Flin Flon, contracting then at Inco.

There was nothing in Sudbury. Inco wasn't hiring. MacIsaac
made some kind of excuse. Suggested Paddy Harrison and a
new shaft somewhere. Pretty vague, Jack said afterwards. Giving us the brushoff. Dropped by Falconbridge. Nothing.

"Where to now?" I asked.

"Flatten her for Toronto," Jack said.

On the way down to Toronto we got drunk in the car on
cheap Ontario beer, and Uncle Jack was figuring it was really
because he was too old.

"Forty-four isn't old," I said.

Coughing on the drag of his cigarette. "Lately I feel a hundred and forty-four."

"You should quit that," I said.

"I s'pose," he said, eyeing the cigarette. But the face was saying why bother.

We were heading for Toronto because we heard there was
work driving a tunnel there for a subway.

———

Coming back into the kitchen, Sextus shuts the door carefully behind him.

"Jesus, it's cold out there," he says.

"I thought you got lost," I say. I pour tea.

The mood lighter now. Everything cooled off. Like the weather.

"I walked down to the end of the lane—you can't see MacAskill's old place anymore," he says. "Was thinking about the old man. How he ended up. In the kitchen of that place. With Angus for company. The old cocksucker not even aware that there was a dead man in front of him.

"Then there was poor Uncle Sandy," he adds.

Oblivious to my silent withdrawal.

"Everything linked together," he says. "The three of them. This queer symmetry in the way they lived. And died. Here's to them," he says.

I raise my cup.

———

In Toronto, the contractor on the tunnel job had a shift boss from Glencoe. Jack called him on the phone. We arranged to meet him at a tavern called the Rondun, in Parkdale. We hit the place about five in the afternoon. Everybody there looked like from home. "We're going to like Toronto," Jack said, winking. A lot of local fellows drinking there. Ironworkers from Mabou. Miners from Inverness. Tunnel men from Judique, with stories from places with names like Amos and Wawa and Flin Flon. Places I heard about in Tilt Cove. Wasn't long before we were both pretty full.

In the can, a MacIsaac from Port Hood said out of the side of his mouth I could probably get something with the ironworkers at the new TD Centre. Whatever that was. "You look like you could climb," he said.

I gave it a second and a half of thought, then said, "Nah . . . the old fellow and I are partners. We're looking for work underground."

Toronto was something else. We stayed in a run-down hotel not far from the tavern.

Going to bed, I was looking at a newspaper. On page three there was a story and on the top, the name A. Sextus Gillis.

"Cripes, Jack," I said. "Look at this."

"Well, well," he said. "He's moving up in the world."

"We'll call the paper in the morning," I said. "Go see him."

Jack had his big paw on my shoulder, standing on one foot shaking off his shoe.

"Nohoho," he said. "Wouldn't want to bother the young fellow at his new job."

Then put the light out. Jack always took his pants off in the dark.

"He'd shit if we showed up," I said.

Jack laughed and laughed. "I imagine he would," he said.

Next morning, when Beaton took us down to the subway job, I knew somehow there would be nothing. Something about Toronto. The clamour of noise seemed to be saying: You two don't belong here.

Beaton took us to see the super. A New Brunswicker. Remembered Jack from Niagara Falls. But had no openings. Maybe in a week or two. Fellas were always moving around.

Jack looked at me, and I at him, and he said, "Thanks, anyway."

When we left Toronto, we drove all the way along Bloor

Street and out Kingston Road, everything thinning out as we progressed eastward. Jack looking tense.

"Look," Jack said. "Christ. There's the Scarboro Foreign Missions."

Bunch of fancy brick buildings in a field near the lake.

"Sure we could go down there and get some frigging feed," he said. "All the money the wife's poured into that place. Well. Well. That's what it looks like."

Of course we kept on going. Took forever. Watching the map, turning northward at Napanee.

"A few miles further on is where the Pen is," Jack said. Kingston Pen. "Fair share of people I could visit there." And laughed.

"We'll give 'er a miss for today."

Heading for Quebec then. Beaton had given us a name there. Cousin of his, underground captain in a place called Bachelor Lake. Coniagas Mine. Base metals and silver. Assured us that if there was nothing there the cousin'll know somebody in Chibougamau, a hundred miles or so farther up the line.

"Getting near Santa's country," Jack laughed.

And, Beaton had said, there's something starting in Matagami Lake. You'll get something. Somewhere.

Whacked the roof of the car with his big thick hand and we were off.

We spent a weekend in Val-d'Or on the way to Bachelor Lake. In a hotel. Six bucks a night. Imagine. There was a tavern in the basement. We spent Saturday afternoon and evening there. Jack went off to bed early. A pretty girl named Scotty talked to me. Told me she was a prostitute. Just like that. Came right out with it. Had a husband, working underground in Cadillac. Am I interested?

She had a heavy Scottish accent. Maybe, I said. How much?

Ten bucks. She asked if I had a room in the place. I did but Jack was in it. Could always get another one. Yes, wouldn't kill me to blow another six bucks plus the ten for her. Figured, I guess it's about time. After hearing so much about it in Tilt Cove. And I still hadn't even considered anything with Effie. So why not? Rehearsal time.

Just as we were about to leave, Jack staggered in and sat down again. Sizing her up, tuned in to her accent. Started asking her where she was from in Scotland!

Peterhead, she said.

Never heard of it, said Jack. *Bheil Gaidhlig agad?* Asking her if she could speak Gaelic! Soon she excused herself and left, laughing at us.

Some things Uncle Jack didn't have a clue about.

———

Bachelor Lake. The middle of nowhere. Tilt Cove without the ocean. In a nearby lumber camp, the inmates were worse than us. And an Indian settlement, but they avoided us. You could expect trouble any time the communities made contact. Lumbermen and Indians. Miners and lumbermen. Indians and miners. At each other's throats if there was booze around, which there always was.

There was a little French place called Miquelon about twenty miles away. I remember it only because there's an island with the same name near Newfoundland. There was a ramshackle roadhouse there. Sold booze and had a jukebox. You'd go out there now and then, looking for excitement. Hookers from Val-d'Or or Chibougamau would set up shop out there now and then.

I think mostly of blackflies and unreal sunsets. Just getting from the headframe to Ikey Ferris's beer hall, you'd be half eaten.

Jack would say: "Blackflies so bad they sit on the limbs of the trees, then fly down and bite a hunk out of you. Then fly back up and eat it."

Everybody laughing. Even the French guys. Even after they'd heard it a hundred times.

Sun set late in the north, but you'd always go out to watch. The drizzle of blood from a bruised sky.

4

"You've changed things a lot since she was here," Sextus says.

"Yes."

"So how long did she live here before you guys, you know . . ."

"Got married?"

"Yeah," he says.

"I don't know. Couple of years."

Ma went out to Squint's spring '65. Then herself moved in here. Early summer.

"Seems to me Christmas '66 you spent at our place. Or some of it," he says, winking.

"She was here," I say. "I couldn't very well."

"Absolutely," he says. "No shacking up in those days."

Grandma was gone by then.

———

According to the letters, Effie and Grandma were getting along great. "She wants to talk Gaelic all the time," she wrote. "It's nice. Makes me think of Mom though I hardly remember her now." She can call her mother Mom because she never knew her. If she'd known her longer it would be more natural. Like Ma or Mama. She was free of Angus but, according to the letters, he was dropping in unexpectedly from time to time. Always sober, she assured me. "Seems to have cleaned up his act a little bit. Grandma has a good effect on him. He's afraid of her. Like everybody else. But she has a heart like you wouldn't believe. She always insists he eat with us when he's here. Duncan doing well in the Sem."

Things become a blur after the summer of '65. Jack and I in Bachelor Lake. The drinking became habitual there. Not a problem, at least not compared to most of the other fellows there. Not like later. But looking back from now, Jack and I, pretty well every day, after work. And on weekends, a lot.

Millie has this theory: In some people, the life spirit dominates; in others, it's the death spirit. Or they alternate. Then one day the death spirit says, "Enough."

"Then she pulls the plug," says Millie.

Looking back on those days in Bachelor Lake, I can see the death spirit already taking hold of Uncle Jack. The way she claimed my old man. Only Angus seemed exempted from her attentions.

———

Effie wrote: "I think something happened during the war. Something that involved them, together. There are different stories. I talk to your grandma about how different they were after. She said they were just 'dear boys' going away. Friends with everybody. Then they came back, friends with nobody, except, eventually, when we moved over here, each other. I think Duncan knows more than he lets on."

That letter was one of the things I got rid of after she left. I've never told her what I know.

Another letter. Late '65, I think: "He landed here again the other night, drunk. Grandma put the run on him. Living with Grandma is so great. I think it's the first time I can remember feeling safe."

She had that right. Grandma made you feel safe. I think now Grandma was the only reason I survived with my head in one piece for as long as I did. She was tough and direct. Except for the clothes, she even had a mannish look. The way people get when they age naturally, men and women blending into one neutral gender. Like weathered hardwood. You didn't mess with Grandma. Hard, she was. Yet you'd never be afraid of her.

Grandma once talked to me about when Ma and Pa got together, when he came home from the war. They were going out a bit before the war.

"They'd come home from the mines. You'd think they were from Boston, the clothes on them. On the go all the time. Hardly see a hair of them one end of the visit to the other. Except for the meals. It was like feeding the army."

Ma said: "Before the war, they'd be at the dances. And we'd see them around. They were pretty conspicuous. The latest styles. Had an old car. We'd get a ride home. It was nothing serious.

"Then when he came home for good, after the war, I came up from Judique for the party in the hall. Everybody had heard Sandy'd been shot. Coming home. We were all curious. We expected everything to be like before. The old Sandy, full of fun and teasing. Then when I saw him, I just got this feeling.

He was pretty frail for a while. Then he'd come to the house, all the way down to Judique. And, well, I don't know. We just eventually decided."

I figured it out once that Ma and the old man had to get married because of me. She felt sorry for him. One thing leads to another. Before you know it there's a bun in the oven. Those things don't matter anymore but I suppose it was a bit tricky back then. You'd never ask her about something like that. Hard to imagine them the way they were. Especially my father. God forgive me, but it's easier to picture her and Squint.

———

"Do you think you'd ever do it again?" he asks.

"Do what?"

"Tie the knot."

"Ho-ho-ho," I say.

Had this conversation with Millie once and she told me we'd be damned fools and I agreed.

"Sometimes I envy those who can," he says. "I'm like yourself. Shouldn't even have done it the first time. But there you are."

He can think that if he wants to.

"Women are funny," he says. "You first meet them, the sun rises on you. Can do no wrong. A fellow gets high on it. I swear . . . Then after you live with them for a while you realize you're like anybody else. Familiarity and contempt. The two faces of matrimony."

He lights another smoke.

"The trick is to get out before they get needy. That's when everything gets sticky. Start looking for a relationship. That's the big word now. Relationship."

5

Then Grandma died.

Uncle Jack was coming along the drift. You could tell it was him by the light. Low. Hand-carried. And he always moved slowly and deliberately. No mistaking Uncle Jack. Accustomed to walking around in the dark. Spoke briefly to my partner, Proulx, a Frenchman who didn't have much English. Signalled me to follow him for a bit. I did.

"Grandma's gone," he said.

––––––

"I shouldn't have been surprised, that time I came home for Grandma's funeral. I knew for sure Effie had something in mind for you."

"Right," I say. Uncomfortable.

"Struck me funny at first," he says. "Off-putting. Like if you heard about a guy having a fling with your sister. Then I got a good look at her. Dolled up at the wake. She was really fond of you . . . You should never doubt that."

"Hardly worth talking about now," I say.

"In all the talking we've done, herself and me, she's never said a negative thing about you. You've gotta believe that."

––––––

I badly wanted to go to Grandma's funeral.

"So I suppose I should go along too," I said to Uncle Jack. "Poor Grandma." Thinking of Effie.

"I don't think so," Jack said. "We're way behind here. Counting on you and Prunes there to drive another couple of hundred feet in the next two weeks. You two manage that and you can get a good break at Christmas."

———

"It surprised me, the way she'd become one of the family already. If there had been any doubt in my mind . . . But you came at Christmas. That would have been '66."

He's waiting for me to respond.

"You stayed at our place a lot," he says. "For appearances."

I feel the heat in my face.

"Didn't fool anybody, of course," he says, smiling softly. "Creeping in at daylight. You kept forgetting that creaky stair. Fifth from the top. I had that one cased for years. Ma knew when you were getting in. You rascal." He's smiling broadly.

"Ma figured it looked queer for Effie to stay on in the house after Grandma. But they decided it should be up to you. And of course your ma, Aunt Mary, thought she should stay. Keep the pipes from freezing. Don't remember you raising any objection."

"There were other factors," I say.

"I betcha," he says. "She kept *your* pipes from freezing that Christmas."

That's all he can think about.

I told myself I was protecting her from Angus.

"He sneaks around over here too," she said to me.

"I'd like to catch him at it."

You wouldn't think we were talking about her father.

"If it isn't too much trouble for you," I said, "I think we'd all appreciate it—me and Ma anyway—if you'd stay on here. At least until the summer."

Of course come summer '67 we were talking about getting married.

———

"Women are fundamentally needy," Sextus says. "Of course you can't say that anymore in mixed company. Even a lot of guys will get all huffy if you talk like that. Sensitive types. Make me want to barf. Women aren't happy unless things are changing."

"There are lots of good women," I say. Thinking of Grandma. Ma. Jessie. Millie. Lots more good ones than the other kind, in my experience.

"Only woman you can live with is a woman who likes things the way they are. Or who's got enough clout to change things."

"You're over my head," I say.

"Not when you think about it." He splashes more rum in his glass. "It only takes one frustrated woman to make a cock-up of everything."

———

The first person I told we were thinking about getting married was Jack. Still in Bachelor Lake. Past the two-year mark by 1967.

"Thinking of tying the knot," I said.

He got that look on his face. Same one that came over him every time her name came up.

"Well, that's great," he said, fishing for his pack of smokes. "When?"

"Next summer," I said.

"Fellow'll have to start getting ready for that."

Not asking when I'd be leaving.

Weeks later he asked: "You got a date yet?"

I said, "Duncan is getting ordained in the spring. We're figuring on having him do it maybe in June. Around the middle."

"Let me know," he said. "I'll be going. If I'm invited."

Laughed at that.

That fall they made Jack underground captain, so he moved into the staff house. He could have lived in the staff house all along because he was a shift boss. But he chose to live with me in the bunkhouse. But things were changing. Distance opening up. And would continue to open up, even after he moved home, fall of '69. Something to do with me marrying Effie MacAskill. Making a Gillis of her.

It took a long time for him to get around to telling me. And when he did nothing would ever be the same again.

6

"The *tihng* is," Jack says, "a fellow never knows what you have to know or want to know. You know?"

Studying a spot on the table between us. In Ikey's place at Bachelor Lake. It's late. Everybody else gone and Mrs. Ikey giving us the eye. He's been rambling on about the early days in northern Quebec. Bourlamaque. Cadillac. East Malartic. Amos. Noranda. Good times, hungry times.

Ikey sitting with us for part of the evening, telling stories about prospecting. How he staked the Royal York Hotel in Toronto during a prospectors' convention once. Laughing his head off. Me and Jack wondering what the Royal York Hotel was all about. Ikey leaves us alone then.

Jack crushes his cigarette as if he's finished for the night.

"Poor Sandy. And Angus."

Shakes his head, thinking hard about something.

"But it doesn't seem to be a problem between you and his young one," he says.

"I don't know what you're talking about," I say. Feeling something in my gut.

Picks up his bottle, lifts it to his mouth, and empties it. Burps loudly. Making up his mind.

"One thing I always gave your dad credit for. Putting a lot behind him like he did. Except maybe when he'd have too much to drink."

"Putting what behind him?"

He shrugs, avoiding my eyes.

"Wait now," I hear myself say. "Are we talking about . . ."

He sighs. "I imagine we are," he says.

He pulls a package of tobacco and papers from his shirt pocket and begins to roll a cigarette. When it's packed, he runs the fine pink point of his tongue along the glued edge of the paper and with his large, rough yellowed fingers smooths the cigarette carefully. Then points it at me.

"I'd just say this, then. If your dad was man enough to put something like that behind him, then there's not much that any of us have to complain about."

I wait.

"It was just something that happened. Nobody will ever know why. Probably just an accident."

I say, "Just tell me straight. How did my father get hurt in the war?"

He lights the cigarette and when the flare dies from the end says: "Angus shot him."

7

Early seventies, a year or so after Angus died, Duncan came to see me. I was living alone. Here, on the Long Stretch. It was on an Easter Sunday. I remember that. You could smell the booze on his breath. He'd been working hard through Holy Week in Hawkesbury.

He asked if it was okay to come in. I figured it was about Effie. He had a bottle of Glenfiddich. I declined.

Of course he wasn't here to talk about Effie at all. He was here to talk about my old man. And about his, really. Beating around the bush. Me with the upper hand, knowing just about the whole story of our fathers by then, but him not knowing what I knew. He was writing something about the war and his father, and seemed to want to clear things with me.

Nothing to clear up, far as I was concerned.

"Actually there could be," he said.

"Not really," I said.

"The day Sandy got shot," he said. "Overseas. Do you believe they actually were together?"

"What's the difference?" I said, testing him.

"Your father wasn't shot in Germany. He was shot in Holland."

"Germany, Holland," I said. "Hardly made much difference to his skull."

He poured half a water glass full of the Glenfiddich.

"You heard about the sniper," I said.

He looked at me with that look priests learn.

"People don't realize," he said finally, "how unlikely it was that they could have been together. At any time during the war." He studied his glass for what seemed like a long time. "But, somehow, it happened. Them together. By some fluke. No doubt about that part."

I nodded, waiting.

"And the sniper? The letters you gave me back . . . when. One is quite explicit. A sniper. He states it unequivocally. And I've confirmed what he said, what Dad said, about shrapnel and snipers being the greatest dangers. In Holland. In April of '45.

"But I guess the real point is, nobody knows anything for sure. And in a few years there won't be anybody left to speculate from any first-hand knowledge."

"I guess that's one thing we know for certain," I said.

"And in the long run, what does any of this really mean?"

He stood then, studied me for a moment, his face weary. "Effie's well," he said. "And always asks about you. I hear from them, of course." Studying me with a hint of apology. "He's still my friend. She's my sister."

I was just watching.

"I don't approve," he said. "But I believe the situation calls for . . . compassion."

I nodded again.

"Compassion," he said, "is a . . . quality . . . that defines true . . . holiness. For the living. And for the dead."

He wanted eye contact. But I couldn't.

"God bless you," he said finally, raising a limp hand. Gesturing, the way they do.

Shortly after that visit he disappeared for a couple of years. Went to Honduras to do mission work. And maybe to dry out. Finished his little memorial about the war down there.

We lost track of each other after that. Until recently.

———

In the book *The Day They Killed Kennedy,* the character who is me says to a priest, "Maturity begins at the moment you know that everything you've learned up to then is probably a lie. Including this."

The priest, who is a nice post–Vatican II guy, probably Duncan, says: "There is much to be hopeful about in the word 'probably.'"

The main character in the story is a schoolteacher, the father of the troubled character who everybody thinks is me. This teacher is an unhappy fellow who, because of teaching about the Second World War, becomes obsessed with it. Gets the kids interviewing local guys who were in it. One of the kids gets all screwed up over a story some local guy tells him. The guy is full of anger and bitterness about the Germans. Turns out this kid's mother is a German lady, married to one of the Swedish newcomers working at the new pulp mill. The kid has a crisis. The teacher gets involved. Then gets mixed up with the German wife. Et cetera, et cetera. Old story. Big affair. Inner conflicts. Then people find out. He kills himself. November 22, 1963. Exactly at the moment Kennedy is being killed in Dallas. The place is still old-fashioned, in spite of the new mill. Superstitious about suicide. All the time the story is going on, nobody can say the word *suicide* or speak directly about what the teacher character did. They refer to everything heavy as "the day they killed Kennedy." The end. Got pretty steamy in places. Everybody wondering where he got all that stuff. Looking at me funny. Coming out only five or six years after the old man did what he did, the day they killed Kennedy. It hit Uncle Jack really hard. The book itself was neither here nor there. But what happened to Jack—that, I couldn't forgive.

Part 6

1

Summer 1963. The old man started acting out of character. Gentler in his own rough way.

I was helping out. Haymaking. I was suddenly almost as tall as he was. Surprised to discover I was starting to look like him too. People would comment: especially around the eyes. Getting those Gillis eyes.

Also getting the odd day working for pay. Usually on a pulp truck. People stockpiling pulpwood then. The new mill was starting up. Hard work, hauling pulp and haymaking, before the mechanical revolution around here when everybody went crazy for gadgets. Now a lot of them just shrinkwrap the hay and leave it in the field. And haul pulpwood without ever touching a stick of it. Back then it was forking the hay and slinging wood with a pulphook. Building muscle. I'd catch the old man sizing me up.

July was always hot. Evenings you'd want to go into the village. It was cooler there, alongside the strait. Sit out in front of Mrs. Lew's canteen, have a soft drink, watch the world come and go. Lots of cars roaring around then. Money to burn, for a change.

A Friday night, Effie and I are sitting side by side on pop cases. You can tell she's giving the eye to a car parked in front. A '58 Mercury with Ontario plates. A continental kit on the back end. Big whip aerial. Two guys in the front gabbing and laughing in loud bursts. Their radio blaring *Out in the west Texas town of El Paso I fell in love with a Mexican giiiiirl* . . . Good old Marty Robbins, helping us all pass the balmy boring summer evening.

Paddy Fox is inside. He's leaning out through the open hatch where people buy things. His eye has a permanent red blob in it, like some eggs you open up. Burst blood vessel, I guess. A reminder of my old man.

There there's the crunch of gravel as a big black Chrysler pulls in and slides to a stop. A ghost gets out: white skin, white-blonde hair, white blouse open down to there, and tiny tight white shorts. Three strides and she's up the steps, standing near enough to smell, and ordering a pack of Kools and a bottle of Lime Rickey. Our eyes meet. She's like nobody from around here. And as she turns she stops and looks at me again, almost staring. Smiles and says hello. Then asks what my name is. Has an accent.

I struggle to stand up and say, John Gillis. And she says, Is that a common name around here? Gillis? And I say, Pretty common. She smiles and says, Nice to meet you, John Gillis, and she trots down to the car. And is quickly gone.

"There you go," says Effie. "An older woman for you."

She looked to be about mid-thirties. Little thrills ping in my midsection.

"What do you think, Paddy?" says Effie.

"That's eatin' stuff," says Paddy.

Mrs. Lew is at the window, wiping her hands on a ragged dishtowel.

"That's one of the new Swedes," she says.

———

The old man took his vacation for our haymaking so Grandpa and I didn't have to do it all ourselves. That was weird. He usually only took a vacation in hunting season. Hated haymaking, he said. From the time he was a kid. We still used a horse back then. Mostly to humour Grandpa. We could have had a tractor. But Grandpa like harnessing old Tony, cutting and raking the way he'd always done it. Used Pa's half-ton to haul it to the barn. My father and I did the heavy stuff. Grandpa and Tony both knew they didn't have much more haymaking left in them.

The work Pa did, the way he lived, kept him lean. When he was stripped to the waist under the baking July haymaking sun, you could see the long stringy muscles tense under the milky skin. Uncle Jack tended more to bulk. You'd never notice his physical power unless you got to see his bare back when he was moving his arms around. Like taking off a pullover. You'd see the thick muscles knotting behind the shoulder, neck bulging. Jack was stronger than the old man, but the old man was quicker.

"The old man was kind of like a big friendly dog," Sextus said once. "Uncle Sandy was like a cat."

Near the end Pa seemed to be trying to open up. By then, of course, people were conditioned by his isolation.

Haymaking that summer, my father would have a case of Schooner behind the seat of the truck. Would sip one between loads.

"Want one?" he asked me once, grinning.

Me wondering if he meant it, or was setting a trap.

"No thanks," I said.

Grandpa watching cautiously.

"Here. Take a sip," Pa said, holding the bottle toward me.

I took it, raised it carefully to my lips, watching his eyes as I did.

The beer stung the tongue, hot and sour.

I grimaced and handed the bottle back.

He roared laughing.

———

The evening closed in quickly behind the Chrysler. Seemed to leave everything moving gently and rustly, like a flag stirred by a sudden breeze. You felt an absence. The music coming from the car with Ontario plates had gone gentler, a mournful Acker Bilk tune, "Stranger on the Shore." Effie kind of swaying, sitting on the pop case, looking dreamy. Then the door of the Merc swings open and one of them calls out, kind of rough, "Hey, Eff-ay. Come 'ere."

She stands, stretches, and says, "What."

"We're going to the dance in Creignish. Wanna come?"

"Sure," she says without a moment's hesitation and is gone, door slamming and engine starting simultaneously, tires popping gravel then hitting pavement with a little screech. The continental extension on the rearend almost touching when they accelerated. Then gone, taillights disappearing up over the graveyard hill. Me left with Paddy and his bad eye.

Got up and stretched, like nothing mattered.

Before beginning the long walk home I said to Mrs. Lew, "Give me a pack of cigarettes."

"What do you want?" she asked.

"Gimme a pack of those Kools," I said.

―――――

Two days later I saw the Chrysler in town. I was standing with Pa and Squint on the sidewalk near the old town hall. Noticed them staring at somebody walking along the other side of the street. Squint saying, *"Tha i muineil . . . ,"* laughing strangely, gawking. Pa looking nervous, knowing I was near. Watching the Swede's wife crossing the street wearing tight pants called pedal-pushers. Me knowing what *Tha i muineil* meant. Figured it out.

Me. Too young to understand that grown men remain randy adolescents.

Except Pa was looking like he was seeing a real ghost.

―――――

"They say the worst thing the father can do is make himself hard to forget," Sextus says, puffing smoke.

"Who said that?"

"Who knows? Sometimes the less they say the more they leave behind."

"I never had much of a problem forgetting the old man," I say, feeling the ghostly presence of him again.

―――――

A Saturday evening, the day we finished putting the hay in, Pa said to me, "What are you now, anyway? Sixteen, is it?"

I nodded. Seventeen in October.

"I suppose you'll be wanting your driver's licence soon."

"I'd like that," I said cautiously.

"What's stopping you?"

"Well," I said, allowing a nervous laugh, "I'd have to learn first."

"Bullshit," he said. "You can drive. You've been practising."

I'd been at the wheel, putting the hay in. Could see him watching closely.

"Well," I said, "just in the yard. And around the field. Nowhere with traffic."

"Not on the road?" He looked skeptical.

"No," I said.

"Well. It's about time, then. Let's go."

"But I don't have a beginner's," I said.

"Fuck the beginner's," he said.

A word he rarely used around me before that. His way of opening up, I guess.

We drove out through Sugar Camp. At the turn off to West Bay Road he said keep going. When we got to Glenora Road, he said take a left. I figured I'd turn back at Dan Alex MacIntyre's lane but he said keep going again. Alex Lamey's then. But he said no, hang a left on the Trans-Canada.

"The Mounties will be around," I said. "It's the weekend. We can turn up MacIntyre's Mountain."

"Fuck the Mounties," he said.

Me driving along about forty miles per hour, hands leaving imprints on the steering wheel, eyes bugging out of my head, blood pressure through the roof, and a feeling like sexual excitement right in the pit of my groin. Wanting to pass somebody I knew. Toot the horn, wave casually at people. Especially Effie. Imagining the half-ton as a Monarch. One better than a Mercury. With Hollywood mufflers gurgling.

Near the General Line, Pa said, "I want you to turn up there. I want to show you something."

By then he had a pint bottle in his hand. Must have been in his pocket. Or stashed under the seat.

A couple of miles up the dirt road he said, "Keep left at the intersection, by the old John H. place. Towards Creignish Rear." Going by Shimon Angus's place he nods toward the old farm: "Did you know that Shimon Angus had twenty-seven kids?"

I said I didn't know that.

"From three wives," he said. "The pope gave him a medal."

I think he expects me to laugh.

"Jack's Jessie was saying they should have gave the medal to the women."

A mile or so past Shimon Angus's the road breaks out of the trees and suddenly you can see you're on the top of Creignish Mountain and St. Georges Bay is spread out in a great blue sheet in front of you. At the foot of the mountain, the houses of Creignish are strewn along Route 19, with the church among them. Stella Maris, Star of the Sea. Stuck on the top of a fold in the mountainside, the graveyard rolling off to the right, and the dancehall in front, just across the road, back to the windy gulf. This is where everybody goes on Friday nights to dance and drink and fight and pick up women.

He swigs straight from his bottle and screws the cap back on.

"This is the prettiest place in the world," he says, staring out into the bay.

I'd pulled over to the side, on his instruction.

"I've seen a lot of the world, you know," he said, looking in my direction.

I nod.

"You know that," he said.

"Yes."

"So you know I know what I'm talking about."

"Yes."

"There were places I've seen . . . would have been nice. Holland was too flat. But France. Belgium. Even Holland, though. You should see the nice farms there. Big meadows. Dikes holding the water back."

"And windmills?"

"Big jeezly windmills. Like the books. Canals too."

"Nice people?"

"Oh, yeah." Then, looking back out toward the bay: "But this here's the place, hey?"

White clouds are turning pink, like smoke over a fire.

"Over to the right," Pa said. "You can't see it from here. Used to be a fellow they called Wild Archie. Fished out of Gloucester, Mass." He takes a swallow. "One night he's in a barroom, Wild Archie. In Gloucester, Mass. Gets into a tangle with another fellow. The guy shoots him."

"Shoots him?"

"Shoots him. Bullet passes an inch from his heart. Last thing Wild Archie did was kill the guy who shot him. Bare hands. Before he died. They brought him home, Wild Archie. Buried him down there somewhere."

He's looking out, toward the rest of the world. Face tight from booze.

Not thinking it through, I said: "You got shot once, Pa."

His hand went to the side of his forehead.

"Made quite a mess, eh?" he said.

"How did it happen?"

It'd been years since I asked.

"A long story." Then he said: "You really want to know?"

Shocked. "Sure," I said.

"Well," he said, real slow. "You're going to have to ask somebody else."

Oh.

"I don't know a thing about it," he said.

Then looked straight at me.

"That's okay, Pa."

"Right," he said, looking back toward the bay. "Some man, that Wild Archie."

2

You can tell Sextus is drunk, finally, by the way he almost knocks over his chair standing up. Pushes it back with the backs of his legs, hands pressing on the tabletop.

"There was a reason for . . . Angus and Uncle Sandy. You know?"

He sits down again and seizes the rum bottle resolutely. Pours a shaky dollop into his glass, then looks at me, his face set with purpose.

"You're going to listen to this," he says. "Away back, a few years after Uncle Sandy . . . Duncan came to Toronto. Must have been between '68 and '69. He was ordained. My old man was still alive. Duncan stayed with me. We got into it, pretty serious, a couple of times. And one night, pretty far into his cups, he told me the whole story. Oh, he beat around the bush quite a bit. Asking things like, 'How is a person supposed to react when he discovers somebody close is guilty of something really, really bad?' Him the priest, asking me? I mean, spare me."

I say: "Hey, guess what. I already know the whole story. Okay?"

He takes a long drag on his cigarette, not sure whether to believe me.

"You know? What happened in the barn? In Holland?"

"Yes."

"No sniper?"

"No sniper."

"How Angus . . . ?"

"Yes."

"Who? Where did you find out?"

"Uncle Jack told me."

"Fuck off."

"It's true."

"The old man knew?"

"Uncle Jack knew."

"Holy Jesus."

———

Pa just kept staring out over St. Georges Bay, shaking his head. Occasionally sipping from his flask.

"I hear the Swedes put the mill here because it reminds them of home," he said finally.

"I never heard," I said. The mayor of Hawkesbury said it was because of the harbour.

"Interesting people, the Swedes," he said. "Different ways of looking at things."

"How long do you think they'll be here?" I asked cautiously.

He looked at me full on for a moment. "However long the trees last."

After a while he said, "I suppose you have a girlfriend." Seemed to be killing time. Waiting for something. The sun was hanging just above the horizon. Lights were sparkling on the distant blot of shore. The mainland.

"Not me," I said, laughing nervously.

"Sure you have," he said quietly.

Me thinking: this is weird, for your father.

"It's different now than when I was a young fellow."

"How?"

Then he was watching the sun for a while.

"Nowadays," he said, slouching farther down, "you can afford to be young."

Then, after a long silence in which I thought he'd dozed off: "You need the rig any time, after you get your licence, you just ask."

I stared at him, wondering if he realized it was me he was talking to. He drifted off sometimes. The plate in his head. Often forgot what he just finished saying.

"You hear what I'm saying," he said, looking at me directly.

"Wow, thanks."

Probably the liquor talking, I thought.

"You won't be young for long."

———

"I can't believe the old man knew," Sextus said. "When did he tell you?"

"I don't remember exactly," I said. "We were in Quebec."

"So you knew all along too?"

"Yes," I said.

"And did you ever discuss it with her?"

"There was nothing to discuss."

"Well . . . fuck," he said. "What about the Dutch woman? Or girl, I guess she'd have been."

I raise my hand, cautioning, shaking my head. This is where everything went off the rails with Squint. Bringing the Dutch woman into it. Giving gossip some kind of authenticity.

"That's where I draw the line," I say.

He studies me, face full of sympathy.

"Can't say that I blame you."

―――――

Summer of '63 was when the talk started about my father and the Swede's wife. The Swede was one of the managers at the new mill. She was German. Or so everybody wrongly thought. She was really Dutch. But overheard speaking German at the Auto Parts. And looked like one. The blonde hair and blue eyes. Some kind of an academic. Unusually interested in things around here. Always trying to talk to people. A lot avoiding her, thinking she was a German.

You discover gossip, when it's about yourself, in the sudden silences that seem to go before you, pushing aside whatever was going on before you got there. A strange feeling, that your presence is suddenly alarming to people you think you know well. Conversations quickly started, out of nothing. You don't discover the substance until later.

I shouldn't have been surprised at the gossip. Once I saw them, near the post office, standing talking. The old man was smiling like a boy, hands in his pockets. She was standing with her weight on one leg, the other angled out, casually. Toe poking at bits of gravel. She was wearing a skirt this time.

But there was no mistaking her. The hair, tied back, showing her ears. The skirt draped over the extended leg, showed it off nicely. Arms folded under her chest showed that off pretty good too. Talking a blue streak. Like old friends. Then they shook hands and she headed for the big Chrysler. I felt relief. Something about the handshake. But it still seemed queer, him that friendly with a German.

———

The sun was almost touching the horizon.

"There's the one over the road," he said. "The little red one at Angus's place."

"Effie," I said.

"Yeah, Effie," he said. "You wouldn't be interested in that, would you?"

"Nah. She's like my sister."

"Yes," he said, nodding. "So. You want the rig for going to dances down north. You just say the word. Nice people down there."

"Duncan's going to be a priest," I said.

"Hah." Then: "You used to be around with that little Effie a lot. All the time."

The sun was putting a warm glow on his face, leaving a dark absence where his skull was missing.

"Just playing," I said.

"That's all right. But you get older, there's no more playing." Took another swallow from his flask. "There's a streak in those people."

"Yes."

"A streak o' misery."

"But there's good in them too," I said.

———

By then, of course, there was no reason for him to caution me about Effie. I had other fantasies. The blonde lady, the Swede's wife. The image of her standing close, at Mrs. Lew's, asking who I was, wouldn't leave me. All the impressions created by movies and magazines and songs on the radio, real. Right in front of you, jangling all the senses. Sight, sound, smell, even touch and taste, if you dared. I seemed to be seeing her everywhere.

I was swimming off the old coal pier one hot afternoon when I noticed her standing watching me. Wearing the same outfit I first saw her in. Real short shorts. There was a kid with her. A boy, maybe nine or so. I was alone in the water so it had to be me they were looking at. I didn't know how to acknowledge them so I didn't try.

She put her hand to the side of her mouth and called out: "You make me want to jump in. Just like I am."

And I suddenly had the completely crazy notion that she was there for me. You laugh now but when you're sixteen and curious such things are possible. Why should it only be between men and girls? Why not women and boys? And I wasn't such a boy. Going on seventeen and almost as tall as the old man. The spit of him, people were saying.

Of course, it's pathetic now, but at the time it gave me power. Effie was the only other, but she had nowhere near the force I felt coming out of the Swede's wife. And Effie had outgrown me. You'd think she lived in that '58 Merc with the continental kit. You'd see it gliding over the Long Stretch from up in the field where I'd be turning the hay with Grandpa, or from a ladder on the side of the barn where I'd be fixing shingles or painting. Cruising through like a jungle animal on the hunt, except you could see the prey already inside, sitting up close to the driver. Going somewhere or returning.

Who cared. I had my own imagery. Day and night. And I'd come to, breathless and wet and relieved and lonely. Not knowing that this was as close as I'd get to normal for a long, long time.

———

On Creignish Mountain I asked Pa, "Did you ever go to Sweden?"

He laughed. "Was no war in Sweden."

"You know some of the new Swedes," I said.

He looked at me a moment. Then said, "Don't know a soul among them."

3

Sextus says: "The old man knew? I'd never have guessed."

"Why not?" I say.

"I just wonder why he never told me. That he already knew."

"You talked to him about it?"

"The last time I saw him, I told him the whole thing. He acted like he didn't know."

"He was pretty sick at the time," I say. "Probably forgot things."

"I blamed myself for a long time. Thinking it was too much for him. Mentioning it to him. Trying to get him talking. The stress."

"All I know is it was him told me," I say.

"If I was guessing who told you I wouldn't be half as surprised if it was Squint," he says, testing. "If you ask me, old Squint's the man with the missing pieces of the puzzle."

———

But the first time I asked Squint how my old man managed to get shot, all Squint said was, "Oh, a lot of good guys got shot. Lots didn't live to talk about it."

"How come he never talked about it?"

"Well, that's the thing," Squint said. "Them who lived to talk about it usually wouldn't. Haw haw. Anyway, what's to talk about? You ever been shot?"

"No."

"It's not actually something you 'know' about. Usually just happened. You might know afterwards. But really, you know nothing. Except you're alive, if you are. Then it hurts like hell. Sometimes. The squealing and squirming around can be pretty wicked."

"You been shot, Squint?"

"No, but I seen lots who were," he said.

"You saw Pa when he was shot?"

Squint studied me for a long time, then said: "Maybe."

"What was it like?"

"Oh well, now," he said, "you're a little young."

———

By this time the sun was a big red-orange ball deflating on the horizon. The bay was turning a kind of lavender. The water had little slivers of light dancing on the ripples. It was getting cooler fast.

He said, after another swig: "I just want to sit here for a few more minutes. You'll see something."

He held up his flask, measuring what was left.

"Now watch what happens when the sun hits the water."

I watched as the great ball of fire settled slowly, spreading flat out over the skyline.

"Now look," he said.

"What?"

"The fire ditch," he said, pointing. "Look. There's a big trench, full of fire, running from the land right out to the sun. Look at it."

I see the reflection of the setting sun in a great streak running up to the shore.

"Now," he said. "That's the sewer that carries away all the shit and misery of the day, straight into the big incinerator on the horizon. Sucks the crap out nice as you please."

It looked just like a molten metal stream.

"Of course the world starts filling up with shit and corruption all over again. But for the next minute or so, everything is clean as a whistle."

I looked.

"Am I right or am I wrong," he said aggressively.

"You're right."

"You hear any foolish talk about . . . anything. You just let it go. All right?"

"Right," I said.

"No telling what you might be hearing around. But you just let it slide right into the ditch there. Out to the big furnace."

I was comforted, somehow.

"Okay. Let's go back," he ordered, and he took another swallow. I started the half-ton and turned it around carefully.

The talk was, of course, already going strong. Just not where I could hear it.

———

Sextus is looking relieved. Suddenly refreshed. Says: "I'm trying to think of the old man coping with knowing that all those years."

"He always held it against Angus," I say. "Not that he'd say much one way or the other."

"Never heard him say a hard word against anybody. They can be pretty wicked around here. With the talk."

"Jack never let things eat at him," I say.

"When did you first know there was something wrong with him?"

I shrug. "Just the coughing."

He fumbles a cigarette out of the package on the table between us.

You could tell there was something bad wrong with Uncle Jack long before I left Bachelor Lake. I lived with his cough for years there and in Tilt Cove. But then forgot about it for a while when he moved to the staff house. But during the winter of '67–'68, he'd scare you sometimes. In the cookhouse. Or having a beer at Ikey's. The coughing fits.

They'd make jokes: "If it has hair on it, swallow. It'll be your arsehole." That's the way he coughed.

Then you'd think: That's just Jack. And there were a lot of people coughing in the bunkhouses those days. Especially the ones who had worked in Newfoundland during the war.

Especially St. Lawrence. The radiation. They were only finding out about the radiation there in the sixties. When we were in Bachelor Lake.

"Ma said it was what saved him from the war. Said the three of them came home in the spring of '40. Going to join up. Went down to Sydney. But the old man got rejected. Something about the lungs. That's what saved him."

"From what and for what?" I ask.

"I guess from whatever it was got into the other two. And for what?"

He thinks about that for a few seconds, then smiles. "I guess for what's sitting in front of you right now."

Sextus was born in '42.

————

One evening a few years ago, after I dried out, I took Millie up to the top of Creignish Mountain to show her the fire ditch. Would never have felt comfortable showing Effie. Millie is different.

After everything went black and you could see the beads of light over the mainland, she said, "Did you make that up?"

I couldn't lie. I told her about the old man taking me up here.

"He had a good soul," she said.

"So where do you think it is?"

She looked out over the bay for a while, then said, "How do you remember him?"

"What's that got to do with it?"

"If people remember you well, that's heaven."

"What if they don't remember you at all?"

"Extinction," she said.

"Like Limbo," I said.

"Like Limbo," she said. "Hell but without the pain. Sorrow instead."

"Better than the real thing."

"For some people," she said.

"So where does that leave the old man?"

"Depends on you," she said.

———

"In one way, the war was the best thing that could have happened to them," says Sextus.

"Didn't do much for Uncle Jack."

"Makes my point, doesn't it? Jack was what they'd all have been if there'd been no war."

4

The final months were full of surprises.

Near mid-August the old man called home from the power commission and asked me to drive in and get him. Me with no licence. Ma didn't object, but said, "Be careful," as I left.

Pulling in to the parking area in front of the power commission, I almost ran into a big fancy black car. The Chrysler. The two of them sitting in it. Himself and the Swede's wife. He didn't even try to conceal anything when I stopped alongside.

Late August, Ma asked me to go upstairs with her. Something ominous. Grandpa and Grandma looking at us, curious. Ma wasn't one for private conversations.

She took me to their bedroom and opened his closet door.

"Look at that," she said.

There was a brand-new suit hanging there.

"Where did he get that?" I asked.

"Who knows?" she said.

It was your basic charcoal wool suit, the kind men wore on special occasions. Or to church. Or their own funerals.

"The man never darkens the door of a church," she said.

"Maybe he's got a girlfriend," I said. Joking.

She looked at me hard. "Aren't you after getting the mouth on you," she said and shut the door.

———

Labour Day weekend, the Friday. Sitting alone in the dark under the big pine tree halfway between our lane and MacAskill's, puffing on a Kool. Home was getting too tense. I heard somebody coming. I cupped the cigarette in my hands and held my breath. It was somebody walking slowly along the shoulder of the road. Crunch. Crunch. Jesus. A woman.

She stopped about twenty feet from me and just stood there, arms folded. She was wearing a pale blue checked blouse and pink pedal-pushers. Effie.

"Where are you heading?" I said.

She squealed. "Cripes," she said, when she saw it was me. "What are you trying to do?"

"Sorry."

"What are you doing out here?"

"Just having a smoke," I said.

"A smoke!" She was grinning at that. "When did you start that?"

"Want one?"

"Sure."

And I jumped up.

When she bent her face into my hands to take a light, the flare of the match made her look like a woman.

"So," she said. "Waiting for somebody?"

"Nah," I said. "Just hanging around."

Then I heard the purr of a car out on the Trans-Canada.

"That'll be him," she said.

"How do you know?"

"A woman's instinct." I could picture the smirk.

"I thought he had Hollywood mufflers," I said calmly.

"Who?" she said. "Oh, you're thinking of him. He's gone back. To Ontario."

"So who's this?"

The headlights were intruding already and the hum of the engine was getting louder.

"You're way behind," she said, laughing at me.

Then the car crunched onto the shoulder and pulled alongside. The driver leaned over and pushed the door open. The dome light came on. Warm radio sounds. *I found my thrill . . . on Blueberry Hill.* I recognized the fellow at the wheel, somebody else home from away with his hair all creamed into a black, shiny tangle like you'd see in the movies. Wearing a black leather jacket. He gave me a limp two-finger wave as she swept onto the seat beside him. I noticed then that she was chewing gum. I hated that.

"See ya round," she said as she slammed the door.

The car wheeled in toward where I was standing by the tree, then backed out swift and smooth. Then whipped away with a rattle of gravel. Leaving her smell and the smells of the car and Brylcreem all mingled in with the night.

———

Labour Day weekend, the Sunday. The old man was restless all evening. Then got up and walked out without a word. I followed him, at a distance. Out of the house and down the lane. Who knows what was going on? Caught a glimpse of him at the end of the lane, just strolling casually, hands in his pockets. Then the shadows swallowed him.

The night was quieter than usual. The summer sounds of insects screaming at each other were gone. The sky was luminous with stars and constellations, a full moon hanging there.

I began to focus on a dark shape near the big pine tree. A parked car. I wanted it to be Effie and a boyfriend. But I knew it wasn't.

The way his step quickened, I got the impression he was expecting it to be there. He walked right up to the passenger side, opened the door. The inside light came on. He climbed in and shut the door. It was only for a flash, but I could see that there was a woman behind the wheel. Golden hair piled on top of her head. Then I could imagine plain old Ma, home. Frowning and wondering.

The car started quickly. Obviously a V-8, probably a 420 engine under the hood. A big Chrysler by the look of it when it pulled out from beneath the tree and turned toward the Trans-Canada. They drove some distance before they turned on the headlights. Which was a good thing because if they'd turned them on pulling out from the tree they'd have seen me standing there like an idiot.

———

I was still living through those days when I met Millie. Memories still feeding on me the night I drove her up the General Line, over the back of Creignish Mountain, and showed her how the sun falls into St. Georges Bay. Except I didn't have his faith in its cleansing power.

"I guess I'll never forgive him," I said to her that night.

She let the statement sit there. Me wondering if it was because it was too much for her to embrace or too silly to be worth acknowledging.

"Forgive what?" she said finally. "Him dying?"

"It's more complicated that that."

"The Swede's wife?"

"Forget it," I said.

"It's possible," she said, "you were just jealous."

"For Jesus sake. That's sick."

"She could make quite an impression."

"What do you know about her?"

"I think I remember her," she said.

Part 7

1

Around Labour Day weekend Ma came down with something. Nobody was sure what. But it was bad. She was losing weight and was generally low. And she was cranky, which was unusual for her. These days you'd think cancer right away.

She refused to see a doctor and by the end of the first week of September she wasn't getting out of bed. Grandma cooked the meals.

Jessie would often be there when I'd get home from school. Up in the room. You could hear them talking. Grandma and Grandpa pretty well ran the house. Which was okay except for the cooking. As time dragged by something about it all made me think I didn't really want to be in on it. Adult emotions. Alien territory for sure. I could imagine what it was about but I more or less tuned out.

The old man was hardly ever around. Of course this wasn't unusual. He'd be out at night a lot working. New power lines going through. Substations being built. There was even talk of a new generation station over by the pulp mill. A couple of nights a week you could expect him to stop at the Legion on the way home. Or he'd be over visiting Angus. When he was home, I'd be out cruising around with the truck. Staying out of the way.

I had my licence by then and he was pretty liberal about letting me take his rig when it was available. He'd even throw in gas money.

———

Sextus is standing by the kitchen window, looking out at the storm.

Maybe Millie was right. Maybe I was just jealous of the bastard. I'd never seen the like of the Swede's wife this side of a movie screen. I remember when the papers and magazines were full of Lana Turner, when her daughter supposedly murdered the boyfriend, Johnny Stompanato. Or when Grace Kelly married the prince of Monaco. They had nothing on the Swede's wife for looks. The thought of my old man, with his caved-in skull and the gloom where a personality was supposed to be, going with her was enough to make me feel like throwing up.

When I was little I'd feel that quick tingle when I'd hear them say Sandy the Lineman. Now they were saying Sandy the Stickman. The gossip about him and the Swede's wife getting loud enough to hear. Even for me and Ma.

Ma told me once about birds conducting electricity through their bones and out. He was like that, I thought. Of course that wasn't possible but it was an image that stuck. The electric man. It gave a funny glow to his eyes. Made his hair frizzy. Kept him lean and tense. Explained the angry flashes. Gave me distance. Ma never talked to me about the trouble. And I wanted her to think I didn't know. Grandma and Grandpa hardly breathed.

I'd just drive around. Out to Hastings. If there was a dance somewhere not too far away I'd hang around outside. The mill was pretty well up and running so there was a lot happening in Hawkesbury. A new by-pass and a shopping centre. There was a new drive-in up on the Sydney Road.

It was historic in a way: first time you could get a proper hamburger anywhere around here. Big and fat and juicy with lettuce and tomato and onion squishing out of them. There would always be people sitting out in front in cars. Later there would be an A&W and a Colonel's, and a Dairy Queen. Prosperity was setting in.

One night sitting in front of the drive-in I saw the Chrysler arriving. This time a guy in a suit gets out. He had the kid with him, the boy. The two of them went inside and came out a few minutes later with a bag of food. When they were gone, I went in, returning my pop bottle. Asked the Newfoundlander behind the counter, "Who was that?" The guy shrugged and said, "Some big shot from the mill. One of the Swedes. Why?"

"Just admiring the car," I said.

"Some car, all right," he said.

Just once I talked to Uncle Jack about it. In Tilt Cove. Or maybe it was Bachelor Lake. You could see how uneasy he was.

"There was bugger all to it," he said.

Me nodding. Regretting I ever raised it.

"People got nothing better to do than talk. I told the wife years ago, keep to yourself. Give them nothing to talk about. You know what I mean?" Started rolling a cigarette. Slow and deliberate. "The wife was only going to card games. But it doesn't take much to get them started." Rolling the tube gently, with great concentration. "Jesus Christ," he said, as if to himself. Licked the paper with the tip of his tongue, sealed it with one hand, between thumb and forefinger. Then just looked at it.

"Only way he could have known her was when his crew ran the power into the new house, the place they built up back of Grant's Pond."

The mansion. It had a big carport for at least two or three rigs.

"Right," I said.

That was my point. There was just no common ground between them. No common meeting place. It was totally illogical. And her a foreigner. Maybe even a German.

"It's an awful thing," he was saying sadly.

"Yes."

"The talk of them."

2

The only time the priest had ever been at the house was one winter Grandpa got the flu. We were sure he was gone so somebody called the priest. I remember Ma meeting him at the door with a lit candle. Them hurrying upstairs quietly, the candle flickering. Me, Aunt Jessie, and Sextus on our knees in the kitchen. Grandpa surprised everybody by recovering. After that he was always joking that he'd had more of the sacraments than anybody else in the house. All but one of the seven.

"Only one left is Holy Orders," he'd say.

"Never too late for that one," someone would inevitably reply.

"Only thing holding me back is getting rid of the old woman," he'd say, winking at Grandma. Everybody would laugh.

The priest came more than a few times that fall. He'd just walk in after the first time, like any old visitor. No candles or formalities. Usually just wearing a sweater or a jacket. I'd never hear what they were talking about. They'd be down in the living room. Ma would get out of bed for it, so it was important. The old man would be home for that. I'd take off with the truck.

For the longest time the only one who said anything to me was Aunt Jessie. One night we were playing cards at her place and she put her hand down all of a sudden, looking at me. Here it comes, I felt.

"You're all right, are you, Johnny?"

"Yes," I said. You always knew, when they called you Johnny.

"They'll get through it, you know," she said.

"Who?"

"Your ma and dad," she said, picking up her cards.

"What's the matter with them?"

"Ach," she said, studying her hand. "Couples go through little problems now and then. It happens to the best of them."

"You and Uncle Jack never have any problems."

"Ha," she said. "He's never around long enough."

———

"It was good," he says, "you and the old man having each other. After Uncle Sandy."

"You don't think of it like that. But I suppose."

"I had nobody . . . when everything went to ratshit for me." He's swishing the drink in his hand. Not noticing me at all. "When my old man pops off. Later. And. Well, you know where I turned. Not that it's any excuse."

"Consider yourself lucky," I say.

"You know I actually picked up the phone once to call you. After she pulled the bung on me. To ask you . . . how long before you start to feel normal again. Is it a year? Two years?

Then I thought, What the Christ do you think you're doing? And started to laugh." A big smile.

"She gave you a pretty good run for your money," I say. Feeling giddy.

———

I remember the house being cold all the time. And damp. As if life had stopped. Which was ridiculous. The old people, Grandma and Grandpa, pitched in like they were setting up housekeeping for the first time. And Jessie was around, trying to keep things normal. Except that her being there so much wasn't normal. And the priest wasn't normal. And the old people acting like a young couple wasn't normal.

Then I had a great insight. What's the worst thing that can happen? One of them moves out. Him. So what would be so bad about that? So people would talk. So weren't they probably wagging their tongues off already? Any change would be for the better. Of course I was wrong there.

My only real friend then was Effie, and she was distracted. By boys with big cars. With duck's-arse haircuts. Sextus and Duncan were away in university. Caught up in new lives. As September limped by, my feelings about the Swede's wife started to change. Boy crush wearing thin. The light dawning. My only claim to fame in her eyes was looking like my father.

I saw her with her husband a couple of times and they looked like they were on their honeymoon. What are these people all about, anyway?

———

"Stop looking at me like that," he says suddenly.

"Like what?"

"Like you're the only fucking person in the world who ever went through hard times."

"I'm not—"

"Don't think we didn't know. We heard all about the detox and the rest of it. Don't think we didn't . . . agonize."

The storm thumps the house again.

"I'd rather not relive it," I say.

He jumps to his feet. We're standing face to face.

"For fuck sake give me something."

"Okay," I say.

Who cares anymore?

———

I was tempted to become a spy. You get that way. Heading to town one night for a burger, I saw the big car on the Trans-Canada. Pulled a quick U-ey and followed it. Caught up and sure enough it was the Swede's and there were two people in the front. The old man was supposed to be at work. Something about the new substation. Said he'd be late. Maybe sleep at the shop. I knew it was him but I didn't have the stomach to follow when they turned up Rhodena Road toward Ceiteag's. I turned and went to town, knowing somehow Ma would know and that eventually, inevitably, they'd be up all night for another marathon harangue. Urgent talking. Quick footsteps. Then the sickening smashing when he wore down. At about that moment I started hating her.

Maybe I should have followed them. Maybe that was what caused me to spy on Effie.

———

Once I hurt Ma. I blurted out: "I'm going to talk to that damned Swede." I knew his name by then. Erik Sandgren. Knew the posh house up back of the pond.

Ma's face was white. Her mouth and eyes perfect zeros.

"You just mind your place, young fellow."

She had a dishtowel in her hand and she slapped the table with it. Now it seems almost a comical gesture. But it didn't seem funny then. Her words were white hot.

"There's nothing that you need to be concerned about, young man."

Young man?

"Good enough," I shouted, and headed for the door. Nothing for me to worry about? Dandy. Screw it all.

Whatever was going on, I guess I was a beneficiary. In a sick way. The truck was practically mine. I'd be on the road all the time. Liberated from the cold ugly house. But it was a queer kind of freedom.

If I did venture into the drive-in for a burger, I'd pull my cap down over my eyes and try to avoid looking at anybody. I'd go to the dances early but I'd stay outside in the truck, where I could see everything. A lot of guys popping the trunk-lids, finding their bottles, passing them back and forth with great joy and loud laughing.

Near the end of September on a warm Friday night, listening to the music from the Creignish hall. A fight exploded at the rear of a nearby car where a group of Judiquers were drinking. Two guys pounding at each other, slipping and sliding on the gravel like cows on ice, one getting the worst of it, stumbling toward the pavement backward, then down in a tangle of arms and legs. The other straddles him, smashing at his face. Then the flash of a dome light from a large car near them and my father materializes. And in one swift motion snatches the guy on top to his feet.

The guy turns, fist up. Sees who it is and instantly opens his hands, hold them flat out in front of him.

Pa leads him away. The other fellow stirs and sits up. It all happened in no more than a minute. Then panic sets in and I start the truck and roar away, sending a shower of gravel skittering along the pavement behind.

Wishing the stones were bullets. Penetrating car doors. People's skulls.

Maybe Pa recognized his own truck. But never said anything to me. Big surprise!

————

"One night I put the kid, Sandy, in the car and we drive right across the city. Found the Irishman's place on the Kingsway. Walked in on them. They were in the middle of a nice candlelit dinner. Not sure what I expected. Maybe catch them in the act. Anyway, there I am, holding the kid by the hand. She goes apeshit. The kid goes apeshit." Shaking his head. "I remember the wood. Fancy panelling. And books. And they had their wine in a fucking crystal decanter."

————

Then near Hallowe'en, Pa was home more often. Sitting in the dining room with the paper. Until bedtime. Everything quiet. Grandpa would listen to the fiddle music program in the evenings at 6:45 with his ear right up against the radio. Ma and I'd watch TV with hardly any sound. Everybody seemed normally tense again.

The Ma started bugging him to go to a masquerade dance with her over in Glendale. A dance? He'd be more likely to go to church than to a dance. Hated dances, he'd say when I'd be going. Can't see people wasting their energy jumping around to music, he'd say. People want to burn off energy, I've got a woodpile out beside the house. That's the place to burn off excess energy.

Excess? There's a queer word.

I of course never mentioned the night I saw him outside the hall in Creignish. Not that he was dancing there. But it was a dance. Then, on the day of the Hallowe'en masquerade, he just announced that they were going. He even dressed up, like a scarecrow. He had fake arms stuck out from his shoulders and a big wad of hay under his hat. And a mask. They won a prize and people nearly died of surprise when they took their masks off. Sandy Gillis and the wife.

Look for yourself.

Well I'll be goddamned. He must be ossified.

He looks sober.

It was the only time I ever saw them going out together in my seventeen years.

———

"People ask me," he says. "Would you ever tie the knot again." Half laughing. Shaking his head. "Only thing I want from a woman you don't have to get married for. You've got a right to ask why I had to fuck up your life before I discovered marriage wasn't my cuppa."

"I couldn't care less," I say steadily.

"We wrote to each other," he says.

All the letters she wrote to me are suddenly in my mind. Everything starts with letters. Ends with letters.

"The letters got intense," he says. "But compared with the kinds of relationships I was used to, it was sort of . . . pure. I thought it was just little Effie, Little Orphan Annie like always. Childhood chum. But she was . . . reaching out to me.

"And when we saw each other here, when the old man . . . with all the conflict, me and the old man, and the whole unresolved mess with Uncle Sandy from back in '63. And it was clear from the letters things weren't the best with you two."

Now his eyes are full and I am mesmerized.

"Jesus. I just. I was like a teenager."

"It isn't important," I say.

Knowing that Effie was drawn to me once not just because of my needs but in an even bigger way, her own . . . she would reach out, again. And why not to him? He was big and famous and he could see things and explain things. And give her things and take her away. That was probably the big attraction. Take her away.

Who knows what the Swede's wife had in mind. Or what the old man might have done. Maybe just gone away. Like everybody else.

———

"It was only when I wrote about it . . . or, not about it, but something based on it. That I realized."

"I read your fucking book," I say, wearily.

"Never mind the book."

3

November 11, 1963. He and Angus went to town that day, as usual. Alone. Don't remember how I got there. Watched the parade alone. Saw them and their comrades marching by in their berets and clinking medals. And afterwards there was the usual retreat to the Legion. Then to MacAskill's, with their bottles. It was all routine by then.

But he surprised us. Came home early. Looked like he'd been sick. Ashen face. Almost as if he'd been weeping. We just stared at him, Ma and me.

"What the fuck are you looking at?" he said.

Then went down to the living room. Sat in the big chair without taking off his coat.

It was the only time I saw Ma flare at him.

"I'm wondering why you came home at all," she said, "if it's just to sit there like a zombie."

I said to myself, Here it comes.

But he just made a strange sound, almost like a sob. He went to bed soon after that. But that was how he stayed until the end. Speaking to nobody. Coming straight home after work, disappearing up to their room. No more absences.

It was like that for eleven days.

Till the day they killed Kennedy.

———

Not nearly as much wind. Some rain on the day. But a tempest in the memory.

The voice has become flat. Stripped of feeling. Out of consideration? Out of fear? I take the bottle and pour into my teacup. Perhaps it will calm me. Maybe restore the good feeling you always remember from other times.

"I'm in Halifax, boarding up on the north end of Windsor Street, near the Forum," he says. "It was Atlantic Bowl weekend, but I forgot. And I forgot Duncan was coming up from Antigonish. St. F.X. was in the bowl game, as usual." He sips thoughtfully. "And I remember I was studying for a quiz, listening to a little radio. Guy breaks in. I think it was about three o'clock. A Friday afternoon. Says, 'We take you now to Dallas.' Wow. It was tough studying after that. I made a pot of tea. On my hotplate."

He looks at me, waiting.

"What do you remember?" he asks.

"Nothing."

Except maybe that in the morning Pa had gone hunting. I jokingly said I should take the day off school, go with him. We were all worrying by then about his mood. Something dangerous and new. But going hunting almost seemed normal.

He smiled at me. That's what I remember.

"I guess it was about five that afternoon," he says. "The phone rings at the boarding house. It was Duncan. Calling from the Lord Nelson. Fuck. I forgot I was supposed to meet him there.

"'Did you hear about Kennedy?' he says.

"'Christ yes,' I say. 'Who do you think did it?'

"'Some Protestant,' he says. I can't help laughing."

———

What else do I remember? There was a dance that night. In Creignish. The regular Friday night. Buddy MacMaster playing, as usual. There had been talk that Father Donald was going to call it off. Out of respect for the president, who was a Catholic. But they went ahead with it and everybody was talking about Kennedy. I was there. Actually inside, standing at the back. Listening to the music, feeling okay in spite of Kennedy.

I'd left home about eight o'clock and Ma was kind of concerned that Pa hadn't come back from hunting. A short time back you'd have automatically thought: The Legion. But he hadn't been going there lately. Not since the eleventh. Probably over at Angus's place. But there had been no sign of Angus lately either. Not since the eleventh. No matter what you thought, there were some things that you'd just never do. You'd never call looking for him. I used to say to Ma, "Why don't you call the power commission, or the Legion, or the tavern and see if he's there?" And she'd just roll her eyes. You didn't do that with him. Not ever.

Effie was at the dance with a gang. Driving by her place, I almost went in to ask if she wanted a ride. The latest boyfriend had gone back to Ontario by then. But of course there were lots of boyfriends and I could tell she'd left for the dance already. The only light was in the kitchen. In any case I wouldn't want to run into the old man if he was in there. I could imagine them sitting there. Himself and Angus. Talking about God knows what. Probably drinking wine.

Sure enough Effie was at the dance ahead of me. And I could tell there were a few guys with the eye on her already. Sniffing and circling. She asked me to dance with her once and I did, though I wasn't very good at it.

"How did you get here?" I asked.

"A ride," she said. Tipping her head to one side.

"I guess the old fellow is at your place," I said.

"Your father?"

"Yes."

"No."

I should have been worried then, but I was distracted by the tilt of her face. Not that worrying would have made any difference.

She said: "You're good. You must have been practising."

I knew it wasn't true. But that raised interesting possibilities. And as the last set started, I spotted a grade eleven girl from Long Point on the sidelines. Asked her to dance and she said yes. Halfway through the third figure, I asked her if I could drive her home. She looked at me with a half-dubious expression, then laughed and said, "I suppose."

Holy mother of God.

———

"We got pretty ripped that night. Drunk college students everywhere. Next day there was a minute's silence for Kennedy before the game. I think about half the St. F.X. team were Americans. Good Catholic boys from Maine and Boston. Duncan was saying he hadn't seen so much emotion in the St. F.X. crowd since the Cuban missile crisis the year before. Them worrying then that poor Kennedy was going to start a nuclear war. Little did they know that the poor fellow had already started the war in Vietnam. Where half of them would end up in a few years anyway. Jesus."

———

Settling into the truck, after the dance, I was trying to find something on the radio. Nothing but serious music. Classical.

"Awful about Kennedy," she said.

"I know," I said.

Wondering where he might have got to if he wasn't with Angus.

"How are you finding grade twelve?" she asked.

———

The way Uncle Jack put it: "He was like a frigging Indian in the woods. Never a sound. Some fellows would be blabbing and drinking rum. Shooting at anything that moved. Not him. He'd go in with one or two bullets and he'd have them coming back if he didn't get something. He was real at home in the woods. Serious about hunting, Sandy."

I discovered later he'd taken a pint of rum with him that day.

———

"After the football game I had to go back to the boarding house. To get money or something. Anyway, there's a message to call home. So I do. Thinking maybe one of the old people. Ma answers, making some small talk at first. But I can tell something is wrong. Then I figure it's the old man. Something in the mine. In Tilt Cove then. I never thought for a minute Uncle Sandy."

———

Driving away from the dance, in the truck, for God's sake, she was sitting away over by the passenger door. Usually they're in the middle, close. So how does that happen? Do they just come over? Are you supposed to drag them over? How do you do that?

"So how are you finding it? Grade eleven," I said.

"Good," she said. And went silent again.

"Buddy was playing pretty good tonight," I said.

"Yeah," she said. "But I wish he'd get a guitar player or something. Or play records once in a while. They do that some places now. For round dancing."

"Yes."

"I like round dancing. The slow stuff. Now and then."

This sounded like a beginning. Intimate disclosures coming out.

"Do you want to go for a drive somewhere?" I asked. Meaning park somewhere.

The classical music grew on you. It was slow, at least. Some of it had a nice melody.

"I have to go right home," she said quickly.

We were passing the end of the Creignish wharf road and I could see taillights going down there slowly. Cars going down to park. Whitecaps flashing on the dark seashore.

"Sure," I said.

———

"Ma says, 'By any chance you haven't been in touch with your uncle this weekend?'

"I thought she said Duncan and I said, 'Yes, we were just at the football game.'

"She says, 'Football game?' Surprised like.

"I said, 'Yeah, St. F.X. won.'

"She says, 'I mean your *Uncle*. Sandy.'

"'Sandy?' I say."

———

Down her lane, up to the darkened house. I stopped, turned out the headlights, and cut the engine. But left the key on accessories. The music continued. Then I put my arm on the back of the seat. My hand came close to her left shoulder. I guessed they must just haul them over at this point. But my arm was frozen.

She said, "I'll have to go in."

"Sure," I said, jumping out my side. Then she slid across, under the wheel and out behind me. Hey. She could have used her own door. But she used mine. A signal of some kind. So I walked with her to the door.

"I hope they didn't lock me out," she said.

I hoped they had, but said: "They should put a key someplace. Just in case."

She laughed and said: "Usually we don't even lock the door. But we've been locking it lately. A lot of new people around."

"That's for sure," I said.

She turned the knob and the door opened.

"Well," she said. Half questioningly. Hand still on the knob, holding the door half opened.

———

"Ma told me then. He'd gone hunting the day before. Never came back. Big search on. Said she was really grasping, calling me. But I should know anyway. He'd been acting strange. Maybe he went to Halifax.

"'Where's Angus?' I asked. 'Right here,' she said. Then I figured: This is peculiar.

"After I hung up, Duncan and I decided to drive down right then and there. Once of the priests at the university had loaned him a car to go to the game."

————

I could tell just by the way she was standing that she expected something. So I carefully put my arms around her waist. She closed her eyes and started to turn her face a little to one side. But I then pressed my mouth against her warm dry lips. She accepted. Then moved her head gently around, working the kiss, thrusting just a little. There was a little bristle under her nose. Then I could feel the softness of her body leaning on me. Then she pulled back and said, "I better go in."

"Yes."

I remember driving home thinking: That was pretty easy.

When I got home the Mounties were in the yard and a bunch of other cars. Some guys from the power commission. West Bay Road fellows from the pulp mill. But it was too late to go looking.

They asked me if I ever went hunting with him.

No, I said.

Did I know any of his places?

Well, I said. He often goes up back of Creignish Mountain, around the old Shimon Angus place.

No, somebody said. That's too far. He went on foot. He'll be out somewhere around Sugar Camp or Queensville.

So that's where we spent Saturday.

————

"I never really took it serious, until I got here," he says. "Jesus, the commotion. Cars and trucks lined up along the road. The house full of people. The old lady in control. Poor Aunt Mary in pretty bad shape. I think that was the end of Grandpa, that night."

Tramping through the woods all day Saturday, I couldn't help thinking of the girl in Long Point. Figuring the next time I'd know what to do. There was a regular Saturday dance down near Port Hood. At Neilie MacDonald's. Should have made a date to go to that. All the time suspecting this was a waste of time. Nothing could have happened to electric man. Sandy the Lineman. A frigging Indian in the woods. Shot in his big thick head in the war and survived that. Could take on any four people and they wouldn't lay a hand on him. Probably holed up somewhere with a crock. But also with a rifle. What if he broke his own rule about hunting and drinking? Then the Swede's wife crept into my mind. And I kept seeing him getting into that big car. Maybe they just took off. For Halifax. Or Sweden. Who knows? The old man always made the world seem small. So maybe that was it. They were gone. And we were wasting all this time. Time better used making plans for tonight and the one from Long Point. And wasting the time of all these people. Pulp mill guys. Linemen. Mounties. Christ Jesus. Knowing that all these people would add the futile stupid search to the rest of the stories about Sandy the Stickman. The Fugitive. It was embarrassing, seeing all the people who were spending their Saturday trudging around the woods. Half the fucking Legion here. We'd pay for it. Bastard. Leaving me to face this.

Then you'd think about Kennedy. Everybody talking about that.

Of course the real reason we were wasting our time was because we were looking in the wrong place.

It was other hunters who found him. Two fellows from Louisdale who didn't even know about the search that was under way down near Queensville. They were hunting up back of Creignish Mountain, a couple of miles to the northeast, at Ceiteag Alasdair's.

It was Sunday.

―――――

"Everything changed then."

"I guess so," I say, pouring a little more rum into my cup.

"Where were you when you heard?" he asks.

"I think everybody was at Mass when they found him."

The priest prayed for him and Kennedy together even though we didn't know Pa was dead. Hearing their names together, I felt panic. Wanted to jump out and shout at Father Hughie: What the fuck do you think you're doing?

"We got in late from Halifax. We had to stop in Antigonish, tell the priest we were taking his car down here. Then when we get out here, herself meets me on the doorstep. Says they found him. Fuuuck."

―――――

Ceiteag Alasdair. An old woman from another time. Stamped her name and character on a patch of woods up in the mountains. By natural selection, her name had overwhelmed the memory of any man who might ever have been part of her life. There were women like that. Henrietta MacInnis. Her descendants were known as Henny's, no matter who their fathers were. Ciorstaidh MacIntyre. Her descendants were known as the Ciorsti's. No matter who their fathers were. And Ceiteag Alasdair. Talk about women's liberation. They're like spruce trees, women like that. Indestructible.

All that was left of Ceiteag's life was a small cellar, crowded by bushes that bore lush berries in the summer but exposed in the winter, at least until the snow came and filled it up. It was lined with careful fieldstones. About ten feet square and you'd hardly notice it. Until you were into it.

That's what they figured. He came along not paying attention. Fell in. Rifle went off. Boom.

You'd never have expected something like that could happen to Sandy Gillis. A veteran of the war. Slogged all the way through France. Battle of the Scheldt. Lots of action in Holland. An experienced hunter. Like an Indian, he was. But then you'd never have expected him to take a flask with him hunting either. He loved a dram, but never when he was hunting. Drinking and guns don't mix, he always told me, and that is what they were all saying at the wake. But there it was, beside him. The little brown paper bag with the empty bottle inside. A pint. Golden Diamond. The receipt said Thursday evening. You could still get a pint of rum for about $2.50 then.

The other thing they were saying was that it was completely unlike Sandy Gillis to have had a bullet in the chamber, unless of course he saw something. Was getting ready to shoot. In any event, they figured he fell in, landed on a rock in the bottom of the old cellar, the rifle under him. The force of the fall broke the stock, right at the hand grip, caused the thing to fire. The bullet went in under his chin and right out the top. A frigging mess.

———

"When I came home for the long weekend in October, Thanksgiving, everything seemed just fine," he says.

"It was."

"Ma told me they went to the masquerade dance in Glendale."

"They won a prize."

"That should have been a sign."

"Of what?" I say.

"Uncharacteristic behaviour. A sign of trouble."

"Don't get started," I say.

"No point avoiding it."

"Just don't."

"John, the evidence was there. He even broke off the rifle-stock so it would fit between his lap and his chin—"

"It was an accident."

"Christ, I can't believe this."

"I'm just not going to discuss it with you."

"Why the fuck not?"

"Because I already know what you think," I say finally. Getting my chance. Hanging on to myself. "I already fucking know what you think. Myself and the whole goddamned world."

"Ahhhh *Jeesus*," he says. Sounding just like my old man. Getting up, clattering the chair. Walking impatiently over to the sink. Leaning, looking like he's going to throw up. Then turning.

"I wrote that with respect. Get it? Respect. For Uncle Sandy. Okay?"

Now he's leaning on the table.

"So it hurt you. So it scandalized the countryside. But it was pretty close to the truth. The truth that Uncle Sandy was a good, honourable man. No matter what went on with the Swede's wife. No matter what happened out at Ceiteag's."

"It's all bullshit," I say. Quietly. The way Uncle Jack would have.

"Right," he says. "Fine. You think what you want."

4

We had a wake at the house. For three days. Had to take the window out of the living room to get the coffin in. The kitchen and the old pantry were packed with women the whole time. People all over the place, telling stories. Stayed around the clock. And every couple of hours, gathering in the living room, flickering with candles. Kneeling in front of that closed and silent mahogany box. Saying the rosary, over and over.

And people watching the Kennedy things on TV. The body coming back to Washington. The big hearse through the lined streets.

"They were almost the same age," Ma said. Her face white and still.

"They had the exact same birthday. Him and our Sandy."

Isn't that something.

And them both wounded in the war.

You think.

And the little fellow's name is John too.

I never thought of that.

You know, Mary looked a lot like Jackie when she was younger. She still does. Mary won't be single long. Will you, Mary?

She could smile.

Uncle Jack was home from Newfoundland. Lots who came

were his friends. Miners. With big thick sloped shoulders, coming in slowly, the way miners walk. Carefully. From always walking in the dark.

"Sorry for your trouble," they'd say, thick hands gentle and slow.

"Yes," Jack would say.

"And where are you now?"

"Tilt Cove."

"And is there much going on?"

"Going to be some new stuff in the spring. Talking about a second shaft."

"I suppose they'll be looking for people."

"Get in touch with me after."

"Anybody with you from here?"

"The Beaton boys from West Mabou. Charlie Angus from Loch Lomond. Philip MacPhail. From River Denys."

"Charlie Angus?"

"Yeah, he's there. Same as ever."

"And poor Philip."

"Okay. Good of you to come."

"Jesus. Sorry for your trouble."

"I know."

Uncle Jack was drinking vodka most of the time. I found six pints of it buried in the dresser drawer where I kept my underwear. Once when I came into my room he was sitting on my bed drinking out of one of the bottles.

I sat down beside him.

We just sat there.

The last evening, the night before the funeral, the Swede came with his wife. The house got very quiet. A lot of the men there worked at the mill. He was dressed in a suit coming in.

Herself was wearing a navy blue long coat and she had a red silky scarf at the neck. Pinned by a little tulip brooch. And a little navy hat on. She didn't look at all like any other time I'd seen her. She looked plain. The hair looked dull and damp. There were bluish crescents below her eyes. No lipstick. And she looked unbelievably sad.

They talked briefly to Ma. Shook my hand. Her eyes were scanning my face, and we nodded at each other. I was remembering the other times I'd seen that face, with its smile and mysterious signals. Ma was overly polite to them. As if the bishop had docked.

Then they went down to the living room together, arm in arm. And they stood there in front of the coffin. Not kneeling or blessing themselves or anything. Just standing there. I was watching from behind. She was hanging on to her husband's arm. Her head actually turned toward his shoulder as if she was going to lean her face into it.

Then they turned and came out. They put their names in the visitors' book and on their way by they stopped in front of us and shook hands again. I noticed that Sandgren took Ma's hand between both of his and he said to her with a little bit of an accent, "He was a good man, Mr. Gillis."

Ma nodded but she was staring at the Swede's wife, trying to say something, or hold something back.

The Swede's wife said: "I come from Holland. My home was Zutphen. Your poor husband. When we spoke. He told me there are people here. Van Zutphens. I hope to meet them. One day."

Ma said, "My husband was there. In the war."

"Yes," the Swede's wife said. "I knew. I remember the Canadians. I was a girl. But I remember." Her cheeks were pink and the eyes flashed, and I think her quick sorrow bumped Ma a little off balance because she then took the Swede's wife's hand and said simply, "I'm glad you came."

"Maybe we can talk sometime," the Swede's wife said.

"Maybe," Ma replied.

"My name is Annie," she said. "Annie van Ryk."

"Yes," said Ma. "It was nice meeting you."

Like it was all over.

There was a wet streak from the corner of the Swede's wife's eye. She turned to her husband and quietly said, "We should go now."

Squint was eyeballing them both, sitting at the kitchen table where I'm sitting now, an odd twist to his face. As they were leaving, he was saying to nobody in particular, out of the side of his mouth: "Good thing the *fuamhair* wasn't here for that."

———

Here's what Millie told me years later, sitting in my car on top of Creignish Mountain, looking out over St. Georges Bay.

How sometime in the early summer of 1963 the Swede's wife arrived at her parents' farm over near Dundee, on the shores of the west bay of the Bras d'Or lakes. Had a big visit with the old people. Talking Dutch. Millie doesn't speak Dutch even though she was born over there and learned it first. She gave it up when she started school. Resented all the reminders: You people don't know how good you've got it here; you don't know what hunger is; you don't know what being occupied by monsters was like; never mind you were little, you didn't know; we protected you.

After the woman left they told Millie she was somebody from home. That she grew up in a place that had been liberated by

Canadians; met some of them; boys from Nova Scotia; one named Gillis; was just curious.

Millie said: "I remember my father saying he told her, 'Good luck. Half the people here seem to be named Gillis. Or Mac-Donald.' Poppa figured she'd had a crush on somebody named that, in the war. You don't think it could have been?"

———

I can remember the sorrow that moved through me then, toward the fire ditch. But feeling none of the relief he'd promised.

Part 8

1

My horoscope, November 27, 1963: *Time ripe for basic changes. Express hopes, ambitions. Check with authorities. Follow expert advice. Continue to be optimistic. Associate due to offer encouragement.*

The funeral is a blur. Sounds of clinking from blazers heavy with medals dangling from coloured bits of ribbon. Legion men from Amherst. And Sydney. Old North Novies. Burying one of their own. The Swede and the wife didn't come.

I see people lining the street all the way to the cemetery but that couldn't be. Nobody ever lines the street for a funeral procession here. I'm getting mixed up with the other one. In Washington. There was a piper, I know that. The same one Angus had, nine or ten years later. He played "Flowers of the Forest." Uncle Jack was standing in front of me at the graveside and when the piper started I saw his shoulders jerking. Ma held her fist under her nose the whole time. The only one you could see actually weeping was Sextus. I came close though when the piper played "MacCrimmon's Lament" as we walked away from the grave, leaving Legion men to fill it in. Grandma was snivelling by then. Ma actually moving like a slow march. Feet stiff.

The hardest days were afterwards.

———

Ma at the wake. Comforted knowing that when all these people in the packed house were whispering they were talking about her qualities. But I could tell.

And Effie. The way she'd take my hand whenever she came close. She knew too. That the majority of these people needed more. Accidental death wasn't good enough. Sandy the war hero who got shot serving his country, now killed falling into Ceiteag Alasdair's old cellar? Not likely. Not Sandy. Not when you put it together with what people were saying about the Swede's wife. Not when you knew he had that streak in him anyway. Accidents like the one that killed Sandy the Lineman were in competition with the TV stories. There had to be more to it. Drama. Romance for certain. That's how gossip starts.

And the Kennedy stuff on TV was a perfect background. Our little spectacle drew significance and drama from it.

When Effie came up to me she'd take my arm and squeeze it a little. Getting my full attention. God, she was getting good looking. Seventeen. No more Little Orphan Annie.

"It'll be all right," she'd say.

After midnight, when the place would thin out, Sextus and Duncan and Angus and Squint and a few others would sit around the kitchen table drinking rum. Uncle Jack would be gone by then. Jessie taking him away gently. Him staggering a little bit. Everybody wondering.

And the day of the funeral, somebody from the power commission came early with an industrial vacuum cleaner and did the whole house. So when the undertaker came and took the coffin out it was as if none of it had happened.

Of course it rained and after the funeral half of them came back for tea and drinks again and stayed late into the evening. Made a mess of the place all over again. But it was different.

The mourning was over, even if the grief wasn't. The old man was gone. Mostly everybody talked about Kennedy. And Oswald. Squint being an old sniper explaining how Oswald did it. Three shots. You had to be real fast. Rifle was bolt action. He was good, Oswald. Well trained, obviously. And Angus saying how Ruby should get a medal. But he shouldn't have shot him. Should have cut his fucking guts out.

It was the one time I felt a bond with Angus. Went out for air once and saw him leaning against the house, like taking a leak. But when he turned and spoke you could tell he'd been bawling.

———

Effie was the first to tell me Sextus had written a book about it. Years later.

"Guess who's written a book?" she says.

"A book?"

She laughs.

Me so surprised I never thought to ask what it was about. Of course I found out soon enough. The *Hawkesbury Sun* wrote it up. Big deal. Book about here by somebody from here. Never mind what was in it.

———

Sextus took me upstairs after the funeral and pulled a pint of vodka from an inside pocket. We were standing in the bathroom. You drank vodka if you didn't want people to know. Jack did that too. All through the wake.

"I don't know," I said.

He uncapped the bottle and took a swallow. Made a face.

"Give it to me," I said.

I gulped a mouthful. It burned my throat and stomach and I felt a sudden sweat and a lightness behind the eyes.

"Not bad," I said when I got my breath.

He was smiling.

———

Downstairs they were making jokes with Ma about being single again. And she was going along with them. Poor Ma. Wouldn't want to make anybody feel bad even if they were being arseholes.

There was a lawyer there. A young fellow originally from down north somewhere. Doucet. Pa must have known him. He introduced himself and asked if he could see me alone for a minute.

Said he was a friend of Pa, and how sorry he was, etcetera, holding my hand in a steady grip longer than I was used to.

"You're the man here now," he said seriously.

I nodded.

"While I'm here," he said, "I have something I have to show you. If it's okay. I could always . . ."

"No," I said. "That's all right."

He unfolded an official-looking paper. "Certificate of Death" was written on the top.

"Somebody had to witness this," he said. It was signed by the Polish doctor in Hawkesbury. "I took the liberty."

"Sure," I said.

I read quickly. I saw the words "severe trauma" and "accidental gunshot wound." There was a jumble of medical terminology.

I felt sick and grown-up at the same time. Handed him back the paper.

"This is just so you won't be worrying about anything," he said. "We can talk in a few days. You, your mother, and I. About the will. And the insurance."

"Insurance," I say.

"Of course," he says, brow furrowed. "It was an accident."

He winked and nodded his head quickly. Assuming I understood. But that didn't matter.

2

"You don't know 'euphemism'?" Sextus says. "Think Euphemia or Faye. Synonym for deception."

Euphemia. Effie's real name.

"The day they killed Kennedy really meant the day Sandy . . . you see. It's hard to say. Even for me. Killed himself."

"That's bullshit," I say quickly. We're not going to get into that again.

"You're right," he says. "Killed himself? Somebody killed him? Circumstances killed him? What difference? The thing was . . . why?"

"Sometimes life ends when you don't expect it to," I say.

"If you believe that," he says quietly. "Something that simple, how come it's been so hard for you to think about, never mind talk about?"

"I've never had any trouble thinking about it."

"Ha!"

Ha yourself.

———

Ma spent a good week writing notes on the little cards she sent to everybody whose name appeared in the visitors' book and on the Mass cards. There must have been hundreds. Duncan took a bunch of the cards back to Antigonish for distribution among the priests at the university. They'd have time to say all the Masses people were offering up for poor Sandy the Lineman's soul.

"Your dad would be awfully proud knowing they'll be saying Masses for him over at the university," Ma said.

Dad?

Even Ma was changing.

———

Sextus says, "Sandy just disappeared. Nobody talked about him. So it was like he never existed. You look around for a trace of Uncle Sandy and . . . nothing. Like you pulled your hand out of a bucket of water. Sandy deserved better than that. To be written out of the memory . . . for something like . . ."

"Like what?"

"Small-town shit."

"If you're talking about the goddamned Swede's wife, then that's it!" I shout, jumping to my feet.

His face is very calm.

"Where does it leave any of us," he says, "if one . . . lapse . . . erases everything else?"

Nowhere to look but at my calloused hands.

"That's all I was trying to say," he says.

———

Before, the schoolbus had rocked and bounced with the noise and carrying on. Guys grabbing at girls. Legs. Tits. Hair. Them screaming. People up and down the aisle. Throwing things. Guys messing up each other's hair. Even mine. People getting pissed off. Hair was a lot of work then. Getting longer.

After the funeral the bus was quiet. You'd catch people watching you. Then they'd look away. A lot of low talking. First I thought it was just them being respectful. Then I realized it was them talking behind my back. Exchanging what they were picking up at home.

We don't know the half of it. Smirking. Words that rhymed with *Swede* and *wife* and *Sandy* made me jump.

Effie would sit with me, which I appreciated. Then I realized she probably knew what was going on and didn't want me thinking she was part of it. The safest place for her was beside me. A kind of loyalty. We were both from the Long Stretch. Screw them.

The teachers. Every single one would say hello no matter how many times I bumped into them during the day. Cheerful as hell. But I couldn't concentrate on classwork. People watching. Teachers talking. I broke out in a swath of pimples. Then I got a big cold sore.

"Johnny's got a dose," somebody said. The way they laughed I knew I wasn't included in the joke, even though it was about me. At recess or noon hour I'd just sit in the classroom. Whenever somebody barged in they'd stop quickly and say "Oh, hi" and retreat. That went on through the end of November and into December.

Then he ceased to be. And I did too.

Over Christmas I decided to quit. Piss on it.

Ma wasn't happy when she heard. She got Aunt Jessie to put pressure on me. And Sextus came down from Halifax early in the New Year to ask how come. I had no answer for him.

"Maybe a few months out will do a fellow good," he said.

"Won't do any harm," I said.

"A fellow can always go back," he said.

"That's what I figure."

He retreated then, back to his life in Halifax. Going to the university. Building his road to the Future.

After that the rest backed off.

Plus the pulp mill was going full blast by then. There would always be something. Cutting pulpwood or working there. Even driving a truck. And there was bold talk about refineries. Petrochemical plants. You name it. The place was going to turn into a frigging metropolis. Who needed school?

3

"There's just the two of us left," he says.

"Plus your kid," I say.

"She's a girl. The name will go."

"Hardly," I say. "There's more Gillises around here than you can count."

"I'm talking about our Gillises," he says. "Our line."

"You're looking," I say, "at the human starter pistol."

"Which means?"

"I just shoot blanks."

He puts his head back and laughs. Then stares at me.

"Maybe," he says.

"No doubt about it," I say.

"What if Sandy wasn't premature?"

Now it's me staring.

"Just something to think about," he says. He takes a swig from his glass, then goes to get his overnight bag. Brings it to the table. "I want to show you something," he says. Rummages inside and pulls out a pistol. I figure at first it's a toy. Something for the kid.

"Not a starter pistol," he says, holding it up.

"That's not real," I say.

"It is." He spins the cylinder.

It's small enough so you could carry it in an overcoat pocket.

"Where'd you get that?"

"It's yours," he says.

"Mine?"

"I meant to give it to you years ago. But I guess I thought it would look odd." He's turning it in his hand. "You might have been tempted to use it. On me."

He laughs and pulls the trigger. Click.

"You never saw this before?"

I shake my head, keeping a close eye on it.

"It was Grandpa's," he says.

"You're kidding."

4

I no longer felt like going to town, even for a hamburger. Every time I looked at his truck, I didn't want to go near it. And dances were out of the question. Even if I wanted to go, people observed mourning periods then. Quaint when you think about it today. Of course when Lent started, in February, social life came to a halt for everybody. Effie started coming over again, to watch TV. They had their own by then. Angus won it in a Legion raffle. But she said she didn't get any joy out of watching TV at home.

Duncan would visit when he was home but he'd be talking mostly to Ma and the old people. Seemed he was studying Gaelic at the university. Wanted to talk it with Grandma and Grandpa. Them obliging, but saying, after he left, his accent was queer. Pronounces his *l*s. Like they do back in the Old Country. Well, his ma was from there, they'd say. And that would explain it.

Ma liked Duncan's visits but I could see he was after getting very distant. Piety setting in. Everybody knew he was heading for the seminary next year.

I spent almost all my time in the house. Watching TV day and night. At least until it went off, after the news. The news was at midnight then. Was following the Kennedy stuff pretty closely. They'd set up a special commission right away to look into it, though I couldn't imagine what there was to look into. Oswald, the Communist, killed him. Jack Ruby killed Oswald. Ruby was in jail, but it seemed that he was nuts. Telling people nothing.

Effie would tell me I should be getting out more. I told her I had to stay home to keep an eye on things, especially Ma. Ma, of course, seemed to be doing fine. Even Grandma. You read that after the shock of something like that there's fatigue. Then sorrow. But I never realized there was also relief.

Grandpa, on the other hand, felt neither relief nor guilt nor much of anything. He'd begun to slip. He hardly ever talked English anymore. Except when Sextus would come around.

———

"Grandpa was probably the first casualty," he says. "He was the most vulnerable. You could see him starting to slide back. I guess when he arrived, mentally, back around where he was travelling in the States, he dug out the gun. Always kept it in an old trunk. Don't suppose that's around anymore."

"Went many a housecleaning ago."

"Told me he brought this from a fellow in a lumber camp in New Hampshire. He was leaving for Boston and the fellow told him he'd need a gun. So he bought it."

He hands the thing across to me. I take it gingerly. I've never held a handgun.

It's heavy for its size. Cold.

"I don't particularly want it," I say, handing it back.

He says, "I think when Grandpa gave it to me he was under the impression that I was Sandy. The way he talked."

A reasonable mistake.

"Said it was a shame how I lost the Gaelic when I got shot in the war. So I just took it. But it was meant for Sandy, so it would have been yours," he says, handing it back.

When I don't take it he sets it down on the table between us.

———

Grandpa became preoccupied with money. Figuring it had become his job to provide again. Like the old days. All winter he was talking about going to the woods, cutting pulpwood. I didn't understand much Gaelic so I was missing a lot of it. It became kind of a joke.

One day in March I watched him from my bedroom window trudging off across the field toward the woods, carrying a pulpsaw and an axe. The old-fashioned way. Ma wanted me to go after him, but Grandma said he'd be okay. As long as it wasn't a chainsaw.

It was the same the next day. And the next. After about a week I decided to check on him. I followed his tracks through the snow and after about a twenty-minute walk I could hear chopping. He'd been busy. He actually had about three cords neatly piled.

I stood there until he saw me.

I could tell by his puzzled look that he wasn't quite sure who I was. I realized then that I really had no choice but to start going with him. I found Pa's power saw in the barn, hardly ever used.

The sad thing was that there was no money problem to worry about. Pa's veteran's pension would continue. The old people had their pensions. And, Ma said, there was the insurance.

"What insurance?" I asked her.

"Oh," she said, "Pa left us well looked after, God bless him."

Then I remembered the lawyer after Pa's funeral.

"Like how well?"

There were two policies, she said. One from work, naming her. The other through the Legion, naming me. Two substantial amounts, she said. I'd get mine when I was twenty-one.

"They've decided somehow it was accidental," she said.

"What do you mean, 'somehow'?"

She just gave me a look.

To me the work was just a reason for going outside, but gradually we had a substantial pile. Maybe a few hundred dollars' worth. I started thinking about how we were going to get it out of the woods. I'd heard that Squint MacDougall had bought a new tree-farmer, planning to get into the contracting business, starting with his own woods in Sugar Camp. A lot of people were doing that now that there was a mill.

The morning I went out to talk to Squint, it was my understanding that Grandpa was going to take it easy. Stay home until I got back. He said something to me, and I assumed he was agreeing with me. But he went off to the woods as usual, and that was the end of him. Curled up on a bunch of boughs and died. And that's how I found him early in the afternoon on a crisp sunny day in April.

——————

"Grandpa hurt almost as much as Uncle Sandy," Sextus says. A fresh drink in front of him. "The old boy had a life and a fellow never really got a chance to know it."

"He was eighty years old," I say.

"Christ. It must have been a shock for you. You found him."

Actually, he seemed to be sleeping. Curled up like a child. And when I realized, I can't say that I felt much of anything. I gathered up his axe and his saw and I headed for home. Of course I checked first to make sure. But it was pretty obvious. He was already stiff as a stick.

At Grandpa's wake Effie draped her arms around my neck and hugged me tightly.

She was wearing a strong cologne that stuck to me for the whole evening.

I remember asking her how things were in school. Her rolling her eyes. "You aren't missing anything," she told me.

Ma saying: "Death always comes in threes." And everybody looking uncomfortable, not wanting to stare at Grandma.

———

"What were you figuring on doing with yourself now?" Uncle Jack asked after we'd buried Grandpa. He'd come home right away. Planned to stay until after Easter. A couple of weeks. Things to clear up. Grandpa, of course, didn't have a will.

"I don't know," I said. "Probably look for something around here."

"I suppose," he said. Like there was something on his mind.

We were sitting in Billy Joe's tavern. I was only seventeen. Four years under the legal age. But tall as the old man and the image of him. So nobody bothered me. Beer suddenly didn't taste so bad. Chilled, at least. I had four. Was feeling better than I had for months. Coming back from a leak, passing a table of guys from the pulp mill, I heard the words "power-pole Gillis."

Swing my face to the table and they're all studying their beer, except the fellow who said it. A bigmouth from Princeville. And without thinking I backhanded him right off his chair.

He must have been off balance or something because I've never been any good at hitting. Don't know why. Maybe because I saw the old man hit Angus once. The old man was a good hitter. He had a knack. Jack was like me. Told me once he'd never hit a person. But Jack never had to. In one flashing, fluid moment, he'd have a guy off balance and his face would be rubbing off on whatever it was pushed against.

The bigmouth is scrambling off the floor and I'm kind of paralyzed. I'm in for it. But suddenly he's a statue. Jack has him by the back of the neck, saying, "Hey hey hey, what's going on here?" The guy tries to swing around, but the shirt twists into a kind of knot, choking him. Jack is just talking to him quietly. And by now there's a couple of waiters over and it's finished. Jack and I leave. Me mouthing off over my shoulder. Jack steering me to the door.

"What got that started?"

I can't. How could I repeat those words?

But if he was a stickman, wouldn't that argue against the theory that he was in a state of torment because of the business with the Swede's wife? And would he do himself in for that? Impossible. Like they say: Being a stickman is never having to say you're sorry.

I asked Millie once if she'd ever heard my father was like that. She just asked, "What if he was?" I didn't have an answer and she said: "If he was, good on him. We only live once." My Millie.

5

Effie was talking about taking secretarial. You could take a course at the convent school in Mabou. Or nurses' aide in Antigonish. Maybe getting on at the mill.

"I hear there's even a newspaper starting up," said Sextus. "So there might even be work for me."

"Ha, ha," she said. "You've got bigger fish to fry than around here."

Always saying he wanted to be a writer. Duncan was going to be a priest. That was normal. A teacher, maybe. But reporting the news was a process you'd never have any contact with around here. Pretty exotic. Of course the reach of his ambition went far beyond the little paper a couple of young fellows were trying to establish in Hawkesbury. Far beyond anything we could imagine back then.

———

"The urge to write a novel really first came to me when Grandpa died," he says. "Seeing all those old people around. I realized I'd kind of forgotten about their existence. Every one of them a connection with a time that had become unreachable and mysterious to us, the time when we were all immigrants around here. I'd listen to them talking Gaelic. Like a secret code. Like they were full of hidden history. Then I remembered the gun. Kind of a metaphor . . . the mystery of their lives. Write a story about a mysterious gun turning up after somebody's grandfather dies. Then I thought: No, it'll have to be something more original than that. It was only later I thought the nature of memory itself. Tricks it plays."

"Maybe it was too deep for around here," I say.

"No," he says. "A good idea badly executed."

That's the trouble with jazzing things up. Ordinary people miss the point.

"Who thought of the name?" I say.

"The editor figured it would get American interest."

"And I suppose it did."

"Nothing that would make any difference."

Good for the Americans.

I drain my cup. And I'm thinking how easy it is to slip back.

The last five years or so, ever since AA and meeting Millie and getting myself in shape, it became impossible to imagine that I would ever slip back, feel as I now feel. That strange belligerence, beneath a numb weariness. But here I am.

———

Wednesday night after Grandpa's funeral Jessie and Uncle Jack came out to take Ma to a movie in Hawkesbury. Ma was worried about people talking, so soon after Sandy. To hell with it, Jack said. The place is full of strangers anyway, he said. So they went. Grandma was in bed. I was watching TV when I heard Effie in the kitchen.

She was wearing one of Duncan's old coats, jeans, and heavy wool socks. She crashed down on the chesterfield beside me.

"What are you watching?" she asked.

"Jack Benny," I said.

"Crikey," she said. "Is that all there is?"

So we just watched.

"How are things over the way?" I asked.

"Not good," she said.

"Duncan's gone back?"

"Yes. Just Papa there." Something in the way she said it.

"You can always stay here."

"Just you and me," she said. I could feel her fingers on my neck. Teasing.

"And Grandma," I said. "And Ma."

"That's too bad," she said.

And the problem is, you never know whether they mean it. Even today, familiar as I am with the little games they play, you feel the same old responses. I crossed my legs, pretending not to notice what she was saying or doing.

"So you don't like Jack Benny," I said.

She took a handful of the hair on the back of my head and gave it a little yank.

She slept on the couch that night.

I put the blankets on her carefully. Hung Duncan's old coat on the back of a dining room chair. And when I came down the next morning she was gone.

School, of course.

Friday evening I decided to take the truck into town. Near their lane I could see there was a car up at their house. Arse-end low from the continental kit. Whip aerial swaying in the wind. Ontario plates almost obscured from salt and roadshit.

———

By March, you could see a difference in Grandma. Starting to go down. Seemed to lose all her opinions. Which was a good thing because Ma suddenly had plenty. Politics. Religion. Housework. Grandma just seemed to be pushed aside by them. Which I didn't mind. Ma was always too easygoing. Easy to a fault, Jack would say. Poor Mary, people had habitually called her.

She opened up. Little glimpses of her long-buried self. Startling stuff, like the fact that she was brought up. That's how people described being adopted. Brought up. She knew who her real mom was. Some single girl from Judique who went away to the States after she was born. Never came back. Her mom's parents gave her to an older couple who had no children of their own. Lived down the shore road in Judique.

Suddenly she was sharing all sorts of little bits.

"Everybody thought Sandy Gillis could have done better," she said, laughing. "They didn't remember what a wreck he was coming home from the war."

"Couldn'ta done better than you, Ma," I said.

"Darn right," she said. "Who'd've put up with him?"

Us laughing. Her eyes wet and sparkly.

Easter weekend Duncan was home. I got in the half-ton and drove over to their place. Their gate was open so I just pulled in like the old days. Evening of Good Friday. Days getting longer. The ground was wet and muddy, so I stopped near the gate and started walking a kind of crescent path, around the mud. Frost coming out of the ground. Spring always smells like catshit.

Then loud voices. And Effie's high above them. Then a crash. I froze. Then the old man's voice, harsh. "You miserable old bastard, if I ever hear the like of that again, you'll be on the road. You hear?"

My father? Then, of course, it registers: Duncan. All anger always sounded like my old man.

Then another crash and the door suddenly opened and it was her rushing out.

Saw me. Stopped dead. Paralyzed. Just staring.

What I did? I waved, a fluttering little gesture with the hand.

She turned quickly and went inside. She didn't look back.

———

"Duncan was the big surprise when the book came out," he says.

Probably liked it," I say.

He raises his eyebrows. "Why do you say that?"

"Duncan was always unpredictable."

He laughs.

"For sure I knew one person around here liked it," I say.

He's smiling in anticipation.

"Guess."

He looks away. "Yes," he says. "She told me."

Her letters.

"I remember it almost by heart," he's saying. "She said, 'I don't know how much of the story is true. It's very touching.' That was her word. 'It's very touching. But the details, in the end, don't matter. The story is really'—get this—'about how we hide from the truth, or let other things get in the way of the truth.' Can you believe that?"

Effie talking about truth. Him writing about the lives of people who called it *thruth*. Makes you want to haul off and . . .

"Wow," I say.

He's back there. And I'm back there. But There is two different places.

"I'm saying, high-priced reviewers didn't figure that out. But there she was, our Effie. Writing to me from the Long Stretch. And getting it absolutely dead on."

Our Effie?

———

Big arguments about it. Right here, where we're sitting.

"A little strange," I said to her, "a fellow cooking up a big pack of lies to make some kind of a bullshit point about the truth."

"You have to read beyond the details," she said.

"Go ahead and take his side," I said, wishing I could think of something clever.

"Let's just not talk about it."

"Why don't I just go to town and talk to people of my own mental calibre."

"Grow up," she said.

I headed for the door.

The worst thing was that she wouldn't tell you to stop and come back. So you'd head to Billy Joe's and get yourself lost in a lot of mindless crap about the mill and the usual pile of discontent from people who were never really better off than right now.

Then you'd try to make up for it with her over a thirty-dollar dinner at the Skye Motel dining room. Of course it was 1970, near the end of everything up until then. Thirty dollars down the drain.

6

On his last Saturday night home, Uncle Jack came over unexpectedly. We were all sitting around the kitchen table drinking tea. Jack was catching the Sunday-evening train to North Sydney. Heading back on an overnight boat.

Out of the blue I said: "I should go with you."

They all looked at me.

"Back to school is where you should go," Ma said.

Aunt Jessie said: "My God. Why would anybody want to go into that?"

"What do you think?" I asked Uncle Jack.

"I don't think you know what you're talking about."

I said, making it up on the spot, "I could make some good money this summer, get myself a car, and go back to school in the fall."

I think it was the reference to school that slowed them down. Ma probably thinking, Well, maybe it would get him out of the house for a while. Aunt Jessie thinking it might be good to have somebody keeping an eye on the old fellow. Jack saying no way I'd last more than a few weeks in that place but not sure if that was good or bad.

Eventually he said, "Where did you get the notion you'd be making good money?"

"Well, in Ontario I hear they can make fifty or sixty dollars a day bonus."

"Ho-ho," he said. "We're not talking about Ontario, where they've got unions and modern technology. We're talking about the ass-end of the industry. You'd be on pick and shovel all summer. Think about it. Pick and shovel. The tools of ignorance."

"So how much do they pay?"

"You'd be looking at a buck forty an hour, probably."

Jesus. They were making twice that at the mill. But it wasn't the money anyway.

"Sounds pretty good to me," I said.

"Right off the top, they'll be taking room and board. Plus you'll have to buy thirty or forty dollars' worth of gear at the store. Before you get started."

"The pulp Grandpa and I cut is worth about a couple of hundred bucks," I said, looking at Ma. "You could loan me that, couldn't you? Squint's already promised to haul it out to the road for nothing. Says he'll take it in to the mill if I want."

Ma laughed. "You really want to go, don't you?"

And at that moment, I did. Really.

"What do you think, Jack?" she said.

"Well . . . I dunno," he said. Which was what he always said when he knew.

———

Squint seemed to be around a lot those days. Dropping in out of the blue. You'd be in the middle of eating at noon. The door would open. Squint would walk in. Hello everybody. Just passing by and wondering. More likely smelling the grub. Squint lived alone. Never married. Nobody would have him, they used to say. Big joke: When Uncle Jack would have been away for an unusually long time they'd be saying to Jessie, We'll have to line you up with Squint. Her howling and pretending to gag. Everybody getting a big kick out of it, including Ma. The old man smiling, saying, Don't be so hard on poor Squint. Of course Squint had been overseas. You couldn't say anything around the old man about anybody who'd been overseas. Not even Squint.

———

"Those letters probably more than anything else opened up the possibility of something between us."

It's me who knows about her letters.

"I know there are plenty thinking it's a lot of crap. But there are enough others saying great things. But there's one thing. It's down home that really matters. And she was the one voice of encouragement from here. Her and, eventually, Duncan, of all people."

"So what did you fucking expect?"

"I don't know. I didn't think it was so outrageous."

"The old man stood out like a sore thumb. And the Swede's wife."

"I heard that," he says. "The lawyers were a little worried about the Swede."

"I wish they'd have been as worried about some of the others. Like your father," I say.

I pronounce the words carefully and aggressively. In his face.

"That's pretty unfair," he says gently.

"Unfair?"

"I didn't think he'd be so . . . sensitive."

"He was a dying man."

"I didn't know that." His face now haunted.

Well, everybody else knew.

"I expected he'd give me at least . . . that much credit for it." He holds thumb and forefinger about a millimetre apart. "You know? You realize . . . Jesus Christ, here I've been doing pretty well. Good jobs. People away acting like I'm a celebrity. But him? Fuck-all recognition from him."

Tugging at me to say something.

Then looks away and says: "That's when I told him about what happened to Uncle Sandy. As much out of spite as anything else."

———

Early in '64, the Swede moved away. We heard New York City. The mill had a sales office there and he was supposed to run it. She and the boy went with him. Then later, there was a story that she and the boy moved back to Sweden. Some local men, sent by the mill to Sweden for special training, saw her at a company reception. Looking good as ever, they were saying. I never saw her again after the wake. He eventually came back for a while and I saw him several years later, when I went to work at the mill myself.

Here's what Millie thinks. The closer people were to the war, the more inflexible they became. You'd think it would be the other way around, but they weren't. And that's why people like the old man and Angus and Squint and the Swede's wife and the whole sorry lot of them were so vulnerable. Your life is battered by circumstances the way a tree is battered by the wind. If you can't bend, you break. And the first sign of danger, like the rot that weakens the tree, is self-loathing. Something she heard about when she was in Toronto. Apparently she went to a therapist there for a while. Then it got too expensive and she quit. Ironically, after she quit, she really started drinking hard. Spent more on booze than on the therapist. But that's a whole other story. So, she says: The secret of survival is flexibility.

7

April 19, 1964. A Sunday night. Jack said the train left at eight o'clock. Stupid time to be heading out on a long complicated trip, but there you are. We'd get to North Sydney just in time to connect with a coastal boat that was crossing the Cabot Strait that night. Jessie drove us to the station. I think it was the first evening of daylight saving, so it stayed bright longer. One of those chilly, crunchy evenings you get in the spring when everything goes kind of blue as the sun sets. Not like the copper colour you get in July when the sun is an incinerator at the end of the fire ditch.

Going up the long crawl of Sporting Mountain, Uncle Jack produced a flask from his coat pocket. Took a swig.

"I'd offer you one," he said, "but you're a bit young to start."

I didn't want one anyway.

"How old are you?" he asked.

"Seventeen."

"Oops," he said, smiling.

"What?"

"You have to be eighteen. To go underground." Pausing for effect. "You'll have to go back."

I laughed.

"When'll you be eighteen?" he asked.

"October."

"Oh well. You look older. Say you're eighteen. If they ask for proof I'll back you up. Say you're sending home for your birth certificate. They'll forget."

He was looking out the window, dreamily, allowing his head and body to rock in alternating rhythms as the train clattered through the night.

———

Sextus is sitting with his chin practically touching his chest. No wonder, the amount of booze in him. Heaped ashtray in front of him.

"That book," he says. "If it did nothing else, it opened my eyes. Made me realize just what it's all about."

"What what's all about?" I say, allowing a trace of impatience.

"You'll be the pride and joy of a place, then you do something that's more about something you care about. Then you realize.

Only reason anything ever mattered to the place all along was because it reflected well on them. You know what I mean?"

"Frankly, I'm sick of the subject."

"Frankly, eh?"

I should have been watching him more carefully.

A stunning blow to the side of my head leaves me momentarily in darkness though I can hear him saying, "You big-feeling sanctimonious prick," and can feel the chair tipping backward as in slow motion.

I still have wits enough to roll off sideways, landing like a cat, hands on the floor in front of me, and stand quickly. Even I'm impressed. He's one arm length away. Oddly, I feel no impulse to retaliate. My head has only one thought: Pa lives! I can see him in front of me, eyes dancing.

I almost smile but instead, I say: "That was fucking clever."

I'm sure he wants something else. Wants me to come flailing at him. Provide closure. Another shrinkwrapped notion. Screw him. Let's leave it open.

He wheels, stomps toward the door, grabbing a jacket as he goes, then outside. Slam!

I have this queer image: him out there in the storm with the Lineman, or Stickman. Me in here with Uncle Jack.

Jack's voice comes to me through the wind. He's saying something like: You did good there. That was the proper thing. You're all right.

Part 9

1

Driving home in the spring of '68. After four years away with Uncle Jack. Three of them at Bachelor Lake. Time past but not past at all.

November 22, 1963, and my father occupy my life as real and present as all the experience I have since. The day seems like yesterday. And the going away with Uncle Jack. The living in Tilt Cove. Bachelor Lake. Just layers.

May 1968. Driving down the long hundred miles of packed dirt from Miquelon to Senneterre, with nothing but trees and low cloud and dirty clods of spring snow to look at. Then pavement to Val-d'Or. Reviewing layers of time. Old people gone. Ma now Mrs. Squint. Effie clinging to me from the distance, me to her. Feeling really good. Thinking: I've got the worst over with and I'm only twenty-one going on twenty-two.

Jack didn't get up to say goodbye. Working graveyard, but I still found it disturbing. Us together most of the time since we went to Tilt Cove, April 19, 1964.

―――

Uncle Jack was right about my age. The doctor in Tilt Cove told me I had to be eighteen. I said I was but that I didn't have anything on me. Jack backed me up and they said send home for it.

Which I did. By the time I got it I was eighteen and they didn't care. I was only a labourer. I got all the worst jobs underground. Pick and shovel stuff, like Jack said. Breaking rock on the grizzly with a sledgehammer. Cleaning the sump in the bottom of the shaft, using shovels and a muck pig to get out the water and sludge that accumulated there. Installing air and water pipes. Laying track. Every shit job that nobody else would do.

I didn't mind at first. I got a buzz going underground. The cage ride down. The cool black privacy below. The pneumatic roar of the jacklegs and the sudden silence when the miners finished the drilling and were loading powder and fuse. You'd be looking forward to the end of the shift then. And there'd be talk, in the quiet. About other mines, the war, the depression. Stuff I knew vaguely about from the old man and Angus at the kitchen table drinking.

Everybody seemed to be a little bit crazy. Everybody but Uncle Jack. And they seemed to know it. He was different. Always listening. Always the first to laugh at something funny. He was a boss, but he'd stand and talk, twirling the safety glasses in his hand. Sometimes he'd even grab a shovel and help with the hand-mucking.

I even got kind of fond of the smell, the dense damp exhaust of the rusting machinery, compressed air, ore dust, blasting smoke. Just as well I didn't mind it since it got into your clothes and your skin and nothing seemed to get it out. Only cheap shaving lotion if the occasion was important, which it rarely was.

I can still remember trudging down a drift at the end of shift, waiting for the snap and thunder of rounds going off. Rumbling guts of granite. And the guys giving each other a hard time.

Hey, young fella, bring that eight-foot steel out to the station when you're coming.

Me doing it.

Asking, when I got it out, what to do with it.

Them saying, Work it up in yeh.

Everybody laughing like mad. Including me.

The whisper and rattle of the cage hurtling up and down the shaft, the snap of signals as it stopped at each level, the clank and thump of heavy wooden doors echoing through the emptying drifts, loading the guys for surface and the shower and a beer at Itchy's or, after '65, Ikey's, and a pile of mass-murdered supper wherever. Compliments of Crawley-McCracken.

I was just a helper. But they were promising that I'd get into production work by that fall. I was related to Jack. And a lot of them knew the old man. From the war.

"You Sandy Gillis's boy?" they'd say, eyes narrow.

"Yes," I'd say.

"We were overseas together," they'd say. As if that told me everything.

———

Letter from Aunt Jessie. August '64.

"So the young fella is on the paper in Halifax," Jack says. "Son of a gun."

But you could tell he was pleased. Aunt Jessie sent a clipping of the first story that had his name on it. It didn't mean much to me. But it was something to see the name: A. Sextus Gillis.

"Great that he's using the A.," Uncle Jack said.

Showing it around the club later, his best friend, Black Angus MacDonald, said: "What the fuck kind of a name is that?"

We were still sharing a room then. Barely big enough for two. In a big rectangular bunkhouse made mostly out of plywood.

Fifty men living in it, yet somehow it always smelled clean. You left the work clothes over in the dry, a change house located right next to the headframe, that perpendicular odd-shaped building that straddles the shaft and distinguishes every underground mining community you'll ever see. The dry had hooks and baskets, raised close to the roof by chains and pulleys. The way campers hang food to keep it from bears. You'd lock the chain since your wallet would be in the basket. Nobody ever pretended that there was much respect for private property in the camp. People came from everywhere.

———

Letter from Effie. September '64.

"Dear Johnny," it said. Dear? That was a first. The letter was full of news, mostly about people getting married. People a little bit older than we were, but whom we'd know from the dances. There must have been five or six couples tied the knot that summer. Even the one from Long Point, the girl I took home that night. In the family way, Effie implied.

She said she was going out with somebody but it wasn't serious. Was thinking of going to Mabou in the fall. Taking secretarial. But there was a new motel opening in town. Maybe getting on there. Said she missed me.

I bet.

———

In August of my summer in Tilt Cove a young MacNeil fellow from Mabou, working in a raise, lost a finger. Sandy MacNeil. I couldn't forget the name. He was on Uncle Jack's shift and

I'd heard Jack warn him half a dozen times about wearing his wedding ring underground. But he'd only been married a few months and wouldn't listen.

"Wife said she'd be checking when I go home," he said. "Wants to see that soft, white little band of skin around the finger, next to the knuckle, where the wedding band is supposed to be. Or I'm in for it."

He laughs the way the newly married do, when it's still okay to be soft.

Jack just shrugged and walked away.

And one day MacNeil tried to yank his hand out of the way of a moving tugger cable but the ring hooked on a single broken strand of wire. Lucky he didn't lose the whole hand, Jack said. Jokes in the club that night, about the finger and the wedding ring. He's real handicapped now, Black Angus was saying. That finger was the best thing he had going for him. MacNeil went home. Jack spoke to the captain and they decided to break me in working in the raise. Gave me MacNeil's job.

Before I left Bachelor Lake, Jack had told me they were talking about moving me up. Putting me to work with the geologists. Maybe paying me to go to the mining school at Haileybury in Ontario. After that, fast track to shift leader. Me laughing, thinking about the way they talked about guys who learned mining in school. But Jack's face was serious.

Uncle Jack was my biggest discovery in Tilt Cove. He had a life there. He had friends. Not just fellows from home, like Black Angus and Philip MacPhail. Young guys too who talked to him the way they talked to each other. He was the only shift boss people seemed to like. Maybe that was because he lived in the bunkhouse instead of the staff building across on the other side of the pond. Guys could sit at his table in the club and talk about anything they felt like over a beer. It was because he was able. They'd say he could operate two jacklegs at the same time. Somebody saw him once. His partner had a hangover and was sleeping behind some old timber in a crosscut. There was Jack, running both machines. And the time somebody lost a tram car down an orepass. The engineers were baffled. Jack got it out. And not just underground. You'd be crazy to arm wrestle Jack. When Itchy, who was the club manager in Tilt Cove, needed somebody to keep the place under control when he'd have a special night he'd get Jack. Nobody fucked with Jack. Nobody ever saw Jack raise a hand against anyone. Jack only had to look your way and you paid attention.

Standing around in the headframe when we'd be waiting to go down, guys giving me the hip into something solid. Or whack my hardhat with a stick or another hardhat. Stun me for a minute. Just joking, but also testing. And judging. You sure don't take after old Jack. But I didn't mind.

And things gradually changed. I got hit in the face with a piece of stone from a rock I was breaking with a hammer on the grizzly. I hardly felt the blow. But when I put my hand up the blood was just pumping out. Coming off the cage the guys in the headframe looked shocked.

"He almost fell down the fucking waste pass," one said. Sounding alarmed. They quickly started making jokes. Figuring I'd soon be gone. But I stayed and I became one of them. A member of the establishment.

"A good man," Jack said to me one night after I'd been there a few months. Looked me in the eye steadily and said it again: "You're a good man."

I grew inches, just sitting there.

———

Letter from Sextus. October '64.

"He must need something," Jack was saying, carefully tearing the end off the envelope.

"Getting along good . . . likes the job . . . awful busy . . . thinks they're going to put him in the Legislature—That'll be something. Maybe swing something for us then, what do you think?—Saw Duncan in a restaurant the other day . . . he was with a bunch of seminarians and they aren't allowed to talk to civilians—You think!—Says hello to you . . . wants to know how you're getting along."

"Getting along good," I said. "Tell him."

Guys would go out every opportunity. To Springdale. Corner Brook. Just raving about Newfoundland girls when they came back. Real broad minded, they'd say. Haw haw. Didn't bother me a bit.

There was a young one working in the company store. She was from Tilt Cove. Actually grew up there. There were a few real families there. Fishermen before the mine came. Now the cove was blocked from the sea and gradually filling in with tailings.

The girl in the store was Norma. I'd call her Normal, joking around. She was pretty in a way. There had been girls around during the summer. The manager's daughter and a couple of other locals. We all played ball but you wouldn't dare try getting anything going. But Norma was different. She'd always talk to me. Chit-chat about the news. Whether or not Canada should have a real flag. She didn't think so.

The only female at Bachelor Lake was Ikey's daughter, Miriam. Young and pretty but the word was out: look at her crossways and Ikey will cut your balls off.

———

Letter from Aunt Jessie in November '64.

"She says Grandma is doing good. Had her in to the doctor last week but she's fine considering. Says your ma is fine. Says the young fellow was down at Thanksgiving. Got his own car now. Got himself a Volkswagen bug—death trap! Doing good at work. Got a story in the paper almost every day.

"Ran into Squint out at your place the other evening. Getting into the pulpwood contracting. Looks like he's going to lease your woods for the pulp. Got a couple of trucks. Himself and Grandma beat the other two at cards."

Squint? Playing cards?

"That'll be a help to Mary. Those woods were ready for cutting for years now. As long as Squint doesn't ruin them. Was always kind of a gwoik, Squint. In the woods, anyway."

Everybody getting on with life, or acting like it.

———

Letter from Aunt Jessie. End of November '64.

"Your ma and Squint were at the card game in Glendale last week."

We just looked at each other.

Finally I asked: "And did they win anything?"

Jack looked back at the letter. Studied it.

"She doesn't say."

"Ma loves her cards."

"Ah well," Jack said. "It's been over a year. Since poor Sandy."

———

I dream about him a lot. I can never remember where we are
or what we're talking about. Always very casual and friendly.
The way I never knew him. Except, almost, once. Up on top of
Creignish Mountain, watching the sun go down.

2

It was starting to rain halfway to Senneterre. Big spatters on
the windshield. I passed a young fellow on the other side of
the road, heading in the opposite direction. Standing there in
his underwear, staring at me. A hitchhiker, changing out of his
good clothes so they wouldn't get wet. Had a big bag of mining
gear on the ground beside the suitcase. Like somebody from
home. Heading in. Looking for work. Me heading out.

———

Letter from Effie. November '64.

Kept it in my pocket until Jack went off to the club. "Dear
Johnny." The words were like a touch.

It was a long letter. Stuff I already knew. Her working
in the motel. Not liking it much. Then a lot of woe. She
never realized she could miss somebody as much as she
misses me! More than Duncan. She could never really talk
to Duncan. And while she never really talked to me either,
she knew she could. Not out for number one like all the
guys she knew. Somebody she knew she could tell anything

to without worrying that it would be all over the place in twenty-four hours. Was I planning on coming home for Christmas? Please say yes. Et cetera.

It was the kind of letter you'd expect to sign off with a love So-and-so. But she didn't. She signed it like this: "Your (best) friend. Effie."

And that was how Christmas '64 happened.

I was asking Jack what his plans were for Christmas.

"I wasn't thinking about Christmas. When is it? Jesus. We're that close. Well. Well."

After some thought he said: "I suppose I should talk to the brass. Figure out what the schedule is like for Christmas." Then: "What about yourself?"

I don't know. "What do people usually do at Christmas?"

"Some go out. A lot stay. No place to go. You make extra, working over Christmas."

"I suppose," I said.

———

At night I'd just lay there, listening to Jack snoring. Or if he had a few in him, coughing. Sometimes expecting him to expire in a great gagging spasm. It was scary. Especially thinking that this could be my whole life. Me, eventually, the guy keeping somebody awake with the hawking and coughing and farting. There had to be something better.

Then I'd think of Effie.

———

Getting gas outside Val-d'Or. There was a car on the other side of the pump. Nova Scotia plates. Two big guys in the front seat. Asked the guy at the wheel where they were coming from.

"Walton," the driver said. A mine down near Windsor, on the Bay of Fundy. Heading for the new development near Matagami Lake.

"Heard of it," I said. "I'm just coming out of Coniagas Mine in Bachelor Lake."

The guy on the passenger side said, "Poor you," and the driver snickered.

"Quite the shithole, that is," he said.

Jack still there. The best damned miner in Canada. Not likely to be working in a shithole.

———

"We need a little break," I told Jack, just before Christmas.

"Whatever you think yourself," Jack said, nursing a beer in Itchy's club.

I was drinking a Coke.

"I wouldn't mind going home for a visit," I said. "It's about time."

"Yeah," he said. "A fellow should make the effort. Check in on Grandma. How she's getting along. And have a visit with the young fellow. Before he's the premier and too busy."

———

Letter from Sextus. Mid-December '64.

Dear Pa.

"He's getting some time off at the holidays," Jack said.

"Great," I said. "When's he coming?"

"Hmmm. I guess he's not . . . Himself and some friend are going down south for the holidays. Bermuda."

The way he said it. *Bermouda.*

"That's queer," I said.

"I always wanted to go to *Bermouda.* They say it's hot down there."

"Probably," I said. "Who's the friend?"

"It doesn't say," Jack said.

———

A week before Christmas Uncle Jack was into it pretty good. Getting his Christmas cheer out of the way before going home, he said. Aunt Jessie was strict about liquor. I was having rum and Coke and feeling the buzz.

Jack brought it up. "Do you ever think of the old man?"

"Now and then," I said.

"You might hear some bullshit around home," he said. "People with nothing better to do." A pause. "You just . . . you just let it go by," he said with a wave of his hand. "Right?"

"Right."

"You're a good man," he said.

Not a stickman.

3

After Bachelor Lake, Val-d'Or looks like a city. Billboards and neon signs and car dealers. The air is different. Hazy. People are all in a rush. Wondering what it would be like working in a place like that, right on the edge of the city. You'd never have a nickel to your name. That's what it would have been like in Sudbury. Toronto would have been a disaster.

Prunes was from Val-d'Or. My partner at Bachelor Lake, Proulx. Nice guy. Always practising English on me. Probably because of him I'll never work underground again.

A Friday evening in January 1968. Men in the dry quieter than usual. Coming and going from the first aid room down back. Somebody hurt, probably. Picked up my lamp from the usual spot on the rack, strapped the battery on. Slung the light around my neck. More people heading for the first aid room. Jack with them. Something going on down there. Went along to look.

First I couldn't see anything. Just a row of broad-backed sweat- and dirt-stained shirts, in a little semicircle, like a singing group. I moved up closer, looking between two of them. I see a yellowish corpse on a trolley, a small towel covering his privates. Everything else exposed. Showing large bruises up the chest. Jawbone askew. Arms stiff and formal at his sides. Jack poking at his side saying Jaysus. He's practically turned into jelly inside. The corpse quivers when Jack touches it.

Prunes. Took a shift on the crusher, hoping to get on there full time. Surface work. Prunes never liked underground the way some do. Me included. Until that moment.

Clearing something from a conveyor belt, he got caught. Went into the hopper. Halfway through before they got to the shutdown.

Coins covering his eyes. New wife in Val-d'Or.

Life's too short. Even if I had to go on pogey.

I think it was the coins in his eye sockets that did it.

I had a number for his wife. He gave it to me before, saying if I was ever in Val-d'Or. But I didn't have the heart for it. She probably couldn't speak English anyway.

———

It was mid-afternoon when I parked my car on the main drag and checked into the Hotel Louis-something, same place Jack and I had stayed on the way up. Got into my room, then crashed. Had been up with some of the boys at Ikey's kind of late the night before. Ikey left the bar open for as long as we were there. A lot of free rounds.

Had a restless sleep. Dreamed I was in my bunkhouse room with Jack and Effie. Effie was sitting on a chair. Wearing her father's old army jacket. A big row of medals across the front. Has her legs crossed carelessly, so you could almost see up. Jack was studying her, saying "Kind of coarse, she is."

Keeps repeating it.

Effie just looking at him like she couldn't care less, but like she expected me to do something.

And I couldn't think of a thing. Then she hauls out a gun. I wake up in a sweat.

Wherever that came from. It wasn't like Jack to make comments like that. A few weeks earlier he had a letter from Jessie. Maybe that caused it.

"Says here she's acting like she owns the old place."

"Who?" I asked.

"The young one," he said. "Your missus."

"Oh, for Christ sake," I said.

He laughed and said: "You'll be having the *fuamhair* in there with you before you know it."

"Not likely," I said.

It was late when I awoke. The hotel room was dark. Down-stairs there was a babble and a stink coming from the beer parlour, so I went in there. Ordered a quart of Molsons and a bag of chips. A couple of pieces of pepperoni. Just sitting there enjoying the beer when I looked up and it was the hooker, Scotty. As soon as she opened her mouth I realized how lonely I had been. It was the accent. In this place. It made me smile.

After some small talk she said, "We never finished the busi-ness we started the last time . . . we don't have to, but."

Looking over her shoulder.

"I'm surprised you remember," I said. Almost three years gone.

"I remember you dad," she said. Pronouncing it like "dod."

I was about to correct her but, realizing it felt good, stopped myself. Then told her I had a room. Alone this time.

She laughed and grabbed my hand.

Going up the stairs I was panicking. Thinking we should have had more to drink. Suddenly not liking the look of her rear end as it swung up the stairs before me. Looking large and threatening. Feeling everything but lust.

At the door she looked in cautiously, then went straight to the bathroom and looked around. Smiled and opened her arms to me. I just stood there. So she came toward me with her head cocked to one side, caught the end of my belt and gave it a tug.

I was suddenly feeling wretched. But Scotty was oblivious, opening my trousers, reaching in and beginning to rub. I closed my eyes, so it would be forever unseen, and unremembered.

When I opened my eyes, she was taking things off as anyone would for any reason. To wash, or swim, or sleep. With no more ceremony that Uncle Jack or Black Angus or Prunes in the dry. It was only when I saw her breasts exposed. They were larger than I would have guessed and they startled me with a primal longing, to put my hands and my face on them.

"You're a miner," she said, after removing the rest of her clothing, and then mine. "Normally I'm afraid of the miners. They get rough. But this is your first time. Paying for it. I can tell. Which reminds me." And neatly plucked my wallet from my trousers hanging on the back of a chair beside the bed. Extracted a twenty, put it in her purse, and was back to me almost without having interrupted what she was doing.

"I could never live with a miner," she said again, busying herself at my neck. "My husband works on the railroad."

"That's queer," I said. "First time I met you, he worked in Cadillac, you said. Underground."

She sat up then, laughed, and gave me a playful slap.

"Never contradict a lady," she said with that accent.

"So what does he really do?"

"Ask me what my dod does," she said, lifting her sentences at the end.

"Your father?"

"Aye," she said. "M'dod is a prison guard. Back home. A screw, they call them. I used to tease my dod, askin', Dod, what's a screw gettin' an hour these days?"

Threw her head back and laughed. She had a lovely long neck.

"M'dod's a hoot," she said.

"So what is it your husband does?" I asked again.

"You really want to know?" she asked, with a wicked look on her face.

I nodded.

"He works behind the bar. Downstairs."

She giggled.

But before the panic got me, she went to work, pushing me back on the bed, then straddling me energetically, one hand holding me by the hair, the other busy where I couldn't see but could feel an avalanche. And I suddenly went spastic, then an explosion, replaced by shame and embarrassment.

"Ooh, what a naughty boy," she said, wiping her hand on the blanket and climbing out of the bed.

She was putting her clothes on as quickly as she had taken them off. Then she said: "Let's go down and you can buy me a drink. Maybe try again later."

And I said I don't think so, thinking about the big fellow in the wrinkly white shirt down behind the bar.

4

I hadn't told anybody exactly when I'd been arriving, so Effie wasn't home. I drove out to Squint's. Aunt Jessie was there. The three of them sitting at the kitchen table drinking tea. Jessie and Squint had coats on. Big hugs from Ma and Jessie. Squint shook my hand, looking glad to see me. Squint seemed okay after all. Then he went out again. Had a big tree-farmer in the yard, a bunch of cogs and gears spread out under it on a piece of cardboard.

"Ask Jessie about Sextus," Ma said when I had a cup of tea in front of me.

"My God, you never know where he's going to be next," Jessie said. "One day he's calling from Ottawa. He was there when Trudeau won the leadership and became the prime minister.

Then it was straight down to the States to cover the uproar over Martin Luther King. Wasn't that awful? The poor man."

The month before, April, they'd been talking about Trudeau at the camp. All the Frenchmen excited getting one of their own in the big job in Ottawa. Jack telling them they were all being sucked in. Some old draft dodger pretending he was a hippy. Only half-French anyway.

In '65 Jack said he voted for the Ralliement des Créditistes. Some fringe party I could never figure out. When their guy came to the camp he couldn't talk enough English to explain himself. Jack voted for him anyway. Then ragged the guys who voted Liberal or Tory. Calling them patsies. Them shouting back at him in English and French: "You're just fucking around, Jack. Makin' a mockery of democracy."

Jack saying: "Bullllllshit. That old Caouette is the real McCoy. An honest man. I bought a car from him in Amos in '39." Then laughing his head off. Jack was always looking for ways to rile people up, then laugh at them.

Ma asked, "Have you seen Effie?"

Exchanging a quick glance with Jessie when I said, "No, she wasn't home."

Then Ma says, "Och, she won't be far. So where will you be staying?"

———

Jessie finally asks, "So. How did you leave the old man?"

"Prospering," I said. "Doing great. Could land home any day. You won't know him."

"Oh," she said, laughing. "What's he been doing? Watching the diet, I hope."

"Getting younger and better looking every day, Jack is."

"Well, he'd better give me a little notice," she said, brushing crumbs off her lap.

"You better be careful," I said. "Jack'll be taking up with some old French one if you're not careful."

"Will you listen to him," said Ma. "The lip."

"No big loss," Jessie said, laughing.

A few days before my last shift underground, I could hear Jack roaring in the washroom of the dry, the spasms deep in his lungs. Imagine windowpanes rattling.

One of the shift bosses tossed his head to one side and said, "You better check."

"Jesus, Jack, is this you?" I said. Standing at the urinal looking at a fibrous red blob the size of a jellyfish.

"Wha'?" he says innocently. Over at the sink drying his hands. The seizure past.

"Mother of God," I said, "somebody left half their guts hawked up in here. Yech Christ."

"Sorry," he said. "Musta had a nosebleed in my sleep last night . . . ran down my throat."

Before I left for home he said: "I don't want you going telling the young fella. Or anybody. Okay?"

"Sure, Jack."

After Aunt Jessie was gone, Ma said: "We were half thinking you'd want to be staying here for a little while. Till you get things ready."

By the look on her face, it had already been decided.

———

"God. Look at you! You're so tall and so thin!"

Me glowing and wanting to eat her.

She asked where my bags were, I said I'd left them over at Squint's.

"Oh," she said, a little surprised.

"I thought it might be best for the first little while," I said.

Then she dragged me half running to the living room and down onto the couch where she covered my face with kisses and messed my hair and told me to stay there while she made supper. And chattered all the while from the kitchen about new projects starting up and thousands working in construction, and everything changing. It was like the causeway all over again. People coming home. Her working at the motel. Assistant manager now but still planning to go back to school. One of the girls from work going to be the bridesmaid.

The wedding had been set for June, right after the federal election, so Sextus could be the best man. I wanted Uncle Jack but she said no, Sextus would be better. He was travelling around the country, writing about the campaign. Coming home as soon as it was over.

After we ate we lay together on the couch, arms wrapped tightly around each other. There was no longer any doubt in my mind why I'd come home, or where I'd spend the rest of my life. Right here. Like this.

But later, when I awoke and found her to be sleeping, her head close to mine, curls tickling my nose, I was suddenly overcome by dread. The faces of our fathers filled the room, beaming their unhappiness all around. And when my stirring woke her she sat up slowly and asked, "Do you really want to? Go through with it? We don't have to, you know."

I said, "I really want to."

Then she told me that she could understand what I was feeling. She felt the same thing. But it would pass.

"We've got the jitters," she said. "I hear everybody gets them."

You want to get married but you don't want to get married. And you finally do because you said you would.

———

I was glad she admitted jitters and misgivings, because the images of her father and mine were jostling in my head all the time, it seemed. The old odours of his work clothes, still hanging on pegs in the porch. His hardhat and utility belt on a shelf. But more than that, I had the awful feeling that I was to be measured against his judgment for as long as I stayed here.

That was fifteen years ago. I have learned to ignore it. But only after recovery from years of absolute failure.

The old people around here used to fear the *cailleach oidhche*, the spirit that threatened their sleep, uninvited and unwelcome, creeping up on them with her smothering weight. I know her well. Not as an old woman, but as a man.

———

The slightest movement and she's fully conscious. Legacy of her father's prowling.

"Where are you going?" she asked, hint of panic in her voice.

"I'm beat," I said. "Gotta go home."

"Home?"

"Ma offered me a place out there. Just so—"

"It wouldn't do any harm to stay here," she said. "I could fix up a room."

"No," I said. "It isn't that."

5

It was late in May. The election was on for June 25. Our day was June 29. It was surprisingly easy to settle in with Ma and Squint. They lived in a big old place that had been mostly closed off until Ma moved in. Within a few days I found a rhythm in the place. Going out in the mornings, checking what Squint was up to. Usually fixing some piece of machinery. He had half a dozen men working in the woods and he spent most of his time repairing vehicles and equipment. The tree-farmer had a major problem. I'd picked up enough general knowledge of machinery working in the mines that I could be useful to him. Knew a lot about diesels.

Squint was easy on the head. He had some of the old man's edginess but a lot of Jack's slow deliberation. And he loved to talk.

So I asked him, "How has old Angus been making out lately?"

He laughed without stopping what he was doing.

"Angus is Angus," he said.

"What exactly is it that's wrong with his hearing? He always acts kind of deaf."

"Who knows," Squint said. "Selective deafness. Hears what he wants to, misses the rest. Pretty useful handicap."

"He's faking."

"No," he said.

September 1944, in Italy. Angus got caught out in his own artillery barrage. Out in no man's land. Coriano Ridge.

"Typical of Angus," I said. "Caught out."

"Well," Squint said, "maybe. But Angus was a specialist. They sent him out on sensitive snooping assignments, lightly armed.

Gathering information about what the enemy was up to."

"Lightly armed?"

"You had to travel light, and the Sikhs taught him to depend mostly on his knife," Squint said. "Lots of stories about what Angus would be getting up to out there. They say he could travel at night like a raccoon. Whenever they wanted to take a prisoner for questioning, they'd send Angus."

―――――

When I finally encountered him, in front of the liquor store in Port Hawkesbury, Angus looked like a wreck. His hand shook when he held it out to me. Still wearing a necktie, but the shirt collar was grimy and the skinny neck scruffy.

Very serious. Asking about Ma and Squint and Jack. I was surprised by the amount of dignity he could muster. What did I think about the election? Was I ready for the big day? Great thing, Effie and me. Hoped we'd have a whole barnful of kids.

Some hope.

Before I left him he dropped his voice and asked if I could spare a five until the cheque came. I dug one out and gave it to him.

―――――

I remember asking Jack, "How did you face Angus, after you first found out?"

Jack shrugged. "Figured if the fella that caught the bullet could put it behind them, who was I?"

Then I blurted: "But what if Pa didn't know? What if he thought it was a sniper like everybody else?"

"That's a good one," Jack said.

———

And each evening I would drive in to the motel and get Effie. We'd go to a movie. Eat at the drive-in. Or a restaurant. Or just drive and talk. Then we'd go home and have a drink of something. Or tea. And she'd ask if I wanted to stay and I'd say I'd better not.

"You're so old-fashioned," she'd tease.

Me mumbling something apologetic.

Her saying, "It's a good thing one of us has his head screwed on right."

6

Getting married is way too easy. A couple of people not yet wise enough to make a sensible decision only have to go along to some church or government person and ask to be married and it's done. So sure of themselves.

Of course it's easy to get out of commitments now. Thanks to Mr. Trudeau! People in and out of marriages like mortgages. Actually a mortgage is a lot more binding. Ending a marriage? No fuss, no muss. But I see lots of fuss and muss at work. People and their personal problems take up half of my time.

June went by quickly. Another Kennedy murdered. Sextus had to leave the campaign for a week to deal with that. Must be the only reporter they've got up there, Ma said. Then Trudeau walked away with the election. I didn't vote. Didn't give a shit one way or the other.

Sextus and Jack both docked on the twenty-eighth, Friday

night. Met up at the airport in Halifax. Drove down together. Both a little wobbly getting here. Then we got together with Squint and Duncan. Father Duncan, at this point. Had a little stag party. Drinking and talking. Jack and me catching up. I never mentioned Scotty.

Effie wanted to get married outside. In the field below the house, near the poplar trees. I was thinking: Not far from where Pa shot our dog. Duncan, who was presiding over everything, got the go-ahead from the bishop on the understanding that we'd all troop off to town later and sanctify the whole performance with a proper Mass. Which is what we did. Effie invented a lot of the ceremony, with Duncan's approval. There was a lot about loyalty and re-spect. She had daisies tangled in her hair. They had to be artificial because the real ones weren't out yet. Only dandelions. I joked she should try them but she just gave me a look. Jack and Squint and Angus standing at the back of the crowd looking very edgy.

Jack saying afterwards: "Jesus, boy. That was some nice."

Me searching his face for evidence of mockery.

What else? Dinner at the Skye. A party at the house. A cou-ple of Duncan's priest friends showed up. One had a fiddle and the other brought a guitar and they were good.

I was afraid to stop driving that night. After it became time to leave the party. I remember Uncle Jack was drunk. On the verge of passing out. I volunteered to drive him home. Sextus took me by the arm. Fairly drunk himself.

"Hey, man," he said. Talking like someone from away. "I think you got something else to take care of." Arm over my shoulder, face close to mine. Sweaty. His arm hot. "Little bit of business over there in the corner," nodding his leering face toward Effie, who was with Ma and Squint, conspicuous in her new suit. Her travel clothes.

"I'll take care of the old man," he says. "You take care of that."

Two hours after we left, near Truro, Effie asked, "When do you plan to stop?"

———

Fortunately I had a bottle of rum with me. I took a large drink when she went into the bathroom. Then a couple more when it became obvious that she was taking her time in there. Sitting on the side of the bed with a quart of rum fighting panic.

Scotty was supposed to be for practice but all she proved was that I needed lots of it. Should have started sooner. Practising. Christ.

The drink helped. I felt suddenly reckless. Undressed. Clambered into the bed. Switched off the bedside lamp. And thought of Angus.

She didn't wait for me to start anything. She took control. All the things that I'd imagined were supposed to happen seemed to happen. But when it was over, I still felt that I'd missed something.

———

Squint and I actually became friends in the following months. No way was he going to be my stepfather. He was no Uncle Jack. But gradually I warmed to him. Occasionally we'd go in to Billy Joe's for a beer. Played a lot of cards. Effie and me, himself and Ma. With a few drinks, Squint was one of the few who'd talk about the war. Places he'd been. Some of the things he'd seen. And I often wondered how much he really knew.

I got work at the pulp mill. Started stevedoring, loading

boats. Then the woodyard, driving a loader. Called into the office one day and Sandgren, the Swede, back from New York, asked if I wanted a permanent position. I said sure. Sandgren had become personnel manager by then. He pointed out that I really needed a grade twelve certificate but he was sure I'd get that sooner or later. And I assured him I would. Before I knew it I was in. Wondering why he smiled at me and acted friendly. But I never got a chance to ask because he was gone soon afterwards. Back to Sweden. Never heard of either one of them again.

7

Squint came by one afternoon on one of my days off shift. Effie was at the motel. It was early afternoon but he'd already had drinks by the look of him.

"Come on to town," he said. Which meant to Billy Joe's.

My choice was to go with him or have him settle in here. Probably had a bottle in his truck. I decided to go. Squint was a binge drinker. Would go on it for a week at a time. No harm in him, though, Ma said.

The tavern was practically deserted because it was mid-afternoon.

"You know what day this is?" Squint said.

Then I remembered. November 11.

"Was there no ceremony this year?" I asked.

"Didn't go this year," he said. "Your ma gets a little tense. For good reason, as I understand."

I felt a tightening in my gut.

"Don't get me wrong," he said. "Your father was a good man. Shame he had to live with something like that . . . considering how everything happened."

I didn't ask. Something told me I didn't have to.

"Nobody ever told you, eh?"

"Told me what?" I said, studying my beer bottle.

"About what happened to your old man."

I nodded.

"Funny thing," he said. "I was there. But I don't quite remember exactly how the two units came to be so close together. We'd never been in the same area before. But out of the blue we heard we were relieving the 9th Infantry Brigade and I remember somebody saying, 'Jesus that'll be the North Novies.' And sure enough, it was. Somewhere close to the German border. Near a place called Dokkum. You ever heard of it?

"I was out all night on a contact patrol. Not a hide or a hair of a German to be found. Near daybreak I'm after coming out of some woods, from the east, into a big polder with an old stone barn in the middle of it. Sun just coming up.

"Then I sees this commotion around the front of the barn and when I pull up, they're taking somebody out on a stretcher. Looks dead to me. Has that orange look. And a wicked smash in his head. Blood all over. I look closer and Jesus Christ, it's Sandy Gillis.

"Talk about surprised, seeing him there.

"'What happened?' I ask somebody.

"'Sniper,' they say. 'Over in those woods, by the sound of it,' pointing to where I just came from.

"'Says who?' I say. I'd been all over that area. Seen nothing. The guy points to the door of the barn and there's Angus MacAskill standing there. Like he was going to pass out.

Almost as far gone as the guy on the stretcher. Soaked with poor Sandy's blood. Tried to carry him, I guess. Making himself look good."

"Look good?"

"Well," he says. "Think about it."

Looking straight at me, face full of insinuation.

"I took off then, heading for those trees. Imagine how I feel. They're saying somebody picked off Sandy Gillis right under my nose. But I never heard or saw nothing. Often when there was a sniper, you'd find signs. Empty shells. Food leftovers. Shit. Clothes. Whatnot. I spent a lot of time in those woods that day. And there was nothing. Not a trace."

I haven't touched the beer. Afraid to look at him. That he'll stop. Or continue.

"The official report said a sniper," he said. "But we all knew different."

"No sniper," I said.

"Oooohhhh, no. No sniper." He started fishing in his jacket pocket for a package of cigarettes. Keeping close eye contact. "So you knew," he said finally, eyes narrowed.

I nodded.

He lit up a cigarette. "When the rest of it started coming out, some of the boys thought we should say something. Or do something. Fella shouldn't get away with something like that. Then the Krauts suckholed. Days later. Maybe a week or so. War was over. And we were thinking about other things."

He was studying me quietly: "You're okay, are you?"

I nodded.

"I often wondered," he said, "how much you knew. Or if you knew anything at all. Especially when that one was around and all the talk was going on."

That one?

"The Dutch one. Who landed here, the Swede's wife. In my personal opinion she was the cause of it, you know."

And he told me, perhaps too eagerly, his theory: that Angus shot my father in a jealous rage over a girl named Annie. Sandy's little Dutch girlfriend.

"How would Angus know that the old man had a girlfriend if he was in a different part of the country right up until they met?"

"I wondered about that. Only thing I can figure was she was there, with Sandy, when Angus showed up."

"In the barn?"

"I'd put money on it. Angus walked in on them. Everybody in Sandy's company knew he was having a little fling with this Dutch one. It had been hot and heavy for weeks. Naturally after he got shot word went around that it had something to do with her. Sure enough, Angus in his cups one night after everything was over starts blubbering about some female being in the barn with Sandy when he got there. And everybody just put two and two together. Sandy and this Annie having a little time in the barn, before the North Novies move out. A little bit of a fare-well. And who should walk in but Angus the *fuamhair* from home.

"Some wicked story, what? Then when she showed up here seventeen years later everybody was talking and wondering what was going to happen. Never expecting what did.

"Queer when you think . . . yourself and young Effie . . . married now. Your old man would've got a wicked kick out of that."

Squint and I drank late into the night. Eventually he delivered me home. Somehow to bed.

I came half awake as Effie was dressing to go to work and I decided then that I would never tell her what Squint had told me.

Whatever happened there no longer mattered.

———

Millie says Squint's story was a load of crap. Admitted that her family had known Annie Van Ryk a lot better than she'd first acknowledged. Squint was talking through his hat. Annie was from Zutphen. Millie had an uncle there.

"Annie was a doctor's daughter and she was seventeen and the likelihood of being overnight in a barn with a soldier, no matter how nice, even a Canadian—I doubt it.

"And if she was! Can you imagine somebody like her who saw something like that happen ever wanting go set eyes on either of those guys again? Not likely. She'd have freaked out, first sign of either one. Run a mile. Wouldn't have stayed around here a day. Never mind getting involved again."

Involved again?

"Well . . . it's not unlikely that they . . . knew each other. Over there. Annie and your dad. Maybe even . . ."

"Maybe," I said.

"And if that part was true, it's possible that they reunited over here. In '63. Isn't it?"

"Maybe."

"Isn't it!"

"Yes."

She only confirmed my own instinct: the Squint story was just over-excited gossip. Long before Millie came along I'd shoved it into the background with all the other myths about

Sandy the Lineman. Some things can never be explained. Explanation requires logic. What happened to my father was as illogical and pointless as the war itself. Not worth talking about. People naturally want to find justifying causes and large purposes in misery, but that day was the beginning of the end for me and Squint. And eventually Ma. It was probably his eagerness in the telling. There was something indecent there. Something real stupid.

Part 10

1

I've forgotten how hard it is to piss in a high wind, propped against a house that won't stop moving. My feet are wet because I forgot to put shoes on before coming out. The ground is soaked and freezing. The storm is passing and there's a cold front moving in behind it. I also forgot that rum always causes some kind of constriction in the chest. Strange. I seem to have forgotten a lot of things. Like how easy it is to fall into the grips of the booze. And how quick you can land back at square one. Wandering around outdoors in your sock feet. All the things they told me at the Monastery the last time. Things Millie and I have told each other a thousand times. But then again. Who wouldn't slip after today.

I'm almost worrying about him. Haven't seen the hair of him for an hour. Ever since he stomped off.

I won't wait much longer. If I'm in bed within the next half hour I should be okay tomorrow. Go for a good long run in the morning. Living like this I'd be worn out in a matter of weeks.

It isn't that these things he seemed so determined to get into haven't been on my mind. It's where they lead that makes me nervous. The old man took the easy way out. But that isn't the hardest thing to deal with. It's going the next step: Figuring, the easy way out of what?

He and Ma were having some problems. But he was always a difficult man, unpredictable ever since the war. But why that particular day? Which made me wonder about the Swede's wife. Was she the "what" he was taking the easy way out of? No way. Not somebody his age. Then you begin to learn more of the details of his life. Eventually you start approaching that age yourself and know anything is possible.

The truth, in the end, was simple. My father had a fling with an old flame from the war. What does it matter now? He never really survived the war. The bullet that killed him at Ceiteag's was, in a way, just a ricochet from the bullet that got him in Holland. Or its ghost.

It is so easy to say. So why is it so difficult to accept? Maybe because I know that those were merely conclusive events. In themselves they mean nothing. The hard part is finding out and coming to terms with what went before. Because if there is anything worthwhile to learn, anything instructive for the lives being lived now, it's entangled in the experiences of lives lived before November 22, 1963. Mouthing endlessly what happened on that day is nothing more than titillation.

2

I knew Jack was a goner the minute I set eyes on him, Thanksgiving weekend, 1969. We didn't expect him but there he was, walking into the kitchen with a big hello and a big smile. Home from Quebec. It was the smile. It was too big for his face. He looked like he was wearing somebody else's teeth and eyes. And the head was too big for the body. Everything out of proportion. Jack had dropped a good forty pounds since the last time I saw him, the Christmas before.

Said he was going to stay around for a while, maybe do some hunting.

Jack? Hunting?

"Jack looks awful," Effie said later.

Effie had quit her motel job. Was home most of the time. She was taking some university courses at night. I bought her a car for the travelling. A '67 Mustang. Kind of an orange colour. You wouldn't miss it. She made quite a picture riding around in that, with her mop of red curls. With sunglasses on her, she looked like a movie star. You couldn't help staring. Even me, and wondering: Wow.

I was enjoying working at the mill. Spending so much time in daylight was a nice change. But sometimes I actually missed the peculiar tang of the underground air, the queer freshness of it, like the smell of new rubber or the inside of a new car. The air at the mill was sour. Some days you'd get a headache.

Between work and home I wasn't seeing much of Uncle Jack.

———

"Jack's in the hospital," Effie announced just after I got home one night around Hallowe'en.

"What hospital?"

"Antigonish."

I called Jessie and she said he'd just gone in for tests. Nothing in particular. Just hadn't been to a real doctor for years. Was postponing his trip back for another week or two.

Then it was Halifax for more tests.

———

Half of the personnel problems I deal with are family related. The other half are what they call substance abuse. We used to call it boozing, though there are other substances in the mix now. I tell the young fellows at work that routine is the source of most of the comfort in a marriage. But it can also become a hiding place and can start stirring up trouble in the best of relationships. People know I'm talking from experience. I didn't realize I was hiding stuff. And I paid for that delusion. Paid big. And they all know it.

3

Effie was pretty rigorous about public routines because of Father Duncan. I'd become more like my father. Indifferent to the rituals and public expressions of faith. Religious in my own way, but private. Effie didn't seem to care whether I went to Mass or not. Ma was scandalized when I wouldn't be there, sitting conspicuously. Later, when everything in my life went to hell, she said it was because I lost my religion. As far as she was concerned that was all you had to know about what happened to Pa. He lost his religion. But he had an excuse, she said. The war. Me? I was just a slacker.

Nature takes care of the routines of intimacy. Eventually you get the confidence to start thinking family. Even though I never entirely lost the feeling that there was something missing.

"I think there were too many dead people in that bedroom."

You can talk about stuff like that with Millie.

"So why is everything okay now?" I ask. "You and me? Assuming it is . . . not wanting to speak for you."

"It is," she said.

"So?"

"Different bedroom," she said.

"I don't think it's that simple."

"You should have had kids," Millie said. "Kids drive the ghosts away."

But Effie wanted to go to university first. Started taking that new pill in spite of what the pope was saying. The pope didn't bother me, but I was suspicious of the pill. Made me feel weird. Impotent.

"I'm determined to prove myself," Effie would say. "Make a contribution to the place."

But the place didn't need it. I had my job at the mill, making decent money. And I had over fifty thousand in the bank.

The university extension courses were one thing. Kept her occupied when I'd be working the long shifts at the mill. But I didn't want her going off to university. People got weird in university. And eventually just put it out of my mind when they told her she'd have to improve her grade twelve marks before she'd be eligible for admission full time. Either that or just keep picking away at the evening courses. Like a hobby. Okay.

———

Life was good. On days off, we explored distant parts of the island, well away from the Long Stretch and the grim places that reminded us of the lives we'd abandoned. She'd drag me off to the university in Antigonish for a concert or a play. All the way to Sydney for a movie. I remember *Midnight Cowboy*.

"Drove a long way just to get depressed," I told her on the way back. "Coulda done that without leaving home." Laughing. You could even tease about that.

And when the trees were turning, in the autumn, and the hillsides oozing lurid shades of rust and yellow, we'd hike for hours in the highlands back of Mabou or the hills that sheltered Lake Ainslie. Kinloch. Gaelic, she'd explain. *Ceann an loch*. Head of the lake. And wonder sadly: Why couldn't we have grown up in a place like this? Usually gazing out over the flashing sea, with me silent by her side, asking myself: What difference could it possibly have made?

"My mother grew up in a place that looked like this, I think. An island called Benbecula. Always in sight of the ocean. The sea has an effect on people. For the better."

And I'd agree, without knowing why.

Once we bumped into Charlie Angus MacLeod in the liquor store in Sydney. Asked about Tilt Cove.

"They've shut 'er down," he said.

I'd get the occasional urge to go back to the mines. Longing for something, not sure what. Maybe something I found there through Jack. Something missing in him now. Last time I'd been talking to Jack he was planning on heading back to Manitoba. Soon as he felt up to it. Or maybe New Brunswick. Up by Bathurst. New mine opening near Springdale, in Newfoundland. A lot of miners from Tilt Cove gone there. But he wouldn't go back unless I went with him. Giving me a wink, knowing that Effie was within earshot. And she said, "Over my dead body," and Jack and I both laughed.

Next thing we heard, Jack was staying around for Christmas.

I was a good husband. I managed that by following one basic rule. To be all the things my old man wasn't. To talk openly. Help around the house. I was one of the original modern partners. And Effie had absolute freedom, within reason. She could come and go as she pleased. And she did. And I was faithful to her above all. The original Stand By Your Woman kind of a man, or whatever they were saying in the song.

Then I noticed she'd get edgy anytime the subject of my father came up. She was really the only person I'd ever been able to talk to about him. What happened. Why. Effie had perspective. But after we were married about a year I noticed she'd try to duck out of certain subjects early on in a conversation. My father was one of them.

"Do we really have to dig through that again?"

Once she said it seemed like I was trying to hang the blame for everything unpleasant on her poor old father. Maybe he was just as much a victim, just by being there. In that barn. In Holland.

Sooner or later people get sick of other people's problems. No matter how real or how serious.

4

"There you are," I said. "I was starting to wonder."

Sextus is standing half in shadow, hands jammed into his jacket pockets. Looking cold.

"Walked over to the old MacAskill place. Starting to look run down," he says. "Can't imagine what . . . Faye! . . . would think of it."

"It isn't so bad in the daytime. Duncan's done a lot. New windows. New chimney. I think he put a fireplace in. Deliberately didn't paint it. Copying something he saw in the States. Cape Cod or somewhere."

"How's the head?" he asks.

"No damage done."

He sighs. "I must be losing it. The least I'd have expected was to knock you over backwards."

"You were sitting down," I say.

"That's true," he says. "But so were you."

In profile, half in shadow, and with a lot of cockiness gone, he'd pass for Uncle Jack. In appearance.

He follows me inside. When I sit to peel the wet socks from my feet, he sits.

"One more," he says. "A nightcap. And sorry I called you sanctimonious."

"No problem," I say.

"It's an awful word, isn't it? A hell of a thing to call anybody."

"What about . . . prick?"

"Och," he says, half laughing. "That's nothing. We're all pricks now and then."

That's what somebody at work called him, just before Christmas '69, when the book came out. It was a fellow from Inverness who didn't know the local situation too well.

"Did you see what that prick from Hastings wrote? That Gillis fella? He's probably related to you?"

"No. Afraid not."

Of course I knew all about it. He'd sent a copy home before it was released in the bookstores. And Effie had been talking about it.

Jack was back and forth but never mentioned it. They were probably all talking about it among themselves. Just not in front of me. One night at Jessie's I just picked it up and took it. She didn't say anything. It looked like about a hundred people had read it already.

A quickly written book with that name wasn't going to upset me by itself. Just the arrogance that it represented. That's what got me. Plus the feeling that everybody was looking at me and talking about me all over again. Like I had something to do with that day. Like I pulled the trigger.

I just put my head down and carried on. Still working in the woodyard where I didn't have to talk to people if I didn't want to. Just roaring around the yard on my loader, moving the pulpwood from here to there. Off the trucks, into the grinders, around the yard. Working harder. Truckers complained that I was bashing their flatbeds and generally surly. But nobody made an issue of it. This is a small place. Everybody knew.

Effie seemed to have become a big fan of his. And of the book. Just before Christmas the stores were full of them. Everybody seemed to be getting the goddamned thing for Christmas. By the new year I was still keeping my head down, taking a bit of vodka to work in the Thermos. And noticing a bit of new attitude in the wife. The birth of Faye, maybe. The book exposed another fault line in the marriage. She didn't want me to know she'd read it and liked it. And admired him for it.

I figured: If you can deceive somebody close about what you're reading, you can do it on any level. And I started to watch her more carefully.

———

"I was real stupid, bringing up the book like that." He looks away. Suddenly distracted by his need for another cigarette. Patting pockets. "Where's my fucking jacket?"

"Over there," I say.

He goes to it. Digs into a pocket, discovers a new pack of cigarettes. Waves it at me, hand like a claw.

"Feeling sorry for yourself," he says. "Every human failure can be explained, to some extent, by the tendency to feel sorry for yourself. You follow?"

"Maybe."

He lights a cigarette.

"You're right," he says. "There I go again with my big statements. That's what happens to you in TO. You learn to talk like a wanker. You know what a wanker is?"

I shake my head.

"Good," he says. "You don't want to know. The minute you know, you can assume it's because there are too many of them around."

"Too many of what?"

"Wankers." Then fondles his cigarette for a few moments. Sips from his glass.

"Thing I always admired about you," he says. "You've never been a wanker."

"If you say so," I say. Take a sip of my own.

"Same for Uncle Sandy. And my old man. Not a trace of wanker in them. Not a wanker hair on their body. Wherever they were was a wanker-free zone. You know what I'm saying?"

I nod and take another sip.

Raises a hand. "Don't say a word. Just sit there and shut up till I finish." Then he smiles at me and says: "Or I'll fuckin' slug you again and *this* time, I'll see that you land on your arse."

You have to smile back.

5

Jack finally told me. It was early January.

"I got the big one," he said.

He was chewing tobacco then. Gave up cigarettes shortly after he came home. Always had a tin can near where he was sitting. Disgusting to some people but I was used to it. A lot of the fellows in the mines chewed. Controlled the dust, they said. Jack should have been chewing long ago.

"Cancer," he said.

———

"Did I ever tell you about the time he came up to see me in Halifax," Sextus says, clearing his throat.

"No."

He picks up Grandpa's old pistol, which is still on the table between us. Studies it for a moment, then holds it under his chin. And he pulls the trigger.

Click.

"You have to wonder why Uncle Sandy wouldn't have used this thing. It's a lot simpler."

"Throw that fucking thing away," I say.

Still fondling the gun he says, "The old man came to see me in Halifax. In my third year, I think. Tracked me down in the Lord Nelson Tavern. That's where we all hung out those days. Landed in. Comes right over to the table. Everybody's looking at him, wondering, 'who the fuck's that?'"

"Why?" I ask.

"He was just so . . . out of place."

"In a tavern?"

He shrugs. "Sat there for a while. Couple of guys tried to make small talk with him. Then he left. I followed him out. Asked how long he was there for. He said he was just heading back. Gave me twenty bucks. Christ, I felt weird. Took a long time to admit what that feeling was."

The mouth works silently for a moment, no words coming. Then, squeezed from somewhere deep in his chest: "I was ashamed. Of him."

Staring at me, awaiting my judgment. Exhaling hot smoke.

"Ashamed of your own father, hey," he says. "Pretty sick. I never even asked him to the graduation."

"He wouldn't have gone," I say. Remembering. Jack and me celebrating the day at Itchy's, in Tilt Cove. Getting drunk for the first of our Gillises to ever get a university degree.

The wind has gone silent for a moment.

"I spent a lot of time wondering what your secret was," he says.

"What secret?"

Then he points the gun at me, holding his arm fully extended, sighting down the arm and along the short silver barrel. One eye closed in a wink.

"Pa-khew," he says. Then: "The way you keep everything locked up. Say nothing. There's gotta be some big secrets in there."

His face is very serious. Then he smiles.

Grow up, for Christ's sake.

"You wonder how anybody does that," he says. "Blow somebody away . . . looking right at them."

"Put it away."

"You can understand a sniper. Like in a war. Or Oswald. You're just shooting . . . abstractions. But up close like this," he says. "I couldn't do it. Yourself I could see. Just . . . quick like. No thinking. Just swing it up. Pull the trigger. Bingo."

He puts the pistol barrel to the side of his head. Pulls the trigger. Click.

"For Christ's sake," I say.

6

Even when you're ready, it takes the wind out of you. Cancer isn't just a word but a proclamation that everything you know is about to change. And death will only be the final, and in some ways gentlest, change. It's the certain prospect of intense suffering, and the terrifying anticipation of all the unpredictable changes it will bring. And loss.

Jack squeezed a large gob of tobacco spit through his lips and into his can.

"The lungs," he said. "Told me in Halifax there's a ninety per cent chance that I've had the biscuit. Said they could fight it but. It was up to me. I figure it would be a losing battle. Just prolongin' the agony. Wastin' the time a fella has left. *'Bheil thu tuigsinn?'*"

"Did they say how long?"

"Could be a year. Maybe more. Maybe less." Then he grinned. "But it'll be a good year, hey? Livin' home. Pesterin' the wife. Gettin' waited on."

Then we just sat.

I decided to make Effie pregnant. Call the kid Jack. No matter what.

But she had her own ideas.

———

Ma once butted in. Just once. "You should see the priest," she said.

It was getting that obvious. Her spending more and more time with the other people who were taking courses. Talking about going back to work. Showing up here and there in public when I'd be working nights. Or in at Jack's place.

"The priest," I said, almost laughing in Ma's face.

"Yes," she said. "Don't act like such a know-it-all."

"Well," I said, scuffing a foot impatiently, not wanting to hurt her.

"You could do worse than talking to Father."

"I'm sure."

"I can tell you from first-hand experience, talking to the priest can help straighten things out even when you think nothing will. It's me knows."

Me looking at her in disbelief. Saying: "A lot of fucking good it did you."

Things pretty strained between myself and Ma by then. Having nothing to do with Squint at all.

———

Sextus says, "You spend your life becoming something, only to learn that you've lost what you were."

"I don't follow."

"That's because you are what you are. That's your secret. Who you are. And have always been."

"You're talking in circles," I say.

"You're absolutely right. I've just given you a class-A demonstration of wanking."

———

Once fertility becomes an issue it isn't long before it becomes an obsession. I asked Effie to stop taking those pills and I think she did. You could never be sure. But nothing seemed to be happening. I even inquired about getting special drugs. The doctor laughed at me. Told me the best drug was a bottle of good French wine. So I tried that. And in January and February, when it was her time, I'd be snooping in the bathroom trash basket. Even the kitchen garbage. To see if maybe she missed. But she was regular as clockwork.

And he thinks she made him pathetic. I could tell him about pathetic.

———

Every day on the way home from work I'd stop in to visit Jack.

"It's a friendly cancer," he said. "I feel better than ever."

"When do you think you got it?"

Laughing. "It's one of those things you always have. Near died when I was little," he said. "So I've done okay. Getting this far. Considering everything." Then: "It was the bron'ical trouble that kept me out of the army. In '40. Who knows what kind a mess I'd have got into if it wasn't for that?"

Mostly we'd just sit and reminisce about Tilt Cove and Bachelor Lake.

Or just sit.

———

Sextus can't keep his hands off that gun. Keeps turning the cylinder. Clicking the hammer on the empty chambers.

"You wonder about the Americans. With so many of these things around, I'm surprised there aren't more people blowing themselves away down there. Or each other. It seems like such an easy solution sometimes."

"What stopped you?" I say.

He looks up, surprised. "The kid," he says. "I swear, if it wasn't for her . . ."

———

I actually went to the doctor myself once. Arranged a checkup. But the real motive was to ask him about Effie. Find out if she was secretly on the pill. Or whatever.

He looked at me sharply and basically told me it was none of my business. But when I was leaving he said, "If you're worried about getting pregnant you'd better have Effie come and see me again."

"What do you mean?"

"You never know with that old Vatican roulette you two have been playing."

"So if we don't want babies we should be doing something," I said.

"Damn right," he said.

Then winked.

So I figured she was on the level.

But nothing happened.

One night I suggested she was taking some prevention secretly.

"Oh fuck off," she said.

All I could think to say was: "Nice talk!"

7

Near the beginning of February 1970, there was a terrible storm. Blew hurricane gales for a couple of days. Lots of rain. Hardly a flake of snow left by the time it was over. But one night in the middle of it a rusty old Greek oil tanker called the *Arrow* wandered off course coming up the bay and ran onto a reef near Arichat. Smack into a well-known hazard called Cerberus Rock. The papers said afterwards the reef was named after some Greek dog that guards the entrance to Hell. The tanker was carrying nearly four million gallons of bunker C, crude oil bound for the pulp mill.

Two nights after that I had a phone call from Sextus. He was in Hastings. The paper had sent him down from Toronto to cover the story. He was staying at the Skye. Had to stay there because of the story, he explained. I thought it queer, anyway, him not staying home. Effie was working at the Skye again and she actually spoke to him before I did. Told him to call me. The motel was full of reporters and government people, down to watch the tanker break up and spill its cargo into Chedabucto Bay.

He wanted to know how the old man was doing.

"Not great," I said. "Good time for a visit."

"Gonna be pretty busy," he said. "But I'll try."

I didn't see much of him during the first few days of his stay. The *Arrow* story seemed to get bigger and bigger every hour. It was on the national news. Oil spills were becoming big news other places. This was a first for Canada.

Effie was night manager at the motel and she was seeing a lot of Sextus.

I was still up waiting when she came in from work at about three on the Thursday morning of the following week. I'd had some rum. A few big ones.

"Where you been?" I asked.

"Working," she said. "You know that."

"I expected you a lot earlier."

"I finished at midnight. But I had a drink with your cousin and some of the other reporters. I wasn't in a hurry because I figured you were at Jack's."

"At Jack's?"

"Well, you're practically living there now anyway."

"Jack's sick," I said.

"I know Jack's sick," she said. And as she started walking away said: "Jack's probably going to die. Another ghost from your tragic past to come and live with us, as if there weren't enough of them here already."

God and the ghosts only know what happened in the next two seconds but somehow I was suddenly staring into her face from up close and my head was bursting. She made no sound. Then I realized she was actually trying to say something. And I felt her hands, on my wrists, tugging, and then I looked at my own hands, which were locked on her throat.

When I released her the only thing she said was: "Oh my God."

And ran upstairs howling.

———

Coming home from work on Friday evening, I stopped at Jack's. He was saying he expected Sextus for a visit later.

I wanted to talk to him about home. About what had

happened with Effie. I knew Jack would make it seem okay. Normal. Would help me get past it.

He was kind of nervous. Said Sextus had been staying at the motel pretty well full time to be available for the briefings, which were happening all hours of the day and night. But he was going to take a break that night. Come by for a *ceilidh*.

"Wonder what we'll talk about," he said.

Me thinking: The damned book.

Jack had never mentioned it to me, nor had I to him.

It was Friday the thirteenth. Uncle Jack died the next day. Or night. We're not sure.

I remember Effie coming in from work some time in the early hours of Sunday. She woke me up.

"Uncle Jack's car is over home," she said, sounding confused. She smelled of liquor. Over home is what she called Angus's place.

"Can't be Jack's," I said.

"It is. Maybe coming here."

I rolled over and went back to sleep.

Next morning it was still there, so I went over. Knowing something was wrong even before I went in. And Jack was dead there, sprawled on the floor of the kitchen, half under the table. There was no doubt. I knew what dead looked like. And Angus, not dead, was flaked out on the couch, snoring. Rum bottle on the table, half full, cap off.

The doctor said he died of a massive heart attack.

Aunt Jessie said Uncle Jack had rheumatic fever as a child.

Romantic fever.

The doctor said that could have done it.

8

He keeps sipping his drink, then adding little splashes. Like he's trying to finish the bottle.

"Over there at MacAskill's, I was thinking I'll never be able to look at that place without thinking about the old man.

"When Effie and I were married we'd often fantasize . . . putting a few dollars together and fixing it up as a summer place. Give the kid some contact with her roots. But just thinking about it would always give me the willies. I knew I'd never be able to darken the door."

"Nobody could figure out what he was doing there," I say.

"Oh, I knew," he says sorrowfully. "I knew. It was because of me he was there."

"You?"

"Sure. That night . . . I went to see him. Just a casual visit. The subject of the book came up. Things got kind of tense. For some reason I blurted the whole story, about Angus and Sandy and what happened in Holland. I don't know what got into me. But I was pissed off at him. He was making slurs about the book and I guess I just lost my cool. Said: 'You think the book was bad? The book is fiction. The truth is a whole lot worse.'"

Sips from his glass.

"You should have seen his face. It'd scare you. He got that upset."

"I thought that little run-in happened at a different time. Earlier. In the fall. Or."

"No," he says. "I tried to fudge it. So it wouldn't look so bad. But we had our set-to the day before he died."

"Well, even so," I say. "I'm not sure why he'd be so shocked. He already knew the story because he'd told it to me more than two years before."

And then something frightening occurred to me. "Unless you included the silly speculation about the Swede's wife."

He looked at me head-on with a perplexed frown: "The Swede's wife?"

9

There were no Legion men or flags for Jack's funeral. The church was only about half full. Duncan celebrated the Requiem with Father Hughie, who preached a brief little homily. About working men and St. Peter and how Jesus always wanted to hang out with the working class. Even working girls, which was a sly reference to Mary Magdalene. The congregation murmured its amusement. I was angry. Where were the representatives of Jack's end of the working class? In mining camps in the bush. In graveyards in places like St. Lawrence, Newfoundland, that's where.

Some of the reporters covering the *Arrow* Disaster, which was what they were calling it by then, came along out of respect for Sextus. Pencil-pushers, I thought. Can't believe Jesus would have much time for that crowd. Jesus, or Jack, when you get right down to it.

Wid and rain and everybody thinking of the big blobs of jel-lified crude oil sliming the shores of the bay and the rim of the Inhabitants Basin, moving right up the strait toward us. At the graveyard Duncan's prayerbook almost blew out of his hands.

Ma on one side of me and Squint on the other side of her. Effie was standing close, clinging to my other arm, but I could tell that her mind was somewhere else.

The two nights of the wake, at the funeral home in Port Hawkesbury, Effie was stuck to him like a burdock. They sat knee to knee, whispering until everybody was gone. Then she and I would stop at Aunt Jessie's on the way home for tea and a drink. The drink would be for me. Maybe a few drinks. Not that they'd notice because I had my own flask out in the car, under the seat. Sextus, the poor fellow, was being pretty moderate for some reason. Have a quick one with me, then back to philosophizing with herself. Talking about his awful book, I figured.

———

"The Swede's wife," he repeated, shifting in his chair and looking away from me. "What did she have to do with what happened in Holland?"

"Some people think she was there. In that barn."

"The old man told you that?"

"No."

Confusion in his eyes now.

"Who told you that bullshit?"

"It doesn't matter," I say.

Then he says with a sarcastic little laugh: "The Swede's wife! That says it all. Wife! The poor little girl in the barn never got to be anybody's wife." Then kind of sneers.

Outside the wind is grieving, gently.

I can only ask: "Little girl? What little girl?"

"I thought you said you knew."

"Nothing about a little girl," I say weakly.

He picks up the rum bottle, then puts it down.

"It came from Duncan," he says. "During a night of booze and confession in Toronto."

10

Angus went a little crazy after Effie and I left our wedding reception. Sextus came back after driving Jack home and found Angus ranting at people. Raving about Sandy Gillis. He knew things that nobody knew. About Sandy. Sextus was about to confront him when Duncan removed his father firmly. Took him to the glebe house.

Didn't come back.

Duncan had a hard time with the story, relating it to Sextus during their piss-up in Toronto. Afraid he was committing a grave sin, breaking confessional secrecy. But he couldn't contain it any longer.

In the glebe house, Angus demanded that Duncan grant him absolution for a terrible sin. On the night of April 22–23, 1945, near Dokkum, he'd discovered his oldest friend, Sandy Gillis, in a barn. In the dark Angus wasn't sure who it was at first. Had his knife at Sandy's throat before he realized. Nearly died himself when he saw who it was.

Sandy had a bottle. Borrowed it from a farmer, he said. They were celebrating when they made a startling discovery. They weren't alone. There was a girl. Hiding there. You couldn't tell how old at first. By the look of her she'd been through hard times, probably from her own people. Hair mostly chopped off. A collaborator. Bad bruises on her face and body. Which they saw while she was naked. She seemed to be really young. Maybe fifteen or sixteen.

She was afraid they'd turn her over to the resistance.

Duncan pleaded with his father to stop. Declared he couldn't hear this as a confession. This was not about a sin. This was about something that a son cannot hear about his father.

But Angus was in the time warp then. Back there. Desperate to confess.

They reassured her. She was safe. No matter what she'd done, they promised not to hand her over to her people. They knew what was happening to collaborators. She told them in her broken English she'd done nothing wrong. Of course they didn't believe her. Resistance people didn't make mistakes. Not about collaborators.

It's okay, they told her.

They gave her food, shared their booze. It was no more than that. Two boys from home, meeting up by some bizarre coincidence. Everybody relaxed. Her most of all, since there was just one of her and two of them.

Everybody happy when they went to sleep.

Duncan wept. Face in hands. Sobbing.

Then told how she got her hands on Sandy's rifle and shot him while he slept.

"It could as easily have been my father," says he. "It just happened to have been Sandy."

Then she went looking for Angus, not knowing that he was like a raccoon in the dark. And before she found him, he got her, with his knife. The way he learned from the Sikhs.

Cut her throat. Took the head half off her.

Buried her deep in the hay. Then went for help, soaked in a

mix of her blood and Sandy's. Stained right through to his skin. Tore his shirt open there and then, showing Duncan where the blood still marked him. Duncan, of course, could see nothing but sagging pasty hairless skin.

Angus told them that a sniper got Sandy while he was opening a barn window. The sun was just rising. His last words, Angus reported, were that the sun felt good. So he stood there one second too long.

———

The night has become still.

"I'm asking Duncan if he thought his father had ever told this story to anybody before.

"'Yes,' he said.

"'Who to?'

"'Sandy Gillis,' says Duncan. Then says Angus figured Uncle Sandy never knew what happened. Just what everybody else thought they knew. That Angus did it. All recollection of the Dutch girl seemed to have disappeared. Last thing he remembered was Angus holding a knife at his throat. Angus decided to clear it up once and for all.

"So I ask Duncan, 'When did he spill the beans to Uncle Sandy?'

"'At the Legion,' he says. 'November 11, 1963. The last time he saw poor Sandy alive.'"

He studies me for a while without speaking. Lights a cigarette.

"You didn't know this?"

I shake my head.

"What were you starting to say about the Swede's wife?"

"It doesn't matter."

"No wonder the old man had a heart attack," he says.

I just nod.

"Not that it excuses anything but maybe . . . adds perspective."

"It doesn't matter."

11

Uncle Jack is dead. Dead and buried. This is the first thought that enters the mind with consciousness. You are waking up on a strange chesterfield. Well, not strange. Aunt Jessie's. And reality floods back in. The reality you so successfully postponed with the bottle you had hidden in the car. Never mind the eyebrow-arching implications of hiding bottles. Uncle Jack is gone. Died hard. What the f. What else matters. Uncle Jack is gone. And so are you. Mouth cracking in the heat of Jessie's electric-heated living room. She got that in for Uncle Jack. When he was sick. Cold all the time, he said.

The house seems empty. Creep upstairs to empty the indignant bladder. Jessie snoring.

Time to go.

Oustide the air refreshes. Close the door carefully coming out.

Do not disturb. The house seems empty.

Halfway home I'm saying to myself: I guess he drove her home, decided, wisely, to leave me where I was.

A drunken zombie.

But when I got home, she wasn't there.

Next day they disappeared. February 19.

After they were gone, I showed Ma the little note she left.

The note wasn't really necessary and it didn't say much. Just that she was sorry, which I didn't really believe.

"All I can say," Ma said, "is thank God poor Jack didn't live to see this."

And I can't help wondering what the other old fellow would have thought. Sandy the Lineman. Or the Stickman. Whatever.

———

"Sextus the Killer. You could read it in all the faces at the old man's funeral," he says wearily now. The aggression gone. "People thinking: 'That book killed his poor father. Writing all that garbage, and poor Jack already sick.' As if I knew. When I wrote it. How sick he was."

"Would it have made any difference?" I ask.

"No," he says.

"Well," I say. "Thanks for the honesty."

The truth, Millie is always saying, is real simple: Life is a sequence of mistakes and consequences and a process of getting smarter because of them. Most of them, anyway. The hard part is those rare, big ones. They're the ones that either destroy you or make you wiser.

It is time for my confession. How I killed Angus.

I didn't hit him or shoot him or scare him to death. But in a moment of choice, I accepted responsibility for ending his life. Partly because of what happened to my father. Partly because of what happened to Effie. Mostly because of what happened to me through them. By dying, Angus freed me from the anger which surely would have carried me away before him.

One night I was coming home drunk from the tavern in Port Hawkesbury. It was in February '72, and it must have been 25 below zero. Angus was sitting on the shoulder of the Trans-Canada. One hand raised. And I just said: Fuck him. That's all it took.

The biggest revelation was how little it bothered me. At first, at least. The regrets came later, when I was well again. After Millie.

Angus dead?

Waking up the next day, head splitting and somebody pounding on the back door. Ma downstairs, calling me. Squint sitting out in the car. Ma all worked up.

"Did you hear about Angus?" she said.

Me looking confused. Which was a truthful look.

And Effie didn't even come home for it.

Until the funeral was over I somehow thought she would. And that it would have made the whole situation worth something. Maybe allow a fresh start even though she had a kid by then.

———

I run some water into the sink, just covering the dirty mugs and glasses. He's giving no sign of moving away from the table. Contemplating the bottle.

Well then, I'll just leave him there.

He's pouring two very stiff drinks and I don't even try to prevent him. What possible harm could they cause now?

"I've always been amazed," he says, "that one death in a war that claimed what, fifty million people or more, one death could matter so much. One anonymous death in a barn in Holland could cause so much havoc."

Then he says: "Guilt is right up there with self-pity in the toxicity department."

And I say, impulsively, "If you're guilty . . . of Uncle Jack, then I stand guilty of murder too."

"Oh yeah," he says, half laughing. "Who did you murder?" Mocking, the way he's good at.

And so I told him about Angus, watching the colour draining out of his face.

My unilateral gesture of reconciliation.

———

"You're a good man," he says eventually. Everything is out of him. He's slumped on his end of the table.

"I have no guilt or anything. Not anymore. Only thing missing was . . . saying I'm sorry. To you. How did it used to go? Heartily sorry for having offended thee . . . I detest all my sins because I dread the loss of heaven and the pains of hell, but most of all because I have offended thee."

He reaches his hand across the table. I hesitate for a moment, then take it in mine. We sit like that for a moment, limp hands lightly clasped.

———

I am standing at the foot of the stairs. My foot is on the first step, my hand on the banister.

"What are you going to do with this?" he says.

I stop and look at him. He's standing there with the pistol in his hand. Unsteady.

"What am I supposed to do with it?" I say. "It's all yours."

"No," he says. "It belongs to you. Where will I put it?"

Work it up yeh, I think. Smile in spite of it all.

"I don't want it around here," I say, letting my weariness through. "There are no guns or rifles in this house. Do what you want."

He walks to the door and out. I hear the storm door slam. He's gone, I figure.

Then he's back.

"There," he says. "That's done."

"What did you do with it?"

"I got rid of it," he says. "That's all you need to know."

"As long as I don't run into it with the lawnmower."

"Don't worry," he says. "You won't find it."

"Okay." I resume my ascent of the stairs.

"Look," he says, stopping me again. "I don't think I want to sleep up there. Could you throw down a blanket?"

It is getting chillier.

I fetch the down comforter and a pillow from the spare room. I bring them to him. He is still looking lost. For a moment it's Uncle Jack's face I see.

He is smiling. "I guess I'm a little scared of the ghosts."

Uncle Jack's face is gone.

"I thought I was the only spook around here," I say.

His face is saying something like: There is so much more.

About the author

About the book

Read on

Ideas,
interviews
& features

Linden MacIntyre

About the author

Author Biography

LINDEN MACINTYRE was born on May 29, 1943, in St. Lawrence, Newfoundland. His father, Dan R. MacIntyre, a hardrock miner, and his mother, Alice Donohue MacIntyre, a schoolteacher, were both natives of Cape Breton (MacIntyre's Mountain and Bay St. Lawrence, respectively).

MacIntyre grew up in Port Hastings, Inverness County, Nova Scotia, where he attended local and county schools in the villages of Port Hastings and Judique. He earned a B.A. in 1964 from St. Francis Xavier University in Antigonish after four years of studies there and at Saint Mary's University and King's College in Halifax.

From 1964 to 1967, he worked as a reporter for The Halifax Herald Limited, publishers of *The Chronicle Herald* and *The Mail-Star*. He spent most of that time as a parliamentary correspondent in Ottawa. Between 1967 and 1970, he was a reporter for the *The Financial Times of Canada*, also on Parliament Hill.

In 1970, he returned to Cape Breton following the sudden death of his father. He worked there as a correspondent for *The Chronicle Herald*, covering northeast Nova Scotia and provincial political affairs until he joined CBC Television in 1976. Based in Halifax, he worked for the CBC for three seasons, hosting a regional current affairs program called *The MacIntyre File*. In 1979, on behalf of his program and the CBC, MacIntyre successfully initiated a legal action to clarify public access rights to documentation regarding police search warrants. The case, *MacIntyre v. the Attorney General of Nova Scotia*, was eventually heard by the Supreme Court of Canada and resulted in a landmark decision affirming press freedom and the principle of transparency in the courts.

Eventually, MacIntyre became an associate producer for the CBC television network. As a producer-journalist for CBC's groundbreaking national current affairs program *The Journal*, he was assigned to documentary reporting in various parts of the world, including the Middle East, Central America and the USSR. From 1990 to the present, he has worked as a co-host on CBC's flagship investigative program *the fifth estate*.

MacIntyre has won several Gordon Sinclair Awards for his work in journalism and broadcasting, as well as eight Gemini Awards from the Academy of Canadian Cinema and Television. He has written and reported for numerous other award-winning projects, winning an International Emmy, a Canadian Association of Journalists Award, the Michener Award for meritorious public service in journalism and several Anik Awards. He has also written and presented award-winning documentaries for PBS's *Frontline*.

MacIntyre holds an honorary Doctorate of Laws from University of King's College, Halifax, and an honorary Doctorate of Letters from St. Thomas University, Fredericton.

The Long Stretch was first published in October 1999. MacIntyre's first non-fiction book, *Who Killed Ty Conn* (co-authored by Theresa Burke), was published in 2000. His latest work, *Causeway: A Passage from Innocence*, will be published by HarperCollins in fall 2006.

Finding Truth in Fiction, by Linden MacIntyre

A STORY has two beginnings: a seminal event inspires the imagination; eventually there is the beginning of a narrative structure. *The Long Stretch* elaborates the consequences of an imaginary event in the very real and tragic circumstances of a war. Someone should have told me just how dangerous this approach to fiction can become.

The narrative begins with a chance encounter on a rainy day in 1983 outside a liquor store in Nova Scotia. But the real beginning is a singular incident many years earlier, during the final days of World War II in the northwest of Holland.

I've always been intrigued by the extent to which lives are shaped by collateral consequences. Decisions or unconsidered actions by individuals we could not have known contribute to who we are or will become. What then, I wondered, lies in store for the descendants of the generations of people who lived through the most violent part of arguably the most violent century in the recorded history of humanity? What turmoil lies waiting in the unlived lives of the children, grandchildren and great-grandchildren of the twentieth century?

The seminal story here is set in war-struck Europe in 1945. Two friends, separated by the evolving strategies of the war, are reunited briefly near the end of it. Something violent happens. It alters their lives. Their subsequent pathologies, in turn, create distortions in the lives of their children who will, in all

> ❝ I've always been intrigued by the extent to which lives are shaped by collateral consequences . ❞

4

likelihood, convey the consequences of that wartime encounter to future generations. Personalities yet unformed will be marked by an event of which their generation will have no knowledge.

The two men who meet outside that liquor store after nearly three decades are cousins, the son and the nephew of one of the two men involved in a deadly encounter that took place in the spring of 1945. The son of one soldier was once married to the daughter of the other, a marriage doomed by the secrets of their fathers. The woman abandoned her husband for the cousin who has suddenly materialized as if out of nowhere.

The narrative opening in this book is a common occurrence in most lives: people resurfacing unexpectedly. Defences are down, memory is momentarily unclear. The moment is defined by a spontaneous emotion. The emotion is confused: the two men were children together; there is the intimacy of a common history. But the most recent common experience was a callous betrayal. There is an automatic impulse to abort the meeting before it starts. But a deeper primal need prevails: the need for reconciliation between two men who share a common bloodline.

I've seen the results of war first-hand, and I have studied and reported on violent conflicts in many places. Wars begin with large ideas that are, inevitably, articulated in simple words and virtuous sentiments. Freedom. Patriotism. Protection of a moral order. Wars begin with promises of justice. How else can we understand the readiness of people to suppress an innate fear of violence, to ▶

> ❝ Wars begin with large ideas that are, inevitably, articulated in simple words and virtuous sentiments. ❞

Finding Truth in Fiction (*continued*)

authorize the destruction of life, property and, occasionally, entire civilizations? Virtuous beginnings quickly mutate into the brutality of conflict. Through propaganda, violence and suffering become normal, banal and ultimately tolerable for the participants. The deviance of what people do in war becomes appallingly clear only to the survivors. It is in the aftermath of war that the greatest disfigurement occurs in the human soul.

This is what I have learned from having grown up among the survivors of two great wars, from having listened to hushed stories in refugee communities in the Middle East, in alleyways and morgues in Central America, in the silent aftermath of slaughter in Central Africa. It is in the eyes of the orphans and the refugees that you see the spark destined to ignite the violence in our futures. Growing up, I realized that I would one day learn to tell a story. As an adult I realized that it would have to be about the legacy of war.

I've never been a soldier, but the limits of experience become irrelevant in storytelling. To reconstruct an important moment in a distant war, I relied on research. I read extensively about the war in Europe. The compilations of Canada's renowned war historian, Colonel C. P. Stacey, were invaluable. My own work in journalism—reporting on the effects of war and retrospective documentaries on World War II—also helped in a general way.

I chose northwest Holland, or Friesland, as the location of the encounter between the soldiers for the simple reason that, for many of the war veterans in the area where I grew

> ❝ It is in the aftermath of war that the greatest disfigurement occurs in the human soul. ❞

up, this was where the war ended in May of 1945. The two soldiers were from different battalions of the same regiment, the Nova Scotia Highlanders. That they could meet up near the end of the war and engage in an impromptu celebration seemed to me to be more historical likelihood than fictional device. I was wrong.

As I began to learn more about the particulars of World War II, it became clear to me that history was in conflict with a crucial part of my fictional scenario. I discovered from my research that an encounter in 1945 between two soldiers from those particular battalions was, to say the least, improbable. I knew that one battalion, the Cape Breton Highlanders, had spent much of the war in Italy, while the North Nova Scotia Highlanders had fought mainly in France and Belgium after the D-Day landings. I was aware that both battalions saw action in Holland in the final days of the war. But everything I read in the official histories made it highly unlikely that the men I depict in my novel would ever have been close enough for the fateful encounter that I imagined in April 1945.

I decided to invoke the privilege of creative licence. It occurred to me that while a handful of old soldiers might find the discrepancy annoying, most readers wouldn't know enough to spot it. Those who did would suspend their disbelief if my story was shaped and told with sufficient skill. I hoped. But in my heart I was afraid. Strong memories from my origins and from a long career in journalism told me that accuracy in small details makes the difference between a storyteller and a liar. ▶

> " Small details makes the difference between a storyteller and a liar. "

Finding Truth in Fiction (*continued*)

And then—one of those peculiar moments which, for people far more pious than I, confirm the reality of great and essentially benevolent forces in the universe, deities with a soft spot for storytellers. On a chilly summer evening, somewhere between a first and second draft of the manuscript, I was standing in a bookstore in a town that isn't far from a real place in Cape Breton called "The Long Stretch." The town is Port Hawkesbury, and in the Volume One Bookstore there, on a rack loaded down with local literary produce, there was a book with a glaring red dust jacket. The name of the book was *The Breed of Manly Men*, which I knew to be a translation from a Gaelic slogan: *Siol na fear fearail*, the motto of the Cape Breton Highlanders. The book was a history of the battalion during the period of World War II. Because this was one of the units mentioned in my story, I took a second look.

There was just one copy of the book. At first glance it confirmed what I already knew. Cape Breton Highlanders … heroic in Italy. I bought it anyway.

Days later, as I browsed, I discovered among all the military jargon and terse accounts of combat what was, I'm sure, to the authors a rather unremarkable disclosure. It was remarkable to me because it involved operations in Northwest Europe. Holland, to be precise.

On April 18, 1945, the battalion was involved in the liberation of some villages and towns near the shores of the Zuider Zee. In a letter home, a Lieutenant Roy described the reactions of the local people:

> **On a chilly summer evening, I was standing in a bookstore … that isn't far from a real place in Cape Breton called 'The Long Stretch.'**

The underground laddies came out and armed with German rifles, grenades, British sten guns and such, whizzed around on their bicycles rounding up collaborators. Any women who had relations with the Jerries had their hair completely cut off and were slapped and such by other women. Dutch SS traitors, trying to sneak away in civvy clothes, were rounded up and forced to go on their hands and knees through the main streets to jail. They were shot forthwith. Huge bands of men and women marched through the streets, arms linked and ten to fourteen abreast, singing their national anthem over and over. People everywhere were laughing, singing and shouting for joy. We were mobbed with kindness.

And then, after that dramatic personal account, the text returned to a recitation of military activities, including this seemingly unimportant disclosure:

*The unit moved off again at 0630 hours on the 21st (April, 1945) and moved to the area of Dokkum, northwest of Leeuwarden, where it **took over from the North Nova Scotia Highlanders of 9 CIB and 3 CID.** . . .*

I read it again. *The North Nova Scotia Highlanders.* I wasn't dreaming. The Cape Breton battalion had somehow linked up with the other half of the Nova Scotia regiment ▶

‘Huge bands of men and women marched through the streets, arms linked . . . singing their national anthem over and over.’

9

Finding Truth in Fiction (*continued*)

just long enough to validate the imaginary encounter I had invented to reflect on war's long-term consequences. Just as two imaginary soldiers stumbled on each other in the darkness of an imaginary barn, the blundering imagination had somehow stumbled upon truth.

❝ The blundering imagination had somehow stumbled upon truth. ❞

Excerpts from Linden MacIntyre's *Causeway*

WE ARE standing in an open field overlooking the strait, just to the north of the village. There is a chilly mist that occasionally turns to drizzle and blows away like smoke. Then you can see across to the other side where the activities are taking place, although it is impossible to see exactly what is going on there. You know the premier, Angus L. Macdonald, is over there, along with a certain Mr. Chevrier from Ottawa, and that before long they will do something important. They will push a button or pull a lever or light a match. It is not clear in my mind. It is what happens next that is important. What happens next will "change everything," will be written down in history. But all you can see by squinting through the occasional lapses in the fog is a marshalling of large machines that vaguely look like giant dump trucks.

I've read about them in the newspaper—the forty-ton Euclids that can carry as much as a railway car in a single load. Now they're gathering around Cape Porcupine for the big job they've talked about for fifty years.

That is why we are not in school. Miss Morrison and Mrs. Gillis have told us that September 16, 1952, is a day we must experience to the full because it is a day that will affect our lives forever. It is a day we must remember in its smallest details, for what we will witness will be as important to our education as anything we will learn in books. September 16, a Tuesday. It is the day they start the causeway.... ▶

❝ September 16, a Tuesday. It is the day they start the causeway.... ❞

Excerpts from *Causeway* (continued)

We stand silently and wait. The murmur of adult conversation filters through the fog. I already know what they are saying because I have heard it at the Hole, where I gather most of my knowledge about the strange ways and mysterious interests of grown-ups. This opening was originally designed for a stovepipe, I think. It is near the chimney, and it allows the heat to filter up from the kitchen. The only heat in the house comes from the kitchen stove. The Hole is my connection to the larger, older world....

At the Hole I heard them talking about the blast that would "change everything." That was last September. An explosion of dynamite that would instantly knock tens of thousands of tons of rock from the stubborn brow of Cape Porcupine. September, 1952, the beginning of the change; the beginning of the future.

❧

THERE WAS nothing but the sound of cars and people talking when I awoke on August 13. When I looked out the window, they were everywhere. I suspect the conversations were all about where to park. The roads were lined with cars. They packed the yard in front of the school and the church, and they lined the back roads up as far as you could see. People wandering around looking for the best places from which to see the big event. The strait seemed to be filling up with boats. Down near Mulgrave, HMCS *Quebec*, a navy cruiser, crouched in the misty morning, a dark grey ghost.

> ❝ I heard them talking about the blast that would "change everything." An explosion of dynamite that would instantly knock tens of thousands of tons of rock from the stubborn brow of Cape Porcupine. ❞

When they weren't talking about where to park, the other conversation was about the weather. The skies were gloomy. People studied the clouds, looking for the hopeful glow of sun behind the murky billows.

Then they'd shrug. Rain or no rain it'll be a great day, anyway—a day to talk about for the rest of your life. The day that Canada joined Cape Breton. Ha, ha.

By mid-morning you could see the big buses manoeuvring past all the cars and pedestrians that packed the roads—yellow school buses and brownish army buses and big blue and white Acadian Lines buses. People in Highland dress pouring out of them. And then you'd hear the skirl of pipes. Men and boys and girls walking slowly by themselves, facing away from everybody, tuning up. The air filled with the brave, doomed cries of history.

I suddenly remember business—the *Post Record*. I'd been told there would be a special edition of the paper, and it would cost more. And, this being a Saturday, my share of the price was larger than on weekdays. I'd make a killing—more than enough for the rides and games at the carnival down in Newtown. And best of all, with all these people and because it was a special day, the papers would be gone in a flash.

I had time to spare and so, when I bumped into Mr. McGowan and he invited me to go out on his boat to see all the vessels in the strait, I said Thanks and Sure.

Mrs. Lew's husband, Lew Reynolds, built Mr. McGowan's boat and we watched him as it all came together over the course of nearly a year. It was like watching the unfolding ▶

" The air filled with the brave, doomed cries of history. "

of a mystery, Mr. Lew quietly going about the task, shaving and bending boards, tapping and chiselling as if he had all the time in the world—never uttering a word. Lew is hard of hearing, so, quite possibly, he wasn't aware that we were there watching. Or maybe it's because boat builders are like artists and, when they're at work, they're conscious only of the job they're doing.

He built a beautiful boat. It looks like the smack that comes around to buy lobsters, a little cabin on front and a long, open area behind. And though Mr. McGowan is a storekeeper, he was unusually generous in letting kids aboard the new boat and taking us for rides around the strait. Sometimes he even let us fish over the side or from the stern as the boat was moving. And sometimes we'd catch mackerel or pollock.

That day the strait was full of boats. I read afterwards that there were a hundred. And in the middle of them, this big grey giant, HMCS *Quebec*, now moving closer to the causeway. With her massive guns pointed at the sky and sailors in their white hats and bell-bottoms lined up along the rails watching and waving as we slowly sailed around them, nobody said a word, we were so amazed.

Mr. McGowan was going to watch everything from the boat, but I had work to do, so he brought me ashore.

And sure enough, when I arrived at the canteen, the papers were there ahead of me. A massive stack of them—each one weighed a ton. I'd be able to carry only a few at a time—a minor problem on a day like this.

> **That day the strait was full of boats. . . . Nobody said a word, we were so amazed.**

Then I started noticing a lot of people wandering around with the newspaper under their arms already. And they hadn't bought any from me.

It didn't take me long to figure things out. Not far from the canteen, a group of grown men who should have had better things to do that day were milling around a whole truck-load of newspapers shouting POOOOOST RECK-ERD ... COME AND GET YER POOOOST RECK-ERD ... SPECIAL EDITION, ON SALE HERE ...

I felt sick, and I wanted to ask them what they thought they were doing, taking over my turf without so much as telling me in advance.

Frustrated, I went back to the canteen and just stood there, looking at the stack of giant papers and, in the background, listening to the city guys hollering as if they were back on a street corner in stinking Sydney, where everybody is too loud and pushy anyway.

And I said: "To Hell with them."

I walked away and left the papers where they were and joined the crowd and the historic day.

It's all a blur when I try to remember details. They say there were more than 40,000 people and I believe it. One reporter writing in a Toronto paper afterwards said 50,000, and I can believe that too. The reason I know about the Toronto story is that everybody was saying the reporter is actually from here— William MacEachern from Judique. And how exciting it is that one of Johnnie and Phemie MacEachern's crowd is a famous newspaper reporter in Toronto, where people from ▶

> ❝ I wanted to ask them what they thought they were doing, taking over my turf without so much as telling me in advance. ❞

15

here usually get work only in factories or digging ditches.

The sun never broke through, but nobody noticed. Neither did it rain. The roads and hilltops were packed everywhere you turned. The air was filled with a dull rumbling, and I eventually realized it was the sound of excitement. All those people talking at once—and cars and buses coming and going.

The speeches and the formal ceremony were on the mainland side. I couldn't get near it for all the people packed on the causeway. C.D. Howe, a big Cabinet minister from Ottawa, cut a ribbon with an old claymore— a sword, and Angus L.'s widow later cut a cake with it. They said the claymore was used in the Battle of Culloden more than two centuries ago. I don't know a thing about the battle, but they say we're all here because if it. I was wondering about all the blood and rust, and how they got it sharp enough for the ribbon or clean enough for the cake.

There were loads of big shots making speeches. Mr. Donald Gordon from the CNR seemed to go on all afternoon. But the only speech the people here were talking about afterwards was the one by Angus L.'s brother, Father Stanley Macdonald.

They asked Father Stanley to say a few words in Gaelic, but they gave him only a minute. After he complained, they backed down and gave him two minutes. And from what I hear, he used the whole two minutes to talk about how ignorant the people from Ottawa were, trying to limit the one speech of the day in the language of Adam and Eve to a

❝ The air was filled with a dull rumbling, and I eventually realized it was the sound of excitement. **❞**

minute or even two minutes. But how he forgave them because you had to remember that Ottawa was still a young and unsophisticated place compared to here.

Half the crowd was laughing and applauding because they understood, and when the dignitaries on the grandstand saw this enthusiasm, they all started applauding too, because, I guess, they figured he was flattering them the way they were all flattering each other in their speeches. And that made the people in the crowd laugh even harder.

They were saying afterwards that surely Angus L. and all the other Gaelic speakers, including Adam and Eve, were up there in heaven laughing their heads off too. And that, if Mother Nature had her way, it would have rained on everything, but that Angus L. put a stop to that, even if he couldn't arrange sunshine.

And when it was over, HMCS *Quebec* shattered the sky with a salute from her massive guns. And, suddenly, air force jets were screaming out of the clouds and roaring down the strait, causing the birds hiding on the naked flank of Cape Porcupine to scatter in a panic.

Then a pipe band struck up a lament for Angus L. Macdonald. And, when they were finished, all four hundred pipers there stepped out in their kilts and sporrans and spats and their cocky little hats, cheeks bulging and faces red. And, with chanters and drones a-howl, they walked across the road to the isles as if marching into battle with the whole world walking behind them.

Although I'm only twelve, I think I can say there has never been a day like this in all ▶

❝ Although I'm only twelve, I think I can say there has never been a day like this in all of Nova Scotia. **❞**

Excerpts from *Causeway* (*continued*)

of Nova Scotia. Nor will there ever be again. The crowd crossed the causeway and, where it joins the road to the north, they turned left and marched all the way to Murdoch MacLean's field in Newtown, where thousands more were waiting to begin the party.

And then it was Sunday morning, as though it had never happened. Everything was gone, except for the causeway and the expectations.

❧

> **And then it was Sunday morning.... Everything was gone, except for the causeway and the expectations.**